JUDGE BURNHAM'S DAUGHTERS

JUDGE BURNHAM'S DAUGHTERS

JUDGE BURNHAM'S DAUGHTERS

ISABELLA ALDEN

LIVING BOOKS®
Tyndale House Publishers, Inc.
Wheaton, Illinois

Living Books is a registered trademark of Tyndale House
Publishers, Inc.

ISBN 0-8423-3185-9

Printed in the United States of America

01   00   99   98   97   96
7   6   5   4   3   2   1

CONTENTS

WELCOME

➤◄ ═╪═ ►◄

by Grace Livingston Hill

As long ago as I can remember, there was always a radiant being who was next to my mother and father in my heart and who seemed to me to be a combination of fairy godmother, heroine, and saint. I thought her the most beautiful, wise, and wonderful person in my world, outside of my home. I treasured her smiles, copied her ways, and listened breathlessly to all she had to say, sitting at her feet worshipfully whenever she was near; ready to run any errand for her, no matter how far.

I measured other people by her principles and opinions, and always felt that her word was final. I am afraid I even corrected my beloved parents sometimes when they failed to state some principle or opinion as she had done.

When she came on a visit, the house seemed glorified because of her presence; while she remained, life was one long holiday; when she went away, it seemed as if a blight had fallen.

She was young, gracious, and very good to be with.

This radiant creature was known to me by the name of Auntie Belle, though my mother and my grandmother called her Isabella! Just like that! Even sharply sometimes when they disagreed with her: *"Isabella!"* I wondered that they dared.

Later, I found that others had still other names for her. To the congregation of which her husband was pastor she was known as Mrs. Alden. And there was another world in which she moved and had her being when she went away from us from time to time; or when at certain hours in the day she shut herself within a room that was sacredly known as a Study, and wrote for a long time, while we all tried to keep still; and in this other world of hers she was known as Pansy. It was a world that loved and honored her, a world that gave her homage and wrote her letters by the hundreds each week.

As I grew older and learned to read, I devoured her stories chapter by chapter, even sometimes page by page as they came hot from the typewriter; occasionally stealing in for an instant when she left the study to snatch the latest page and see what had happened next; or to accost her as her morning's work was done with: "Oh, have you finished another chapter?"

Often the whole family would crowd around when the word went around that the last chapter of something was finished and going to be read aloud. And now we listened, breathless, as she read and made her characters live before us.

The letters that poured in at every mail were overwhelming. Asking for her autograph and her photograph; begging for pieces of her best dress to sew into patchwork; begging for advice on how to become a great author; begging for advice on every possible subject. And she answered them all!

Sometimes I look back upon her long and busy life, and marvel at what she has accomplished. She was a marvelous housekeeper, knowing every dainty detail of her home to perfection. And a marvelous pastor's wife! The real old-fashioned kind, who made calls with her husband, knew every member intimately, cared for the sick, gathered the young people into her home, and loved them all as if they had been her brothers and sisters. She was beloved, almost adored, by all the members. And she was a tender, vigilant, wonderful mother, such a mother as few are privileged to have, giving without stint of her time, her strength, her love, and her companionship. She was a speaker and teacher, too.

All these things she did, and *yet wrote books!* Stories out of real life that struck home and showed us to ourselves as God saw us; and sent us to our knees to talk with him.

And so, in her name I greet you all, and commend this story to you.

Grace Livingston Hill

(This is a condensed version of the foreword Mrs. Hill wrote for her aunt's final book, *An Interrupted Night.*)

1

AFTER SIX YEARS

MRS. BURNHAM stood by the west window of the long, low-ceilinged room, looking out into the grim and desolate twilight. The day had been rainy, the clouds having hung low and gray ever since the early morning, and the faint gleams of crimson and gold with which the west had tried to lighten the scene just at sunset had been quickly overcast, and gray mist was fast enveloping the earth once more.

On the street were to be seen only the hurrying umbrellas of a few belated people and the fast-running water from overcharged gutters by the roadside.

Certainly nothing in the prospect need have held Mrs. Burnham's steady gaze, yet she stood quite still and looked outward with far-reaching eyes that did not seem to see what was spread before them. She was not alone; a small boy in kilts and curls hovered restlessly from her side to the grate, to the south window, to the niche which held the piano, where the firelight made fantastic shadows, back to her side again, ever steadily plying her with questions the while:

"Mamma, isn't it time to light the gas? Mamma, why don't Seraph and Minta come? Mamma, can you see Papa coming down the street? Mamma, isn't it almost time for dinner? Oh, Mamma! won't you please not look out the window anymore and come and amuse your little boy? He's so tired!"

With the last appeal Mrs. Burnham turned, a faint smile appearing on her pale, grave face.

"Is my little boy's tongue tired?" she asked. "Mamma doesn't wonder if it is, you have kept it so busy today."

But she moved from the window, waiting only to draw the curtains close, then crossing the room with the boy by the hand, dropped into an easy chair in front of the fire, which suddenly shot up gleams of light, revealing the fair head of the child as he leaned against her knee. His thoughts had taken a new turn.

"Mamma, tongues don't get tired like hands and feet, do they? And they don't have to be washed and have clothes put on them. Wouldn't it be a funny thing if they had to wear clothes?"

He laughed merrily at the queerness of his own conceit, and the mother smiled on him and played lovingly with the curls about his head; but after a moment it was almost as trying to the child as the position by the window had been, for she fixed her steady gaze on the fire and seemed to go on with thoughts which were apart from him.

To his great satisfaction there was an interruption in the shape of a quick tread down the hall; the door swung open, and Judge Burnham appeared, being greeted by the boy with a shout of delight.

"Glooming in the dark?" he asked as he came forward and touched his lips lightly to his wife's cheek.

"What is the matter with the gas? Young gentleman, why didn't you light the gas for your mother?"

This to the happy boy, who was promptly perched on his shoulder, and, under instructions, flooded the room with soft yellow light. A beautiful room it was; evidences of cultured taste and unlimited means were apparent on every hand. A long room, which might perhaps have looked narrow had not its length been broken into here and there by graceful alcoves and niches; carpeted in tints of green which bordered on the yellow just enough to suggest the sun at its setting; reveling in couches and easy chairs and low rockers, and abounding in books and magazines and the late papers; a perfect home room: not stately nor elegant, only easy and graceful. The gaslight revealed more plainly the pallor of the lady's face, and her husband, who studied her closely for a moment, seemed to notice it.

"Are you well tonight, Ruth? I believe you look paler than ever."

"As well as usual, thank you."

Her voice was low and quiet; composed, rather than cheerful.

"The weather is wretched enough to make people feel miserable," he said, standing with his back to the glowing grate and bringing the boy to a sitting posture on his shoulder; "and you keep housed up altogether too much for your health. Where are the girls?"

"They went to Madame Reno's reception."

"They did!" spoken in a slightly startled tone. "With whom?"

"They went quite alone, Judge Burnham. I was given to understand that such was your pleasure."

The husband laughed slightly.

"Well, hardly my pleasure; I should prefer, of course,

that they have company. I had forgotten that this was the afternoon for the reception. However, I could not have left the office today if I had remembered; and since you did not go, of course I suppose there was nothing left for them but to go alone."

Mrs. Burnham looked up at him half deprecatingly, then gave a significant glance at the deep black of her dress.

"You surely did not expect me to attend the reception, Judge Burnham?" The sentence closed with the rising inflection, yet had hardly the tone of a question.

The judge turned on his heel with a gesture that might have meant importance, opened his mouth as if to speak, then seemed to think better of it. After a moment came this sentence with a half laugh:

"No, I cannot be said to have expected it" (with a marked emphasis on the word "expected"). "What I may have desired is another question. Has this boy been out today?"

The boy answered for himself.

"No, Papa; it has been an ugly east wind all day, and Mamma was afraid of my cough."

"Nonsense! You haven't enough cough to hurt a mosquito. You coddle him altogether too much, Ruth; you will have him as frail as a lily."

"He was quite hoarse this morning, Judge Burnham."

The mother's voice was almost beseeching now, but the husband did not notice it.

"What if he was? A child has to breathe, even when hoarse; and to breathe heated air all day vitiates the blood and weakens the lungs. Get your coat and hat, my boy, and I'll take a run with you on the piazzas; that will be better than nothing."

As he spoke, he placed the little fellow on his feet.

But the child, instead of running, turned anxious eyes on his mother and hesitated.

"I'm afraid it will worry Mamma, and I can stay in the house a whole week if she wants me to."

"Nonsense!" in a sharp tone now. "Get your hat at once; it is not necessary for you to decide these questions."

Then Mrs. Burnham's voice, lower than before, quiet and perfectly controlled, "Don't keep Papa waiting, Erskine; your little coat is in the lower drawer in Papa's dressing room—the gray one, dear."

It was a heavier garment than had been worn as yet this fall, and Judge Burnham laughed at the boy for being bundled up like a little old man when he came back presently robed in the gray coat.

"I suppose you will not come with us," he said, his hand on the doorknob.

Mrs. Burnham shook her head and smiled.

"Not tonight, thank you; I don't like the east wind; it seems to me unusually penetrating."

"That is because you have toasted yourself beside a coal fire all day."

Then the door closed and she was alone. She sat still, staring straight into that coal fire with wide-open, grave eyes; staring away beyond the fire; seeing images that drew no smile to her face; listening the while to the boy's merry voice, broken by an occasional cough, as with rapid feet he tried to keep up with his father's long strides. The dinner bell pealing through the house interrupted the promenaders, and at the same moment a carriage returned the young ladies to their own door. A little later the family gathered in the dining room. If you have read *Ruth Erskine's Crosses* you possibly remember the first family gathering in the Burnham dining room. If you do not, may I ask that you will look up the book and glance over its history that you may have the pleasure of contrasting the two scenes?

A more marked contrast, having to do with the same house and the same people, could hardly be imagined. Yet I call it the same house more from courtesy than reality. The framework was the same, and the old-fashioned ceilings were the same, but the house had been added to and taken from, until Mrs. Ferris, whom you will possibly remember, recognized it no longer as "the old place." An ell had been built on here, and a bay window thrown out there, and a side porch added to the south door, and broad piazzas surrounded the house. Within, windows reaching to the floor, and paint and paper and furniture had so changed the original scene that the dining room of the present, though having the same floor as the one that belonged to the past, had no equal. A lovely dining room, with the table set with every possible modern appointment and served by a trained waiter with exquisite care. To these things Ruth Burnham had been used all her life. But of the three she was really much less fastidious than were the young ladies, Miss Seraph and Miss Minta. What pretty girls they were! Mrs. Burnham, glancing at them across the table, could not help thinking so at this moment. Graceful, well bred, faultlessly dressed in the very extreme of fashionable attire and voluble, after the fashion of society young ladies, over the last excitement of the day.

"And, Papa, that young Pole was there whom we met at the Harpers', you remember. Seraph made quite a sensation promenading with him. I assure you she was the center of all eyes."

"That is not surprising," Judge Burnham said, bestowing an admiring glance on the tall, graceful girl with a wealth of reddish yellow hair arranged with reference to the latest ideas concerning hair, which ideas chanced to be very becoming to her face.

She received her sister's charge and her father's compliment with equal composure.

"It was all because of the Pole, Papa. If I hadn't been honored with his attentions, I should have been lost to view entirely. Minta was the favorite most of the afternoon. That massive Dr. Dorchester, who offers compliments much as an elephant might, assured me that 'your sister is even more brilliant than usual today, and that is unnecessary.'"

The "brilliant" young sister, whose bright eyes flashed fun and fire at once, went off into a series of graceful little giggles over this ponderous compliment.

"Papa, I didn't say a witty thing this afternoon. I was studiedly stupid, and they laughed over the stupidest things as though they were very amusing. I do think people can be the silliest when they get certain ideas into their minds."

"You see what it is to have a reputation, my daughter."

Nothing could be fuller of satisfied pride than Judge Burnham's tones. Indeed, it would not have needed close observation to discover that this father was both fond and proud of his two beautiful daughters. Whether he occasionally remembered the frights they were when he brought home his bride, barely six years ago, is doubtful; men forget so soon and so entirely when it is convenient and satisfactory to do so. Yet, remembering, I am not sure that he would have thought it very surprising. He might have looked upon it as an altogether natural and to-be-expected development from daughters belonging to the Burnham name and blood. Fifteen and seventeen very often give little hint of what twenty-one and twenty-three will be. Mrs. Burnham, however, remembered; recalled often, vividly and in detail, the picture of those two uncouth, ill-dressed, ill-shaped, frightened girls as they came to her in the rag-carpeted front room not quite six years ago. She thought of it tonight; some sudden motion of the head by the beauty, Miss Minta—a motion peculiar to her, extreme in its awkwardness once, softened into an actual charm now—recalled to Mrs. Burnham the hour and the scene in all its embarrassing details, and she did what Judge Burnham in these days never thought of doing in connection with his daughters: She drew a long, low sigh.

The dinner-table talk went on in much the same strain that I have indicated. Who were at the reception; who were conspicuous by their dress or their manner; what the Harpers thought of the entertainment; why the Tremaines were not there; and a dozen other trifles discussed with a zest which belongs only to society lovers. Always the talk was addressed to Papa. Throughout the meal Mrs. Burnham was almost entirely silent, answering the remarks addressed to her by her husband only in quiet monosyllables. Not apparently, however, for any other reason than because the remarks themselves called for no other answer; these being confined almost exclusively to questions as to whether she would have more of this or that delicacy. She gave careful attention to Erskine's wants, but did not talk even with him. This, however, was not noticeable, for the boy had been taught to be almost entirely silent at the table, and he was apparently absorbed in listening to and enjoying his pretty sisters.

Before the second course was concluded, Miss Seraph examined her watch with an exclamation of dismay.

"I did not know it was so late. Papa, we must call on the Forsythes for a moment tonight; Tremaine is to leave town tomorrow morning. I told him we would call. Now, Papa dear, don't frown; you really must be the victim tonight. Horace Wells wanted to call for us, but Minta gave him such a decided negative that he didn't dare to say anything about it to me."

"Well, he is such a bore, Papa. I would much rather have you."

"Thank you," Judge Burnham said with a low bow and an amused smile. "I am not disposed to frown, young ladies; I am quite willing to attend you. I suppose, Ruth, there is no use in asking you to join us?"

Another of those sentences closing with the rising inflection, yet spoken in a tone which makes a negative reply almost a necessity.

"Oh no! thank you. I will remain with Erskine."

Miss Seraph laughed. "What a question, Papa! I should almost as soon expect one of the marble busts in the library to go out with you as Mamma. Oh, Mamma! that reminds me; Dr. Westwood asked today if you were going into a decline, that you were seen so little in society."

"Yes, and I was guilty of the only pun I made this afternoon," chimed in Miss Minta. "I told him you had quite declined society of late; that that was all the decline we knew of."

Judge Burnham did not laugh at this, but bestowed a somewhat sharp, searching look on Ruth's pale face, where a little touch of crimson was glowing now. "Is Joan disabled that she cannot have the care of Erskine?" he asked, and there was a curious sharpness in his voice.

"Joan? Oh no! but I do not choose to leave Erskine with her, you know. Shall we adjourn to the library, Judge Burnham?"

A few moments more and the father and daughters had departed, leaving mother and son alone together.

The boy was very quiet and sweet and loving, exerting all his small powers for the manifest purpose of entertaining his mother; and she smiled on him and allowed herself to be entertained. It was when he was settled in his lace-canopied crib in the lovely pink room which opened out from Ruth's lovely blue one that he put up his small hand and patted her cheek and said: "Dear Mamma, did it worry you to have me go and walk tonight? I couldn't help it, you know; and I'll try not to cough. I wouldn't have gone if I could have helped it."

Mrs. Burnham stooped and kissed the full, sweet lips, and held the caressing hand in a sudden strong grasp; but her voice was quick and firm: "Of course not, my little foolish boy; it is always right to obey Papa. Good night, my darling."

She went away from him at once out into the blue room, and sat down before the open grate, and let her hands drop idly in her lap, and let the great hot tears plash down on the hands. There must be no tears before the large-eyed boy. But there was no one to watch her now.

2

PLANTS THAT HAD BLOSSOMED

NOW you know as well as though I had written a volume to tell you about it that Mrs. Judge Burnham's life had not yet settled into peace. Indeed, it was so very far from peace that her wise-eyed son, child though he was, understood perfectly that his mother was sad hearted and troubled. Yet had Mrs. Burnham been called upon to tell her life story as it had been lived in the past five years, it would have been difficult, perhaps impossible, for her to have explained how she had reached the spot where she now seemed stranded, so insensibly had she drifted thither. You remember with what strong purpose of soul she took up life anew at the bedside of her baby, when God gave him back to her after the last hope had vanished? *She* had by no means forgotten it. Eagerly, I might almost say fiercely, had she tried to live the resolves born in that solemn hour. The sorrowful part of it was that her husband had been through no such experience; had made no such resolves; did not understand his wife; and had no sympathy with the desires that filled her soul. His sorrow had been heavy, his anxiety intense—

or, perhaps, *fierce* would be the best word to describe it—but the moment the strain was over, he was ready to take up life again where they had dropped it so suddenly when their fears came upon them. It perplexed and annoyed him to find that his wife was not ready for this; that a subtle and, to him, utterly inexplicable change had passed over her.

Once more Mrs. Burnham was struggling with the problem with which her married life had begun, namely, "How shall two walk together except they be agreed?" Struggling with it, with immensely greater odds against her than when she first began this divided life.

You will recall the fact that the husband of a few weeks' standing had succeeded, with one pleasant pretext after another, in drawing her away from the prayer meeting, from the Sabbath school, from very regular attendance at church. More than that, he had even drawn her away from her Bible and her daily secret communion with God. Not suddenly, so that it startled her; not consciously, perhaps, on his part; he did not understand these things; how should he? He did not mean to do his wife an injury. But the excuses were so numerous, so plausible; the influence was so steady and so agreeable; it was so hard to break away from his plans, even when they jarred her conscience! The tendency had been always downward, but so slight that it was only dimly felt. Gradually, too, she had been drawn more or less into the whirl of society and found that Mrs. Judge Burnham had a circle of influence which was more fascinating than any phase of fashionable life which had ever been presented to the girl, Ruth Erskine.

Then had come that holy thing into the innermost center of her heart, mother love. You remember how she made all interests, even the Master's, second to this? And you remember, perhaps, how closely the shadows had drawn about her on that evening when the little life almost went out?

Since that time, now nearly five years in the background, there had been kept up a steady struggle between her Christian life and her husband's tastes and plans. Not that she had not tried to explain to him; but the views which could not be explained during those first few months of married life were much harder to explain now. When she tried to tell him that, as a Christian, she must and must not, he confronted her with the statement that she was a Christian when he married her and that she had by no means obtruded her peculiar ideas so offensively then as now. When she tried to make him understand the solemn experience, lived on her knees beside what she had thought was the dying bed of their child, he assured her that that was fanaticism born of fright; and it was beneath a rational woman to make herself disagreeable to her friends because she had been worried, by loss of sleep and the fear of losing her baby, into taking some rash and preposterous vows! And this was quite as much as he understood about it. How could she explain? She ceased to try; and as much as in her lay determined to live her divided life and yet have peace. But peace was not what Judge Burnham was waiting for; he wanted concessions and an agreeable companion always with him in the life which was most to his tastes.

As the days went by, it became apparent that those tastes were almost entirely diverse from his wife's. Indeed, there were hours when the poor wife stood appalled before the thought that they seemed to have no ideas in common anymore. She had not imagined that there could be so many occasions of difference. But if he was in earnest, so was she.

He did not set about winning her as gracefully as he had at first; he had been too successful, during his first attempts, to give him other than a feeling of irritation when he thought of those days and the ease with which he had accomplished what seemed now impossible. I shall have to confess, also, that Ruth's old obstinacy came to her aid, or to her hindrance, as you will; concessions which she could have made she would not; and when she might have resisted gently, gracefully, she often did it sternly, with a determination to carry her point, which was much more evident to her husband than was the reason for carrying it.

Thus the breach between them grew and widened. You are not to understand that they quarreled openly and sharply; both were too well bred for that. They grew cold toward each other, at times almost haughty; they held endless discussions in cold tones, with abundance of ladylike and gentlemanly sarcasm distributed through them; they planned in accordance with individual tastes very often, when each might have planned for the other. Oh! there were constant errors which this poor, blundering Christian wife made. She needed help from the human side, and she had chosen a broken reed to lean upon. Is it any wonder that she made mistakes? Not that they were necessary in view of her position; I am not excusing her; she might even under these circumstances have gone to the Stronghold and received grace sufficient. What I am saying is that she had made life harder for herself than it need have been; in other words, led herself into temptation and was reaping some of the consequences.

Meantime, many outside influences came to Judge Burnham's aid. For one thing, the gay world sought them out in their seclusion; not merely their friends, but the fashionable world itself. The straggling little village to which Mrs. Burnham had been introduced as a bride would not have known itself if it had been shown its own photograph after the lapse of these half-dozen years. The town had received one of those sudden booms common to regions of country near great cities. Two rival railroads had built connecting lines through the place, passing, one of them, within five minutes' walk of Judge Burnham's grounds and making it possible to reach the city in ten minutes instead of two hours. This of itself had established the town on a new basis. Then after the railroads had come speculators—thoughtful businessmen who examined the river rolling quietly through the outskirts of the village with an eye not to the aesthetic, but to business. In a brief space of time, stock companies were formed, and huge factories were rearing their walls toward the sky. Real estate men came, who bought and laid out town lots and advertised them in city markets. And city merchants and lawyers, looking for breathing places for their families, came out to view the land and were charmed. "So quiet," they said, "so rural, so like the country in every respect, and yet within a few minutes of the city."

They invested forthwith, and builders came at their bidding, and great four-storied palaces were reared, and the gas company, and the water works company, and the sewer company, and I know not what other company, followed hard after, and in an incredibly short time every vestige of country life had departed. Men who had toiled until their hairs were white over a few acres, cut them up into town lots, and retired on small fortunes, and thirty trains a day roared in and out to accommodate this sudden influx of city life. And all along the riverbank, for miles out, were rows and rows of tenement houses, built for the factory operatives who had sprung up as if by magic at the first sound of the word *factory*. Judge Burnham's broad acres, which had belonged to the Burnham name for more than half a century and yielded respectable returns from cabbage and potatoes, brought fabulous prices as "city lots." Job Ferris, hands in his pockets, mouth wide open in amazement, stood before two men who were clinching a bargain for a certain knoll, and finally expressed his mind:

"I'm blest if them two city chaps didn't pay more cash down for the wuthless hill, which has nothing but a few trees and grass on it, than I could make out of the field of turnips lying back of it if I was to raise two crops a year for the next fifty years!"

Of course, with all this incoming, Fashion came also. Not a few from the fashionable world were drawn in this direction in the first place from the knowledge of the fact that Judge Burnham's "country seat" was there, and "Ruth Erskine had been so charmed with it that she had gone there immediately on her marriage, instead of taking a house in town, as the judge had supposed she would wish to do."

The lady who used to be Ruth Erskine smiled gravely when she heard this and wondered what her aristocratic acquaintances would have said could they have seen Judge Burnham's "country seat" as it looked when she first came to it. This train of thought always reminded her of his daughters; and then she would go over again their little past since she had known them, with a feeling almost of bewilderment. When was it that these girls, whose beauty she almost felt as though she had created, stepped quietly, even gracefully, yet with an air of assurance—which at times amounted to insolence—beyond her into a life of which they seemed to think she knew nothing? When was it that they began to ignore her suggestions and advice, and go where and when they would, and wear what they would? Often with graceful deference to the father, but with an air of apparent forgetfulness that she belonged to the same household. In the early months of her acquaintance with them their deference to her had been almost painful; it had seemed to her such a pitiful thing that young ladies should appear to have no minds of their own, even in such small matters as how they should dress for dinner in their own home. She had looked forward to the time when they would be able to think and plan for themselves. Now, in looking back, she could not remember just when that time had come, but that it had come was undoubted. In the old days she had been sometimes troubled, sometimes annoyed, because it was always she who was consulted, never the father; on the few occasions when she had sent them to him for decisions, they had been so thoroughly frightened as to vex him almost beyond endurance; and she had therefore abandoned all efforts to force a natural condition of things. Now, as I said, this was strangely changed. Papa was constantly applied to for opinions regarding matters about which he might naturally be supposed to know very little; but as the two bloomed more and more into beauty and prominence in the fashionable world— became leaders, indeed, in their circle—Judge Burnham's long-slumbering paternal pride was nourished with what might almost be called a hothouse growth. He lavished every adornment on them which a fastidious taste could suggest and plenty of money could buy and seemed to enjoy with daily increasing delight their deference to his judgment as to the color of a ribbon or the arrangement of a curl.

The result of their combined tastes was often a picture. Certainly they had blossomed! The lady who had surveyed with satisfaction the result of her hand-iwork on that Sabbath morning when they appeared in the first budding of fashionable attire, looked with a feeling sometimes akin to dismay on the full bloom of the plants she had nurtured. The girls had opinions of their own today and were not timid in expressing them.

Neither were they like their stepmother in their tastes. Ruth Erskine had not been a leader of Fashion, simply because she would not be. Fashion, even in the days before conscience seemed to her to have any-thing to do with it, had not interested her. Nor had she been a blind follower of prevailing styles. Because "they" wore a thing had never been a reason for her wearing it. Neither did she lay aside a style which suited her merely because it had ceased to be "the rage." "I wear what I please," had been a sentence often on the lips of the haughty girl when these questions were being discussed among her friends. "I am perfectly willing that others should wear it or not, as they choose."

Later in life this independence, which in less cul-tured hands might have been somewhat startling, toned down into a refinement that aimed to bestow enough regard to prevailing customs not to be a person of mark in any way in connection with them, and yet to enjoy her individual tastes.

Her stepdaughters, as I have said, were not like her. They were quite willing to be marked in the fashion-able world. The very extreme of the prevailing style was what they aimed to represent, and if they were the first to adopt "something quite new and striking," the more were they pleased.

To be described in a morning paper as having worn the night before at Madame Somebody's reception "the first American representation of a recent Parisian style, which set off their remarkable beauty in a striking manner," etc., would have been a matter of intense disgust to Ruth Erskine; to the Burnham girls it was a pleasure.

Such being the case, you are prepared to understand how constantly they differed even in matters pertaining to costume. And if you understand human nature, you also know that it became natural enough for girls of the type which I think you discover Judge Burnham's daughters to be to say, at first to themselves, then more openly: "Mamma does not understand these things now; she is not in society. Besides, she was always queer; the Tremaines say so."

Other changes had come to Ruth Burnham. Her honored father, after struggling for three years with what was to him poverty in a way which had filled his daughter's heart with exultant pride, and after one year more of such marked business success as to make many watchful businessmen wonder whether, after all, his way had not been the best, and there was such a thing as reward of honor, was suddenly called to that "reward" toward which his heart had tended during these later years. Very triumphant had been that homegoing; hushing the outburst of grief even from the lips of his wife and making Judge Burnham repeat to his heart, unconsciously, the old cry, "Let me die the death of the righteous."

But the desolation the father had left behind him was very great. His daughter mourned for him much more than she would have done in those early months of her married life. With the passing years and the bewildering changes in her own home, she had found herself drawn more and more closely to him.

It was not strange, therefore, that on this evening, as she sat alone in the blue room and let the tears fall unheeded on her clasped hands, the outcry from her lonely heart should be wrung from her with a low moan: "Oh, Father, Father! if you could only have taken me with you."

3

LOGIC AND INTERROGATION POINTS

SUNDAY morning, and a blue sky and sunshine; the rain of the night before quite banished. So were the tears. Mrs. Burnham, presiding at the nine o'clock breakfast table, looked no paler than usual and felt more thankful in her heart than she had for a long time. The reason being that Erskine had coughed but twice during the long night, though the east wind generally set him into a perfect storm of coughing about midnight, and she had lain awake until long after that hour watching for it. The boy was radiant, also, this morning, dressed for church in a deep blue velvet kilt suit, with a white collar and a knot of white velvet ribbon at his throat. The young ladies admitted, when alone, that "Mamma showed exquisite taste in dressing Erskine." The boy was happy over much the same thought that rested his mother's heart. He had slipped his plump little hand lovingly into hers on the way downstairs and questioned, "Did I cough, Mamma?"

"Only two little coughs, my darling; and those were less hoarse than during the day."

Then a gleeful little laugh rang out.

"Goody! I knew I shouldn't; I felt just as sure!"

"Why, darling?"

"Because—this is a secret." And he reached up on tiptoe and whispered in her ear: "I asked Jesus not to let me cough last night and worry you, and he said he wouldn't; and then, of course, I knew he wouldn't."

And then the boy was kissed; long, clinging kisses, which had in them an element of pain. Would he grow up to be a comfort and an inspiration to her, spiritually? Was this lonely mother to have help some-day?

The young ladies were in elegant morning costumes, made in a style which Ruth particularly disliked. Still, she admitted that they looked well in them; that is, as well as persons could look in fashions so devoid of grace as she thought these to be.

"Papa," said Miss Seraph as she helped herself to another muffin, "suppose we go to town to church today?"

"To town? What is the attraction there?"

"Nothing very special; only Patty Hamlin sings at St. Paul's this morning for the first time this season; and I would rather like to hear her."

"I would rather like to see her," declared Miss Minta with a little laugh. "I am never so very particular about hearing her; but if reports are correct, her costume will be something remarkable today; her cousin Harold says it is stunning."

Judge Burnham slightly frowned. "Does young Hamlin frequently indulge in that style of language when conversing with ladies, Daughter?"

"What style? Stunning? Why, dear me! that is a very common word."

"So I think; too common to be agreeable."

"Oh, Papa dear! Don't you go to being a—what is the masculine for prude, I wonder? Seraph and I will be undone if you desert us and get to be overnice."

There was a strong emphasis on the pronoun that referred to him. It marked, even in Judge Burnham's mind, the thought that his daughter wished to emphasize the fact that she considered her stepmother a prude. He felt that she ought to be frowned on for such an insinuation; but she looked so pretty, and her eyes were full of such a winning light, and her voice was so tender over the words "Papa dear," that he merely laughed. After all, she was young; and Ruth was very dignified—always had been. He admired it in her; he would not have her otherwise; but, of course, she should be able to make allowances for girls; and they meant no disrespect; those were not the tones in which disrespect was offered. Nevertheless he smoothed his face into gravity again and said: "I confess I do not like slang, especially when addressed to a lady. I would not allow a young man to say much to me about 'stunning' things if I were you."

"But about St. Paul's, Papa; if we are to go, you must eat your breakfast faster than that; we shall want to take the ten o'clock train." This from Seraph.

"Why, I have no objection, since you young ladies are both of the same mind." His eyes happened to look into Erskine's as he spoke, and he noted the sudden, wistful flash in them; the boy was very fond of the cars, and of the city, and, indeed, of going anywhere with his father.

"Do you want to go to town with us, monkey?"

The child's beautiful face was very bright for a moment, then became grave, and his eyes sought his mother. She was looking steadily at her plate, not even seeming to hear the conversation; so, with a little sigh, he answered: "Not today, Papa, thank you; I will stay with Mamma."

"With Mamma? Well, how do you know but Mamma will come with us?"

"Oh! I know she won't; Mamma won't ride on the cars today."

There was marked emphasis on the word "today." A chorus of laughter greeted him, and the little boy's sensitive face flushed. He looked quickly at his mother to know whether what he had said was a subject for laughter. But she had not laughed. She gave him a rare, sweet smile and said, "Judge Burnham, will you have another cup of coffee?" while Seraph was exclaiming, "The idea!" and Minta added: "You dear little prig! who have you heard say that?"

"Not any more, thank you," said Judge Burnham to his wife. Then: "My boy, what is there wrong about going on the cars to get to church? We cannot walk there, you know."

The child looked puzzled, pained; turned questioning eyes from father to mother, then back to his father's face again. Ruth did not know how to help him without openly showing discourtesy to his father.

"I don't know, Papa," the baby said at last. "I mean I don't know why it is wrong; but I know Mamma thinks so, and that makes it so."

The trio laughed again, and Judge Burnham said, "A loyal disciple certainly; and as good a logician as the majority of overwise people." Then he looked at his watch. "Well, Mrs. Burnham, according to this young champion against error, you will not join the party for St. Paul's? I advise you to do so; I do not believe you are equal to Mr. Beckwith's prosing today. I confess I hail any excuse for getting away."

"Thank you," said Ruth, and she tried to keep her

voice steady, "I do not care to go to St. Paul's today." Then she gave the signal for leaving the table.

An hour later, dressed in deep black, she took her little boy by the hand and went down the wide-flagged street to the handsome new church on the corner that had taken the place of the desolate wooden structure that she had found when she first came. A pretty church it was, outside and in; from the handsome stained-glass windows to the soft Brussels carpet on the floor, there was nothing to offend an aesthetic taste or lead worshipers to St. Paul's for relief. The music, too, if not so artistic as that found in city churches, was cultivated, and the sweet-toned organ was well played. Rested and uplifted by the hymn and prayer, Ruth listened eagerly for the text; she felt so in need of help this morning! It was suggestive: "This beginning of miracles did Jesus in Cana of Galilee, and manifested forth his glory." This heart-burdened woman felt as though almost a miracle was needed to take the jarring elements of her life apart and set them into harmony. No heavy burdens, so-called, but ten thousand little things, or what in our parlance are named little things, weighed down her heart, fettered her lips, filled her with a steadily increasing unrest. If only he would "manifest his glory" by showing his power in her heart and in her home, how blessed it would be!

But, alas for Ruth! she listened in vain for that which would help her troubled soul. The sermon was a well-worded, logical argument in proof of the gen-uineness of miracles! Helpful, perhaps, for those who needed such proof, if there were listeners of that character. She looked about her curiously, wondering if any habitual attendants at that church had doubts in regard to the Bible miracles! The only one who possibly was skeptical in this direction, as in many others, was at this moment listening to the elaborate music in St. Paul's, and Ruth decided that if he were by her side the sermon would not have helped him, for the simple reason that he had not enough interest in the question to care to be helped. As for herself, she had full and abiding faith in the fact that the Christ of Galilee had lavished miracles many and wonderful upon that favored people eighteen hundred years ago; what she wanted was a miracle for her today—in her heart and life.

She went wearily out from the church, bowing coldly to the people on either side, stopping not to exchange other salutations with any; she had held herself almost entirely aloof from the new world which had crowded in on them and hardly more than recognized even old acquaintances who had become her neighbors. The name given to this by many of her old friends was pride; for the sudden rise of property all through that region had made Judge Burnham, who had been one of the rich men of the city before that time, almost fabulously wealthy in the eyes of the community; and Ruth Erskine had always been "a proud girl," they said; "what else could they expect of Mrs. Judge Burnham?" But Ruth's secret heart knew that the knowledge of the fact that her choice of friends would be so entirely opposed to Judge Burnham's tastes and desires troubled her, and she held back the issue by retiring behind her mourning robes.

Also, she knew that this condition of things must soon be changed. Her very mourning was one of the elements of courteous contention, if I may use such a phrase, between her husband and herself. She had not wanted to wrap herself in black for her father. It was true that she felt desolate enough to describe it to the world by the heaviest crêpe it could furnish her; but, lingering over the deathbed scene, remembering the lighting-up of her father's face as earth receded from him and heaven appeared, remembering the smile of unearthly radiance with which he finally "entered in," it had not seemed fitting that she, a Christian, looking forward to the same entrance one day, should array herself in gloom and mourn as those who had no bright side to their sorrow. "If it were wise or kind to make such distinctions," she had said to her sister Susan, "I could wish that society would arrange that those whose friends have gone without a gleam of light into an unknown future should wear the crêpe and bombazine, and let us, who saw the reflection of the glory, signalize it by wearing dazzling white."

But Judge Burnham was emphatically of another mind. He not only approved of the custom of wearing mourning, but he believed that it was a mark of disrespect to the dead not to do so; and for his wife to appear in any other than the deepest crêpe for her father would, he argued, be translated by his acquaintances into a story that there was some hardness between her father and her husband in their business relations; and in this way she would actually, if she persisted in her strange ideas, bring disrespect upon the living husband as well as the dead father.

So Ruth did not persist; she let her mourning be of the deepest, gloomiest sort; and, truth to tell, was glad to hide her swollen eyes and quivering lips behind the heavy crêpe veil.

But as the months passed it was made apparent that no more emphatic had been Judge Burnham's desire to have the mourning worn than it was to have it laid aside at the earliest possible moment. One year, he argued, was as long as they ever wore mourning for a parent;

and poor Ruth, who had always hated to do things for no better reason than because "they" did them, found herself shrinking from this change with a pertinacity which sometimes half frightened her. She could have summoned her Christian faith to the ordeal of facing the customs of society and worn no mourning at all; that would have been a tribute to the fact that her father had gone where they did not mourn; but to elect a certain day and hour in which to appear before the watching world and say by one's style of dress, "Now my days of mourning are over; my father has been remembered long enough; I am ready for the gay world once more——" from this she shrank so persistently and dwelt on the disagreeable side of it so much that she was growing morbid over it.

This was the way matters stood on this Sabbath day, now nearly two years since her father had exchanged worlds; and Ruth, knowing that she must sooner or later yield, still hugged her mourning robes and shielded herself with them from the society which she despised.

Erskine danced merrily by her side, glad that the restraints of the church service were over and he could have his mamma quite to himself.

He and Ruth ate their luncheon alone; the party from the city could hardy arrive before the three o'clock train and would probably lunch in some fashionable downtown resort.

Despite the mother's earnest effort to put self in the background and make the Sabbath a delight to her little boy, she but half succeeded. The afternoon wore away somewhat heavily to the restless child, and he broke into the midst of Ruth's Bible story with this irrelevant question:

"Mamma, what makes it wicked to ride in the steam cars on Sunday?"

Ruth winced. She had no desire to enter into minute explanations with this wise-eyed child. Still he must be answered.

"My darling, don't you remember Mamma told you how the poor men who have to make the cars go cannot have any Sunday—any time to go to church, and read the Bible, and learn about God and heaven?"

"I know, Mamma; but the cars go all the same, and the men have to work, and so why can't we ride on them? They wouldn't have to work any harder because we went along."

The old questions, always confronting those who try to step ever so gently on higher ground than that occupied by the masses; the specious argument which is in the mouths of rum sellers and wine bibbers and grown-up Sabbath breakers all the world over. Surely not so astute a question, after all, since this baby presents it evolved from his own baby mind. Ruth could not help smiling faintly as she answered:

"That is true, my boy, but if we kept on taking the Sunday rides because others did and because the train would go anyway, whether we went or not, how many people do you suppose we would by our actions set to thinking that perhaps it was wrong? And how long do you suppose it would be before the thinking which we set in motion would help to change the customs of Sunday trains?"

Deep questions, these, for a boy who had barely reached the dignity of five years. But he had grown up thus far at his mother's knee and was accustomed to the grave discussion of all sorts of questions. The look in his eyes at that moment showed that he comprehended, at least in a measure, Ruth's meaning. He changed the line of argument: "Papa rides on them."

Ruth could hardly suppress a visible shiver. Here was the sore spot in her life thrusting its sharp point into her very soul, making it at times seem almost impossible for her to be loyal to her husband and true to her child. How was a wife to answer such a sentence as that?

"People think differently about these things, Erskine. You know Mamma told you we have to think about them, and pray about them, and decide what we shall do, not what somebody else shall do."

"Did Papa pray about this and decide?"

"Won't Mamma's little boy leave Papa and everybody else out of the question just now, except his own little conscience, and tell me what he thinks is right?"

"Well, Mamma, tell me this: When I get to be a man, will I think as you do or as Papa does, do you s'pose?"

He will never understand, perhaps, this innocent boy, how his questions probed the mother's heart. "God only knows," she could not help murmuring and arose quickly with a pretense of rearranging the fire, but in reality to hide the starting tears.

"I mean, Mamma," he hastened to explain in a half-apologetic tone, dimly aware that he had in some way grieved his mother, "I only mean I will be a man, you know; and do gentlemen think things are right that sometimes ladies think are wrong?"

"Erskine," Mrs. Burnham said, resuming her seat and taking both the chubby hands into her own, "tell me this: Did God write one Bible for gentlemen and another for ladies?"

"Why, no, Mamma."

"Then let me find a verse in his Bible about this for us to read."

The place was found, and the slow, sweet voice of the child repeated after his mother the earnest words: "'If thou turn away thy foot from the Sabbath, from doing thy pleasure on my holy day, and call the Sabbath a delight, the holy of the Lord, honorable, and shalt honor him, not doing thine own ways, nor finding thine own pleasure, nor speaking thine own words; then shalt thou delight thyself in the Lord, and I will cause thee to ride upon the high places of the earth, and feed thee with the heritage of Jacob thy father: for the mouth of the Lord hath spoken it.'"

The reading closed with a long-drawn, thoughtful sigh on the child's part, but the young logician kept his deductions to himself, for at that moment the party from the city heralded their return with the sound of merry laughter.

4

UNWELCOME RESPONSIBILITIES

MRS. BURNHAM was entertaining a caller in her own room; very few people were allowed the privilege of coming up to that lovely blue room which was the special refuge of the mistress of the house. The daughters understood as by a sort of instinct that they were expected not to intrude here, and the judge himself always tapped lightly before entering; only Erskine was privileged to come when he would.

But the caller was a special one, even Mrs. Dr. Dennis, and the two who posed before the world as dignified matrons were, when alone, "Ruth" and "Marion" still. They did not meet very often. Marion, as the wife of a busy pastor, had, of course, her many cares and her almost overwhelming social duties; and Ruth had fallen out of the habit of going even among these old friends very often. But the old, warm friendship burned strongly, and as often as they met they assured each other, with equal earnestness and sincerity of purpose, that the time between their calls should never be so long again. Still it always was, and there was always, consequently, a great deal to say.

So it was, after Marion had been talking eagerly for nearly an hour, that she suddenly broke off in the midst of a sentence with the words: "But I really have not time to tell you that; it is a long story, and I have stayed now longer than I meant. Ruth, dear, I came to see you for a special purpose today. I couldn't have come merely for pleasure, because we are unusually busy with church work this month; but I knew I was so old and tried a friend that I might venture to say a word to you about that pretty daughter of yours: the younger one, I think she is."

Ruth's face flushed a little; the skeletons in her home—if skeletons they really were—were never brought out for other eyes to behold. Marion Dennis saw the flush and hastened her speech.

"Of course I run the risk of meddling with what is none of my business; but Mr. Dennis said you would forgive because of the motive and because it was I myself. He has great faith in our old friendship, you see. It is nothing very formidable; only to ask you if you know, if Judge Burnham knows, just what sort of person that young Hamlin is with whom Minta rides and walks occasionally? Not quite that, either; for of course you don't know; but my errand is simply to put you on your guard in time."

It was very gently put; Minta's walks and rides with the young man in question were much more than "occasional."

"I know nothing whatever about him," Ruth hastened to say, "and I never heard Judge Burnham mention his name; but I supposed, of course, he knew the sort of person with whom he allowed his daughter to associate."

"Well, perhaps not; indeed, Mr. Dennis says it is more than probable, engrossed in business as he is, and looking upon his daughters as children—all men do that, until they are old enough to be grandmothers—he has probably not given the matter a thought; and, besides, Mr. Dennis says businessmen really know comparatively little about the men with whom they associate intimately. It is so different with a minister, you know; he is the confidential friend of so many people and carries the burdens of others so continually that he learns to keep his eyes very wide open. Moreover, he came very near having a serious lesson of his own, you remember; and that has made him more watchful over all young daughters, I think."

"I remember your anxiety about Gracie. How did you manage it, Marion?"

There was a wistful note in Mrs. Burnham's voice, which did not escape her caller's watchful ear; it said, almost as plainly as words could have done, "I thought I knew all about managing, but these girls of mine are beyond my control, and I don't in the least know how to set to work to right anything which may be wrong."

"Oh! I didn't do much of the managing. I couldn't, you know; she would resent that, naturally. I don't think we ought to expect from young people much that is against nature. Her father had to do the talking; I kept myself as far as possible in the background, only helping with my wits, of course, where I could. It wasn't a formidable thing, though it looked so for a time. Gracie gave me credit for having more to do with it than I had; that was natural, too; but she recovered, and I think she has not thanked me for anything more earnestly than she has for 'helping save' her, as she expressed it, though, as I tell you, I did very little. She went to New York, you remember, and our blessed little Flossy, with her sweet, wise ways, came to the rescue. Then she met Ralph, and that helped immensely. 'The expulsive power of a new affection.' I often think of that sentence in one of our old textbooks. It works magic with the human heart, Ruth."

"How is Gracie?" Mrs. Burnham asked, shading her eyes with her hand and trying to keep a longing sense of envy from appearing in her voice; Mrs. Dennis had very happy relations with her stepdaughter. If Ruth's experiences could only have been like hers!

"Oh! she is well; and happy, and busy. Their letters would fairly make you tired, Ruth, they have so many schemes for their young men and women; and carry them out, too. It is no daydreaming. Gracie, with her young Ralph, not yet a year old, to look after and her housekeeping duties besides, accomplishes more for the cause of Christ in the world than dozens of young wives do, all about her, who are boarding and have not a care in life."

Mrs. Burnham sighed. How much she had meant to accomplish for the cause of Christ in the world! How had it happened that, so young and with so much leisure, she had become stranded?

"But about this young man," said Mrs. Dennis, stealing a glance at her watch and looking startled. "It seems he is very dissipated; drinks even to intoxication, and that quite frequently. Mr. Dennis says he has means of knowing that he is carried helpless to his room three nights out of a week."

"Is it possible?" Ruth said in disgust. She had always shrunk from people who drank liquor to excess, as belonging to a lower order of beings.

"Yes, it is true. Of course Mr. Dennis took pains to verify his fears before he mentioned them; not that it is anything unusual in a society man, but then—"

"Isn't it unusual? You cannot mean that it is common among young men of the higher classes?"

"Oh! you dear child, I am sorry to say it is. The higher classes are the worse off, perhaps, if there is any 'worse' to the scourge; but you know—"

Ruth interrupted her again, glancing around instinctively to see if her child was within hearing as she said fiercely, almost under her breath:

"Erskine shall never taste the stuff!"

("She looked around," said Mrs. Dennis afterward, in detailing this conversation to her husband, "with almost the eyes of a tigress suddenly brought in contact with a danger which menaced her babies.")

"Then you will have to be on the alert, my dear friend; it is none too early to begin with your 'line upon line,' for I do assure you I am appalled at the waste of manhood which is going on in secret. I could almost pray, if I had sons, that I might bury them in their babyhood, lest I should live to see them stagger home.

"But perhaps that is not the worst of this young man's habits. He is a gambler, as well as a hard drinker; almost a professional one; at least he uses his skill to decoy others, it is said. But even that is not what I came to tell you this morning, my dear Ruth."

She drew her chair closer, and her voice sank lower while she told rapidly, with as few words as possible, a story of sin which made the matron's face pale with righteous indignation.

"Now you know," Mrs. Dennis said, gathering her wraps about her, "why I dropped everything this morning and came out to you. I knew, of course, that Judge Burnham must be quite ignorant of facts and that he must be told. And now I have barely time to make my train; I expected to have taken the one that went up an hour ago."

Left alone, Mrs. Burnham gave herself up to painful musings. How should she plan so as to save her husband's daughter from a possible experience of misery? If the relations between herself and that daughter had been what she had planned they should be, the way would have been easy. But now, when she had, in a way which she did not understand, been put to one side, been plainly shown each day that her influence was less than nothing, what was there she could do?

"Her father had to do the talking," Marion had said with a bright smile and a wifely pride in the reference to her husband, and Ruth would not for the world have hinted to another that this father was not in such hearty sympathy with her views as to talk in accordance with them.

Not even Marion, intimate as they had been, should ever know from words of hers that there were any shadows in her married life. Yet all the same she knew that Judge Burnham did not think or feel as she did about many things. Still, in this thing, of course, there would of necessity be agreement. The man was not a fit acquaintance for a lady, and the probability was that her husband would know how to put an end to the acquaintance; she need not borrow trouble over that. But she shrank from telling him. There were so many things nowadays to jar his nerves and spoil their home talks, it seemed a pity to add yet another. Of course he would be terribly angry. What father would not? Perhaps he would even blame her. Yet surely he could see how little influence she had. Her musings were broken in upon by the sound of a clear voice in the hall below:

"Kate, tell Miss Seraph if she inquiries for me that I went to ride with Mr. Hamlin and that I will meet her at Chester's at three o'clock."

"Yes'm," returned Kate, and Mrs. Burnham arose in haste and pulled the bell cord. Kate appeared almost immediately in answer.

"Kate, has Miss Minta gone out?"

"No, ma'am, not yet; she's just going; the gentleman is waiting in the parlor."

"Ask her to step in here a moment, please, before she goes."

Ten minutes passed, and then Minta's tap was answered. She swept into the room—a beautiful girl in her perfect-fitting dress of dark-blue cloth, more plainly made than was usual to her and consequently more becoming. The glow of youth and health was on her cheek, and as her bright eyes rested with a sort of astonished inquiry on her mother, they said almost as plainly as words could have done, "To what am I indebted for such unusual attention?" It was true enough, though Mrs. Burnham did not realize, that she had set, years ago, an excellent example for this indifference on the part of her stepdaughters by being herself quite indifferent in regard to their movements, so long as they were well dressed and well behaved.

"Minta," she began hurriedly, "I want to speak with you a moment."

"So Kate told me. Please be as expeditious as is convenient; I have kept my escort waiting an unreasonably long time now."

"But I do not know that what I have to say can be told in a few minutes."

She was visibly embarrassed and did not know how to commence her appeal. Miss Minta elevated her eyebrows.

"Indeed," she said, the tone being a trifle supercilious; "then perhaps it would be as well to reserve it for a more convenient hour, since I am already being waited for."

"But, Minta, it is about that I wish to speak; I mean about your escort; it is Mr. Hamlin, is it not? I do not think—that is, I feel quite sure that your father would object to your riding with him."

A perfectly foolish way in which to present the subject; no one could realize this better than she did herself. The flush on the young lady's face was brilliant, and her eyes flashed indignation.

"I should like to understand you if I can," she said haughtily. "Pray, why should my father suddenly object to my riding with a gentleman with whom I have ridden every other day for a month or more? And if he objects, pray why does he not tell me so, instead of—"

She paused suddenly, for Ruth was regarding her now with a face calculated to subdue insolence in speech at least. Her voice was less excited than before, but colder.

"I beg your pardon; I was unduly excited in my anxiety and made an unfortunate beginning. I mean I have recently heard that about Mr. Hamlin which leads me to think that your father, when he hears of it, will have very serious objections to your continuing his acquaintance, and in his absence I considered it my duty to warn you."

"And I am expected to be grateful, I suppose? Am I to be treated to a dish of this precious gossip, whatever it is?"

The girl was very angry; there was clearly some reason beside the silly pride of being interfered with which flushed her cheek and made her eyes flash like coals of fire. When Ruth thought it over in more quiet moments she recognized this fact; but now she, too, was angry. What right had this impudent girl, who had belonged only to the backwoods until she brought her forward, to characterize the conversation between Mrs. Dennis and herself as gossip? Still her voice was low and controlled. There had been that trait about Ruth Erskine, the girl: She had never allowed herself to speak with raised voice or rapid enunciation, even when her anger reached a white heat; she had not lost so much power of self-control.

"I have nothing to say beyond the fact that I have such information concerning the person in question as should make a young lady grateful for a warning, presented in time," she said, looking steadily at the angry girl. "What your father may see fit to tell you, I cannot say; but I certainly shall not trouble with details."

"You are very kind and very considerate; I am sure I ought to go on my knees to thank you; meantime, if you have nothing further to offer, I suppose I may relieve the impatience of my friend who is waiting."

I can give you the words, but the tone in which they were spoken and the indescribable manner that accompanied them you must imagine. It was the most decided rebellion against her interference which Ruth had ever received. Even at that moment she thought of Mrs. Dennis and her daughter Grace. What would she have said or done under circumstances like these? Would such circumstances ever have arisen between them?

Probably not. I, a quiet outsider, answer for her; because, in the second place, the two girls were essentially different; but also because in the first place, Marion had gone to her daughter from her knees;

gone with a loving, tender, sympathetic heart, and with infinite skill and patience had touched the sore point between them.

Miss Minta's hand was on the doorknob when her mother spoke again, still in that low, self-restrained voice:

"I have nothing further to say, but I trust we understand each other; the world looks upon me as your proper guardian in company with your father, however unreasonable or silly that world may be; and therefore, in his absence I must exercise my judgment and ask you to suspend further rides with the gentleman until you have your father's sanction; I shall not, of course, interfere further than that."

The hand was still on the doorknob, but its owner turned and gave a look of mingled rage and amazement at her stepmother.

"Do you take me for a complete idiot?"

This was all she said, and as the question did not seem to require an answer, it received none. The door opened and closed with a very decided bang, and less than five minutes afterward, Ruth, standing at the front window, saw the blue-robed maiden carefully lifted into the handsome carriage that stood in waiting, and the costly wrappings were tucked carefully about her by young Mr. Hamlin.

5

"FOREWARNED" AND "FOREARMED"

WHEN Judge Burnham let himself into his own hall that afternoon, it was not his wife who was waiting to meet him but his daughter Minta, attired faultlessly, with a studied regard to his expressed tastes, even her hair done in just the way he liked best; but with traces of tears on her beautiful face and a sort of childlike quiver on her pretty chin which was inexpressibly bewitching to him.

She reached up both arms, put them around his neck, and held up lovely, pouting lips for a kiss, then suddenly drew back and burst into tears.

"What in the world does all this mean?" Judge Burnham asked, dropping into one of the large easy chairs that abounded in the wide hall and drawing his daughter to his side, where she nestled her head in his beard and cried gently and becomingly. "I didn't know such bright eyes as yours ever had time for showers. Who has been bruising my gay little blossom?" and he drew her face away from its hiding place and kissed her tenderly.

"I beg your pardon, Papa, I did not mean to cry; I

know you don't like tears, but I have been so hurt today I could not help it."

"What is it, little sensitive plant? How did you manage to have such troublesome feelings, to be hurt if the east wind blows on them?" And for a moment the father went back curiously to the years that seemed almost centuries away, so great had been the changes they had wrought; the years when these girls of his had been overgrown, ill-shapen, country frights; and he reflected complacently that their appearance then was evidently only an embryo condition, and that the real Burnham blood "told" at last. "In childhood they were like their mother," he told himself complacently; "but as they develop they prove themselves to be true Burnhams."

"Papa," the rosy lips close to his and the voice quivering a little, "I don't like to be talked about."

"To be talked about? Of course not; but I am afraid it is something that you will have to endure, my little lady. Such a pretty face as yours must of necessity attract attention."

"Ah! but, Papa, I don't mean that." He laughed at the sudden sparkle in her eyes, but he did not understand how much a part of her life it had become to be admired and flattered; nor, understanding it, was he well enough versed in the human heart to realize what an element of danger it was.

"I mean, Papa, being gossiped about ill-naturedly, and blamed for little merry things which have no harm in them. You can't think how dreadful it is to a girl to feel that she is being talked over in that way by people who dislike her."

Judge Burnham's face gloomed instantly.

"Of what are you speaking, my daughter? What persons choose to demean themselves by gossiping about you? I should suppose your father's name was sufficient to protect you."

"In society, of course, Papa, I am not afraid of what can be said, because there is nothing to say; but don't you know how two women can get together and pick a girl to pieces if they choose? That Mrs. Dennis has been here all the morning closeted with Mamma, and I can just imagine how she opened her great big eyes, and wrinkled her forehead, and shook her head, and looked owlish and hateful. She was an old maid, Papa, before Dr. Dennis married her, and she hasn't any sympathy with girls, and never had. The Armitages say she made the life of Dr. Dennis's daughter perfectly miserable, and they were really thankful when she married. And now she must come poking herself into my affairs. Do you think I need stand anything of that kind, Papa?"

"Of course not. Mrs. Dennis has nothing whatever to do with our affairs, and her sense of propriety should teach her better than to interfere, even if there were anything for her to try to manage." Nothing could be haughtier than Judge Burnham's tones; his daughter had touched him at a sensitive point. He had always, in a silent way, resented Mrs. Dennis's influence over his wife and had felt more than once that he owed some of the discomforts of his life to the unreasonable degree of deference which Ruth had for the opinions of both Dr. and Mrs. Dennis; he was in no mood to bear patiently with any word from them.

Nevertheless, he tried to speak reasonably to his pretty daughter.

"But, my dear little girl, why should you suppose that the ladies spent their time in discussing you? Certainly there could be no object in their doing so. Isn't that a little bit of imagining on your part?"

"Oh! no, indeed; I have only too good reason to believe that I was the subject of their talk. Mrs. Dennis was no sooner out of the house than Mamma sent for me and read me such a lecture as I never received before; and it was so unlike her that I knew the source from which it came even before she mentioned her caller's name."

Judge Burnham drew himself to an upright posture, and the frown on his face would have frightened Erskine.

"I do not understand, Minta; your mamma lectured you! What was the subject? And she told you that she had been advised to such a course of action by her friend Mrs. Dennis! That is hardly possible; Mrs. Burnham is a lady!"

"Not exactly that, Papa, but Mrs. Dennis had been telling her some tiresome story about Mr. Hamlin— I am sure I don't know what—and Mamma said something about it being very improper in you to allow me to ride with him and said I should not. And he was waiting for me at that moment to ride. I told her that as you had never objected to my going out with him, of course I had no excuse to offer this morning, so I went as usual; but all the afternoon she has been cold and disagreeable; I know she will tell you a long story about me; and I cannot bear to have you think naughty things of me, Papa; and, oh, dear! I am so miserable. If Mamma didn't dislike Seraph and me so much!"

It was put into words at last, this tacit disagreement between the mistress and the daughters, which had been growing up so long and which Judge Burnham had dimly felt, rather than realized. He was man enough to wince under it; he did not like to hear his wife referred to in that manner.

"You should not speak in that way of your mamma, Minta; she is my wife, remember, and it is foolish to say that she dislikes you and Seraph; there could be no possible reason for such a feeling."

The beauty sat erect now and looked full into her father's face with those witching eyes. She must make the most of this opportunity, for on her skillful handling of the subject might hang much of her future happiness, as she, poor silly girl, viewed happiness.

"Papa, you don't know. You are very wise and learned, and Seraph and I are just as proud of you as we can be; but there are some things you don't understand so well as we two girls. Don't you know Mamma is jealous of us? She wants you all to herself; she cannot bear to share you with two young ladies. It was well enough when we were children and she could send us away when she didn't want us in the room; but in these late years it is different, and she— she doesn't mean to dislike us, perhaps, but she almost can't help it, especially when she is influenced in that way by her friend Mrs. Dennis. And don't you see what a temptation it is to find fault with us about every little thing—our taste and our company and everything? Why, she even sets Erskine against us! He told us yesterday that he could not stay up in our room because Mamma would not like it."

She had stated the truth, this truthful young lady, but she had omitted to add what Erskine had—that Mamma would not like it, because the clock was striking the hour when he took his daily lesson in her room.

Judge Burnham sat appalled before these revelations. Was his daughter right? Was this the explanation of his wife's coldness and dignity and persistent thwarting of his plans and tastes? Was she even trying to turn the heart of his little son away from him?

Minta, watching his face, eager over his possible thoughts, suddenly put her lovely golden head on his shoulder in a caressing way, and let her white and shapely fingers toy with the beard that was now plentifully streaked with gray, and said in a sweet and plaintive tone:

"Isn't it hard, Papa, when you are our very own father and we have only you?"

Had they had even him before this mother, whose place the young lady was now trying to undermine, came into his home? Was it possible that neither of them thought of the years of absolute neglect which that father had given them until the new wife roused him, rather forced him, to his duty?

I really do not think that Judge Burnham thought of it; men are very queer—some men; he had let that unpleasant memory drop out of his life as much as possible. These were his daughters now, admired, sought after; even the famous criminal lawyer congratulated him occasionally on their exceeding beauty and grace. Why should he go back into that awkward past? As for Minta, she remembered it well; she was one of those who do not easily forget; on occasion she could have confronted her father with a story which would have made his face burn with shame; but she had, just now, a point to carry; something must be done to forestall her stepmother's story, whatever it was, and leave her free to follow what she thought was happiness. It was not all pride, the motive which pressed her forward; there was an underlying influence that came from a meaner nature than hers, and which held possession of her heart.

They were interrupted; Erskine danced through

the hall, sprang toward his father for the caress which he always claimed, and then delivered his message.

"Papa, Mamma would like to see you in her room before dinner, if you please, and if you have time."

It was a most inopportune moment for Ruth's summons. The meaning look—half appeal, half terror—which Minta gave him, did not escape the judge's notice. He looked stern enough to have charged a jury in a case of high crime, but his manner was kindness itself to Minta.

"I must go," he said, rising and putting her from him gently; "Erskine, tell your mamma I will be there in a moment"; and as the child sped away, he added: "And, Minta, my daughter, I hope to hear no more of this nonsense, born of oversensitive nerves. It is quite natural for you to have them. The Burnhams, unfortunately, are a sensitive race. But your mamma has not the disposition which you imagine. From the very first of my intimate acquaintance with her, she took the deepest interest in you two girls."

His daughter sighed and looked steadily at him with those appealing eyes.

"As for this gossip, whatever it is," he made haste to say, "of course we desire and will tolerate no interference from Mrs. Dennis or from any outsider. You may rest assured that no other commands than mine need trouble your conscience very much."

So saying he ran upstairs to the blue room. Ruth was waiting for him with a feverish nervousness, which was of itself calculated to make her words ill chosen. She felt the importance of speaking at once, for from her standpoint this was serious business; and yet she shrank from it with a degree of timidity which humiliated her. Judge Burnham came toward her with his accustomed greeting and spoke carelessly:

"Erskine said you wanted to see me here. What can I do for your comfort?"

"Nothing for me, thank you; I wanted to speak to you about Minta. I have heard that today which I am afraid will give you great anxiety. Judge Burnham, do you know this young Hamlin with whom she rides and walks?"

"Oh yes! I know him as the grandson of one of the most famous lawyers we ever had in the state. Why do you ask? Has he been so unfortunate as to come under the ban of your displeasure?"

He spoke in a bantering tone, with an evident intention of turning her warning, whatever it was, into ridicule. It did not serve to quiet her nerves.

"I was aware that you knew his grandfather," she said with heightened color. "It was about the young man himself that I was inquiring. I have not the honor of his acquaintance, so my personal feelings are not at stake. What I want is simply to inquire whether you are sure he is the sort of person you desire as an associate for your daughter?"

"As to that, I am not so foolish as to suppose that my daughter is going to gauge all her friendships to suit my individual tastes. The young man is well enough, I presume."

"Then I am afraid you are mistaken. Really, Judge Burnham, I wish you would give me your attention a few minutes. I have that to tell you which is certainly not pleasant for me to repeat but which I think you ought to hear."

For by this time the judge had passed on into his dressing room and was giving attention to his toilet.

"I can hear you," he called, with his face partly submerged in water; "proceed with your testimony."

It was not a comfortable way in which to talk; it did

not lessen his wife's discomfort. She made her words as few and emphatic as possible. By the time she had finished, he emerged again from his dressing room.

"Where did you hear this precious tale?" he questioned, employed, meanwhile, in polishing his shapely fingernails.

Ruth felt annoyed, because with her reply came a deep flush that mounted even to her forehead. She knew by a sort of instinct that he did not like her informant.

"Mrs. Dennis came to see me this morning for the express purpose of warning us of danger," she replied.

"Very kind, certainly."

There was that in the tone which was extremely irritating to excited nerves. The utmost his wife could do was to hold herself in silence until he should choose to speak again.

"Your friend Mrs. Dennis must be kept exceedingly busy if she takes the affairs of all the young people of other parishes on her hands, as well as attending to her own. Isn't she aware that we are out of the pale of her ministrations?"

"Judge Burnham, I did not suppose this subject would impress you as being simply food for ridicule. Mrs. Dennis's sole motive was the desire to do as she would be done by."

"I would not question a lady's motives, but her sources of information may often be at fault. There is a great deal of gossip afloat in this wicked world that true ladies would do well to avoid. I am sorry Mrs. Dennis thought it necessary to pour any of this into my wife's ears."

"I hardly know how to answer you."

Ruth's voice was dropping into a still lower key, and she was struggling hard to maintain her self-control.

"You receive this warning in such a different spirit from what I supposed you would! Is it possible that you do not understand Dr. and Mrs. Dennis well enough to know that they would be sure of their facts before they came to me with them? Do you forget that Dr. Dennis is a clergyman, and that his profession gives him opportunities of knowing what may be unknown to others?"

Judge Burnham shrugged his handsome shoulders in a very exasperating way.

"I knew," he said, "that clergymen were rather given, as a class, to prying into other people's affairs; but I was not aware that they managed a moral sewerage, through which all the scum of the city had to pass. Upon my word, I should want to introduce patent 'traps' into my house to keep out the odor."

And now I am sure you will almost forgive Mrs. Burnham for being exceedingly angry. Up to this moment she had occupied her favorite seat in the room—a low rocker by the south window—but she now arose and, moving a step or two forward, confronted her husband with steady gaze as she spoke: "Judge Burnham, I beg you to remember that you are speaking to your wife about the honored pastor of her dead father and that she will not tolerate such language concerning him even from you."

6

DRIFTING

A MORE obtuse man than Judge Burnham was could have easily seen that he had gone too far. He did plainly see it; he had had no intention of hurting his wife's feelings, but his haughty pride had risen against the thought that Dr. and Mrs. Dennis had been discussing his family affairs and had even drawn his wife into the discussion. This, coupled with his talk with Minta, had made him unreasonably angry. He chose, however, to pass it all off lightly.

He came toward his wife, speaking as nearly as possible in his natural tone: "My dear Ruth, don't go into heroics; sit down and be comfortable. I beg your pardon if I hurt your feelings; I had no intention of doing so; it was your own remark which suggested my unfortunate illustration. Now, let us understand each other. As to the share which your friend Mrs. Dennis had in this matter, I am grateful for her intentions, but not for the fact. She should not have burdened you with anything of the kind. If her husband, as a gentleman, has any information which he thinks I ought to receive, let him communicate with me, not send his wife to gossip with you; pardon the word, my dear, I meant no offense. In point of fact, I attach exceedingly slight importance to the information. Young Hamlin is not absolutely perfect, I suppose; few men are; but he belongs to an excellent family and cannot have gotten very far astray without my knowing it. The truth is that clergymen live very secluded lives—up in the clouds, most of the time; or, if you like the idea better, above the clouds, in air so pure that they cannot understand matters which are of the earth, earthy, and are very poor judges of what is going on. They are continually given to making molehills into mountains. Their ideas of business are simply absurd; might do for the angels, but not for mortals. Now, I hope I have given your friend a sufficiently exalted character and also shown you the folly of depending too much on his opinions."

Ruth had suffered herself to be replaced in her chair and had so far overcome her excitement that she could answer this half-bantering, half-serious statement with quiet voice and manner.

"I did not present opinions to you, Judge Burnham, but facts which can easily be proven; for I gave you names and dates. I was so far impressed with the importance of them that I did what I could to hold your daughter away from association with the villain, at least until you should know the facts, even to giving what was equivalent to a command; but it proved of no avail."

"I am sorry to hear that." Judge Burnham's manner was grave now. "Minta should not have disregarded your expressed wishes. As to commands, we must both remember that the girls are too old to be treated as children; being legally of age, they of course have a right to choose their society; but I trust they are too entirely ladies to often disregard your courteously expressed wishes. Perhaps we must, in this case, make allowance for undue excitement under great provocation. If I am correctly impressed as to family affairs, you do not often notice what callers the young ladies have, and as, in my absence, they are shut up to the necessity of receiving their friends and paying their visits quite alone, perhaps it is not strange that they should sometimes make unfortunate selections, nor, indeed, that they should wince under sudden commands."

"Judge Burnham, am I to understand that you disapprove of having your daughters receive calls and pay visits without me? Are you not aware that they decidedly prefer my absence; that, indeed, they would resent any attempts of this kind as an infringement on their liberties?"

Judge Burnham changed the graceful position which he had assumed before her, with one arm resting on the mantel and his handsome eyes fixed on her. He ran his fingers through his hair in a wary way, walked to the window and looked out a moment, then turned back and spoke as one bored to death.

"My dear wife, it is worse than useless for you and me to talk all these things over; I have no disposition to be a household tyrant toward either my wife or my daughters. I would have them all enjoy themselves in their own way, if they can. That you have chosen a peculiar way, in holding yourself almost entirely aloof from the society which naturally seeks us, is, of course, far from agreeable to me, nor can I fail to see that it does not contribute materially to your happiness.

"That the girls have become accustomed to receiving their friends and visiting them without you is certainly not strange; what else would you have them do? Having perforce educated them to this course it would be unreasonable to expect them to look for, or desire, any other way. You surely know that you have sought your own interests and left them to seek theirs until naturally enough they have done so; and after all, Ruth—it is just as well that we should remember it—you really are not their mother, you know.

"However, as to society, there is no occasion for grievance on that score. I am still in a condition to be glad of having your company; whenever you shall choose to come out of your recluse state, I promise you society enough, and of a perfectly unobjectionable stamp. And now, cannot we dismiss all disagreeable subjects and go down to dinner? I think it must be at least ten minutes since the bell rang."

So this was the end of her honest and painful effort to serve her husband's daughter!

"After all, you are not their mother, you know."

Yes, she knew it only too well. Did she not know by the loving, clinging kisses of her own boy what it was to be really a mother? Yet what had she not done for those girls? Had they known any other mother than herself? There was certainly in their hearts no idol enthroned into whose place she had rudely come. Minta, at least, did not remember her mother at all; and Seraph, but as a dim and flitting shadow. Why could not these girls have given to her the loyalty and attention which a mother has a right to expect at the hands of grown-up daughters? Alas for Ruth that she did not realize, even yet, how surely some of the fault was her own! She had taken hold of duty, it is true, with stern hands and ordered their outward lives in a fashion that she had supposed would mean fairyland to them; but she had been content with this. Into their hearts as a central force, moved under the impulse of love, she had never tried to come. She had not planned to have the sweets of fairyland intoxicate them until their brains were too dizzy to look beyond the new, dazzling outward life; but, left amid its glories to revel for themselves, what wonder that just this thing happened? I want to emphasize the thought just here that the grave mistake in this stepmother's life, even now, was in not recognizing and accepting the fact that part of the fault for this condition of things was her own. She did not recognize it; it seemed to her that she had done her duty—full measure, pressed down, and, indeed, sometimes running over—by these girls. Had she not given up the joy of that first year of married life alone with one's husband, for their sakes? Had she not pressed their claims firmly and triumphantly, even against his will? And how had they rewarded her for it?

She could have wept bitter tears, but she did not; instead, she went down with her husband to the waiting dinner, and took her place at the head of the table, and listened as usual to the chatter of a hundred gay nothings. Apparently, Minta had recovered her spirits; she said not a word to her stepmother, unless her flashing eyes spoke for her; their language was: "You and I have measured weapons, and, if I mistake not, mine are the keenest. There is no use for you to try to poison my father against me; I secured the first hearing." To her father she was all smiles and winning ways, with a pretty little undertone air of gratitude which sat most gracefully upon her.

However, to do Judge Burnham's good sense strict justice, he was by no means so much at ease about the young man who had created this breeze as he chose to have his wife think. Not that he credited a third of the story that had come to him. He had much faith in the statements which he had made that clergymen knew little or nothing about the doings of this world; and he should quite expect that what was considered fair enough in the business world might look black to Dr. Dennis. Knowing nothing, practically, of the lives of ministers of the gospel, being unaware to what extent they are trusted by all sorts of people with inner histories, how, indeed, the faithful pastor becomes, in time, almost a receptacle for all that is sorrowful or terrible in the circle of his influence, and by this very process grows keen sighted, he actually believed that, of all persons, a clergyman was the one most likely to be imposed upon. Still, this young man must be looked after; he admitted to himself that it was true enough that he knew a great deal about his grandfather and very little about him. He must make some inquiries speedily.

Pending these, he detained Minta in the library as the others were passing out.

"See here, Daughter, about this young Hamlin; there is nothing of any importance between you and him, I hope?"

"Why, Papa, how should there be? I have only known him a little over two months."

"True; and that is not time enough in which to develop a special interest, eh?" and he smiled on her pleasantly. "I think you cannot be very seriously inclined, and I should not want you to be, you know, with a stranger."

"Of course not, Papa; nor without telling you about it either. The girls in our set are very fond of riding with him because he drives such magnificent horses, and he seems to be fond of inviting me, and of course I like it ever so much, because it is such fun to have all the girls envy me."

"That is the whole story, is it? Very well; I do not find it alarming. But, see here, Daughter, you must make all due allowance for your mamma. It is genuine regard for your interests that actuates her—nothing else. She was brought up by a father who had exceedingly strict—not to say narrow—views about some things, and of course his opinions color all her feelings; as a true lady, you must respect her views, and even her prejudices, as much as you can."

The beautiful lips pouted a little, a very little, not unbecomingly, and made answer, "Very well, Papa, I'll try; but I should think she might trust me to you." The last pronoun pronounced very lovingly.

The father, fed by pride which was the chief source of his inner strength, smiled on her again and dismissed the subject with the mental determination to look carefully, nevertheless, into this young man's history without further delay. But he did not; the next was an unusually busy day with him in his office, and at the home dinner table Seraph announced in the course of conversation that the Hamlins were to leave that evening for a six weeks' trip to California. The girls had coaxed their cousin into taking them; and beside, his uncle wanted him to go on some business, they believed; but he did not like the idea; he said the whole thing was a "bore."

"And I agree with him," Minta said with a merry little laugh. "I'm ever so sorry to have him go; he is the only real good company there is among the gentlemen; he is so witty, and beside, he is going to send his horses into the country while he is gone."

Her father laughed, asked her if she was certain which she was the more sorry about, the absence of the gentleman or of his horses; and then he told himself that for his part he was glad young Hamlin was going; it would give him time to look up that story more quietly and see if it had any foundation. It was just as well to be careful about these things, though in six weeks, probably, his pretty daughter would have transferred her interest, which was evidently slight, to some other young gentleman who drove fast horses.

As for Mrs. Burnham, she felt indignant that the name which had come to be associated in her mind with disgrace should be so freely on the lips of father and daughter.

And to show you how little progress she was really making in her Christian life during these days, I shall have to confess to you that she said, as she went up the stairs that night, that she at least had done her duty and should not interfere again; no, not if she saw his daughter on the very verge of ruin. She had made an earnest effort and failed. No one certainly could blame her now for holding utterly aloof from it all.

I do not think she meant all this. I think she would have put out her hand promptly enough to interfere if she had seen danger and known which way to move the hand. But that she could harbor these thoughts, even when action was not required, will show you (if you are one of those who desire to be conformed to His image) how feeble the flame was which burned in this poor heart.

⚊┼ ┼⚊

It was Sunday afternoon again, nearly two weeks after the domestic ruffle which Mrs. Dennis's visit had occasioned. Mrs. Burnham was in her own room with Erskine—a thing which was becoming habitual with her on Sunday afternoons. Indeed, the Sabbath had become a day of special trial to this much-tried woman. Very gradually, so that she had not realized it at first, a state of things had crept into her own house of which she utterly disapproved yet found herself powerless to control. Attendance at church had not been a very regular thing of late years, even on her own part. Much of the time either the weather or Erskine's state of health made it necessary, in his mother's estimation, for him to remain at home; and she had made it a matter of principle to remain with him, both in order that his childhood memories of the Sabbath might be sweetly associated with her and because she had no one in her employ with whom she was willing to leave a child.

The young ladies were often so weary of a Sabbath—by reason of the late hours of the night before—as to unfit them for church, even had there been any desire on their part to attend. When they had new suits, or when they could arrange for a trip to the city, or when a stranger was to preach in their church, they could be depended upon for morning service. But circumstances with them were as likely to prove unfavorable as otherwise. And as the days passed, their rule might almost be said to be to lounge through the morning in wrappers and slippers and go to the city for a sacred concert at night, if that could be satisfactorily managed.

Gradually a new program crept into the afternoon. At first it was a messenger from the choir leader, petitioning for special assistance from Seraph, whose voice was worthy of her name when she chose to use it, but who by no means chose to sing often in church. As for being trammeled by a regular engagement there, her father agreed with her that such positions "would better be left for those who had to earn their own living." Yet when emergencies arose, she would graciously lend her aid; and the choir leader, a very aristocratic young man, was, if the truth be told, quite fond of creating emergencies and of being his own messenger to petition. The leading tenor was also very willing to join in the plea, and when they were successful and there was a specially difficult number to render, what more natural than that they should drop in during the afternoon and try their voices together? This being found necessary several times, it was thereby discovered that it would be agreeable to practice occasionally of a Sunday afternoon in order to be ready for future contingencies, and from singing to chatting, the transition was easy enough.

One afternoon the choir leader brought young Sherman with him to hear Miss Burnham render a solo and prove what the leader had said—that her voice ran clearer on the high notes than did the celebrated Miss Hamlin's, though she was a professional singer. And young Sherman enjoyed the afternoon and came again, at first with a flimsy excuse of some sort, and then boldly, with no excuse at all. And he brought Mr. Snowden with him on occasion, who, if not musically inclined, was "away from all his friends and dreadfully bored with Sundays, and it was only a charity to help him get through with the hours." Oh! I cannot explain how it all was. Mrs. Burnham understood only this: If the young ladies had said, "We are going to have a social gathering on Sunday afternoons in our parlors," Judge Burnham would have opened his eyes wide and reminded them that the customs of the locality in which they lived were not in accordance with such gatherings, and on the whole, it would not be wise; and it could have been controlled. But no such thing had been said, or even hinted. It had all come about by the most natural processes. And yet the fact was apparent, at least to the eyes of the lady of the house, that their parlors on Sunday afternoons had become lounging places not only for young but also middle-aged gentlemen and occasionally ladies. Thus much by way of explanation; it is of one particular Sunday afternoon that I wish to tell you.

7

THE UNEXPECTED

TO JUDGE from the sound, a much merrier time than usual was being enjoyed in the parlors: snatches of music not suggestive of worship, mingled with gay laughter, floated up to Mrs. Burnham over the broad staircase, serving to make Erskine restless and inattentive. He stopped frequently in the midst of his Bible lesson to ask: "Whose voice was that? What do you suppose they laughed at then? Mamma, do you think that they will sing that song in church tonight?" and dozens of kindred questions. It was painfully evident that the sounds of mirth below stairs were more congenial to his ear than the Bible story above.

Finally came a gentle tap on their closed door, and the trim young girl whose duty it was to be always in readiness to do errands for everybody entered softly:

"Judge Burnham would like to have Master Erskine come downstairs for a little while, if you please."

The little boy gave a merry spring from the hassock where he was kneeling beside his mother, but she put out a detaining hand.

"Do you know for what, Kate?"

"No, ma'am; he only said, 'Tell Master Erskine to come to his papa in the back parlor.'"

"Mamma, I must go, mustn't I? You said I must always go when Papa called."

There was a little quivering of the boy's chin; he was evidently much afraid that the promised pleasure would be spoiled. Still his mother had no answer for him.

"Who are in the parlors, Kate?"

"Indeed, I don't know, ma'am; Dr. Whately is there, and Mr. Henderson, and I don't know who else; the music room seemed to be quite full."

Mrs. Burnham repressed a little sigh which she did not wish Kate to hear and turned to the appealing eyes of her boy.

"Certainly you will go, dear, when Papa calls; but you will come back as soon as you can, will you not? Remember Mamma is all alone."

He gave his gay little promise, too impatient to be gone to stand still while the tender fingers brushed his curls, too much a baby to detect the pathos in those words, "All alone."

Kate was not deaf to them, however; she gave a swift, searching look at her mistress, and reported it in the cook's room that evening as her opinion that there were "a good many goings-on in this house that Mrs. Burnham did not like, and she didn't believe she was altogether happy, with all her grand ways." And if Mrs. Burnham, careful as she believes herself to be, does not guard her sighs and her telltale face more carefully in the future, before she is aware, the kitchen of her own home not only but many another kitchen will gossip about her household skeletons.

She set the door wide open after Erskine had left her, feeling painfully the loneliness, made so much more deep by the constant hum of conversation which went on below, and putting steadily back the inclination to bury her face in her hands and cry in order to strain her ears to hear, if possible, what was being said or done to entertain Erskine. It was the first time her shielding care of him on the Sabbath had been interfered with. She had wondered sometimes over it, for his father was very fond of him and delighted to hear his steady chatter whenever he had opportunity to "entertain Papa." Now the interruption had come in the shape of a call to the parlor to join in the entertainment, or, at least, the amusement of Sunday guests. Ruth Erskine's father, long years before he was a Christian, had frowned upon any attempt to commonize the Sabbath day. He might read his newspapers, or, if an intricate question was before him, consult his great tomes of law, but he did those things decorously, in the quiet of his own study, and had not been in the habit of inviting even his most intimate friends to share his home on the Sabbath. Ruth had taken it for granted, without giving the matter any thought, that all gentlemen of culture were alike in this respect, and her husband's utter indifference to the recent innovations had been a revelation and an added pain to her.

She saw very little, indeed, of Judge Burnham on Sundays now, and this, too, had been so gradual a process that she had not roused to it until it was an accomplished fact.

Under one pretext and another he was constantly excusing himself from accompanying her to morning service, and his afternoons were generally spent in the library, where he indulged himself in stray fragments from the current books and magazines, doing, he said, the only light reading for which his busy life gave him time. Ruth, who used to join him there, until she found that his constant interruptions and outbursts of laughter over Erskine's quaint remarks made it impossible for her to hold the child's attention to his Bible lesson, had herself set the fashion of going with the child to her room. At first she intended it for but a little while, but on her return to the library, she so frequently of late found her husband absent in the parlors or walking about his grounds that she had dropped the custom of seeking him and remained all the afternoon in her room. He used to lounge in a little before dinner and have a frolic with Erskine, but for several Sundays he had been engaged in the parlor and then had gone to town for an evening service, leaving his wife to absolute solitude after Erskine was sleeping.

Occasionally Judge Burnham pronounced himself to be too indolent for the city; and then this husband and wife, who grew farther apart every day, got through a long evening as best they could. Judge Burnham, doing a little fragmentary reading for himself and a good deal of yawning and sleeping, was generally the one to propose that they retire early, as he had a hard week before him. A good deal of this was genuine fatigue, for it was true that as he grew older he absorbed himself more and more in business, and Ruth heard it from many outside sources that her husband had taken very high rank in his profession.

She mourned much over these wasted hours, but the time seemed to have gone by when she could do other than mourn. She had offered once to read aloud to him and reminded him that he used to like her reading, but he answered laughingly, yet with that undertone of sarcasm which she now heard so much, that that was before such a great gulf fixed itself between their tastes, that he believed each had grown incapable of comprehending the other's literary tastes; and she had felt too wounded to press the question, so they had continued in their separate ways.

A second interruption came to her on this afternoon. Kate began, "Dr. Whately's compliments, and if it was agreeable, he would like to see her downstairs a few minutes."

Ruth's face flushed deeply. She was at a loss to understand the meaning of this. Dr. Whately was not an old friend; he was a comparatively new acquaintance, even of her husband. She had met him by accident one evening in the library and had taken an instant dislike to his face and manner. Since that time his calls had been made almost entirely on Sabbaths. There could not be a shadow of professional excuse for his message, for although he was an M.D., Judge Burnham had laughingly remarked but a few days ago that he wore his title as an ornament rather than a badge of usefulness and had added that he did not believe the man had sufficient energy ever to become a success in his profession. So, although her husband occasionally told Ruth that she grew paler every day and ought to consult a physician, certainly Dr. Whately would not be the chosen one.

Had the gentleman observed her habitual absence from the parlor on Sundays and boldly determined to oblige her to receive him? The thought made the lady so indignant that she almost sent an unexplained refusal. Still, he was her husband's guest. What ought she to do?

"Kate," she asked abruptly of the girl, who was watching her curiously, "is Judge Burnham in the parlor?"

"Yes'm; it was he who sent the message."

"I thought you said it was Dr. Whately. Tell me exactly what was said, please."

"Why, Judge Burnham came to the door and spoke to me, and said: 'Take Dr. Whately's compliments to Mrs. Burnham, and say to her that he would like to see her in the parlor.' That is every word, ma'am."

"Then you may ask Judge Burnham if he will be kind enough to come to my room for a moment; I wish to speak with him."

He came immediately, and with an air of concern. Was anything wrong? Was she not feeling well? She waited for no preliminaries.

"Judge Burnham, will you tell me why Dr. Whately wishes to see me at this time?"

"Why, really, my dear, I am not sure that I can supply a motive beyond the obvious one that it is natural enough for a gentleman to ask to see the lady of the house. Does it strike you as such an unusual proceeding?"

"Very unusual, indeed. Dr. Whately has been here sufficiently often, I should suppose, to have discovered that I do not receive calls on Sunday."

"Upon my word, my dear Ruth, I do not believe it has ever dawned upon him; he is not of that development. I imagine it just occurred to him that the polite thing to do would be to ask for the privilege of paying his respects to Mrs. Burnham, and he immediately did so."

"Then could you not have done me the favor of explaining that this is not the day on which I receive guests?"

Her manner may have been cold and haughty; indeed, on reflection, I am sure it was. She felt very much hurt; whether the guest had intended it as an embarrassment or not, surely her husband was sufficiently conversant with her views to have shielded her had he chosen to do so. She remembered the days in which, thinking very differently from her, he would still have guarded her carefully from any annoyance that he could. I don't think he remembered them just then. He thought only that his wife was making herself very disagreeable about a small matter. He had a way of lifting his eyebrows and smiling slightly behind his gray mustache. It always irritated Ruth, that smile. It seemed to say to her, "You have put yourself in a very foolish position, and the only thing left for you to do is to make your way out of it as gracefully as possible." He gave her at this moment that peculiarly irritating look and smile.

"Indeed, Mrs. Burnham, that is expecting almost too much of me. I do not pretend to be able to explain why my wife should consider it a sin to come down to her own parlor for a moment and say a courteous good-afternoon to a friend of her husband's with whom he has been conversing for the last half hour. The peculiar lens necessary for discovering the heinousness of an action like that, even when done on the Sabbath day, has been by nature denied me, and I must not be expected to rise to the height of understanding it. If you have ever so slight a headache, or are indisposed in any way, I will bear your regrets with what grace I can, but to enter into the metaphysics of the matter, without a direct message from you, ought hardly to be expected of a sinner like myself."

He expected her to turn from him in cold indignation, and he proposed to laugh at her a little— good-naturedly, of course—and then to descend the stairs and say to his guest that Mrs. Burnham was not feeling equal to seeing her friends that afternoon and begged that the gentleman would kindly excuse her.

He knew just how to do it, politely, cordially, and was not troubled by any conscience whatever in the matter. But his wife's nerves were too sore. She turned from him, indeed, and her face burned. But there were other feelings beside indignation, though enough of that element was present, or she would not have done what she did next.

"I beg your pardon," she said; "I did not know I was putting too heavy a strain on your courtesy and kindness; I will give my message in person."

She swept past him like a queen and went swiftly down the stairs. He followed her, still smiling, the uppermost feeling in his mind being one of curiosity as to what she would do. His wife was a lady. What could she do except to receive her caller graciously, of course?

What she did was to move with the manner of a princess down the long parlor to the alcove where Dr. Whately stood by the piano. She acknowledged the presence of the younger guests only by a dignified inclination of the head as she went. Her voice was never clearer nor colder than when she said:

"Dr. Whately, my husband wishes me to say to you in person that it is not my custom to receive my friends on the Sabbath day. It is a matter which is very well understood among all my personal friends. Should you care to call on me at any time during the week, it will be my pleasure to meet you, but I am sure you will excuse me today."

Judge Burnham was directly behind her, veiling his astonishment and chagrin as a well-trained man of the world can do. Ruth turned at once from the amazed, not to say embarrassed, Dr. Whately and addressed her husband:

"Judge Burnham, will you have the kindness to

excuse Erskine from the parlor? I would like to take
him with me to my room."

"Certainly, my dear," the gentleman said, his voice
perfectly quiet; and he called Erskine in his usual tone,
kissed him graciously, and told him Mamma wanted
him now, then attended his wife quite to the door and
held it open for her to pass, bowing as she did so, and
he was never more angry in his life.

Poor Mrs. Burnham! Of all that embarrassed company below stairs—and I will do them the justice of
saying that they were embarrassed—I think none
were so much to be pitied as the angry and humiliated
woman alone in her room, struggling with her passion
and her sense of shame and trying to appear as usual
before the excited boy, who was by no means ready to
leave the parlors and come back to the quiet of this
upper world.

"Why could I not have stayed, Mamma? Papa liked
to have me there, and they all did, I think. Seraph
kissed me and said it was nice to have a little boy to
put her arm around. And I was good; I didn't talk at
all, only when somebody asked me something.
Mamma, I wish I could go back just for a little while.
It is lonesome up here, and I wanted to hear them sing.
Seraph was just going to sing when you came in."

Poor mother! If this baby could only have given her
kisses just then instead of coaxing to go away from her,
it would have helped. It was an afternoon to remember. Poor Ruth was destined to realize fully that one
may shut the doors with emphasis against tangible
guests and yet receive a whole troop of miscreants into
one's heart who make havoc with holy time. As the
storm of passion subsided, she had that hardest of all
feelings to contend with—self-reproach. Reason, being allowed once more to take her seat, accused this

Christian woman of having yielded, not to conscience, but to rage. Possessed with this controlling
influence she had offered to her husband's guest what
he would consider an insult; she had not only given
him an utterly false idea of religion and its power over
the human heart, but she had offended her husband,
and justly. Perhaps this was really the worst sting in
Ruth's sore heart; that her husband would be justified
in utterly condemning her action also. And herein lay
the real point of the sting, for at heart this woman was
loyal. She knew the unbelieving husband would attribute the action to her religion, and persist in doing so,
when she realized only too well that it was the
outburst of a moment's ungovernable indignation.

8

SLIPPERY GROUND

IN POINT of fact that was just what Judge Burnham did. The moment he had closed the door after his wife, he went straight to Dr. Whately and held out his hand with a winning smile, and said, in tones distinct enough to be heard throughout the room: "My friend, I hope you will allow me to apologize for what must appear unaccountable treatment. The fact is, my dear fellow, when religious fanaticism gets hold of a woman she is really powerless before it and, I verily believe, is not accountable for her acts. I am the one to blame; since I understand how completely this strange feeling sways my wife I should not have delivered your message today. I beg you will pardon her and understand that no discourtesy was intended; it would have been the same if you had been a foreign ambassador."

It was the best he could do for his wife's reputation. He knew this, and he did it well; and Dr. Whately, being a gentleman in society, at least accepted the apology with what grace he could muster, and outward calm was restored.

But there were outgrowths from the storm, as there always are when passion holds sway for even so short a time over the human heart. It had been said publicly, as Ruth had feared it would be, that religion must bear the blame for this unladylike action, and people talked, as people will. Those least acquainted said: "What a pity it was that so fine a woman as Mrs. Burnham should be so completely under the control of fanatical ideas; they should think Judge Burnham would almost fear for her reason!" Others of them, less charitable, said it was all very well for the judge to smooth over this little domestic hurricane, and he did it gracefully, but they believed, if the truth were told, that the poor fellow was used to them; and at any rate, if that was the style, when it came their turn to marry, they hoped they might be delivered from a religious termagant, for, in their opinion, they were the worst kind.

The young ladies talked the matter over with their father and said, "Poor Papa," and kissed him; and said they were "so sorry" for him and that he managed it all beautifully; that they felt at first as though they should sink through the floor or, at least, wished that they could, but he was so gentle and so courteous, and they were so proud of him that they really almost forgot to be frightened and ashamed, because of their pride. And he felt himself to be a martyr who had borne himself very well indeed under persecution.

Still, all this did not serve to make his indignation against his wife one whit less fierce. Nor did it serve to help her when, with flushed cheeks and eyes that were red with weeping, she turned to him frankly the first moment that they were alone and said, "Judge Burnham, I owe you an apology for this afternoon's experience; I beg you will forgive me; I ought not to have done what I did."

Judge Burnham was engaged in removing his dress coat and putting himself into his dressing gown; he had not seen his wife since the afternoon. She had sent a message by Kate to the effect that she would like to be excused from dinner as she had a severe headache; and the judge had bowed in reply and had not gone at once to see what he could do for the headache, as his courtesy had always heretofore led him to do. Also, he had gone with his daughters and some of their friends to the city for the evening, merely going through the form of sending Kate to ask if there was anything he could do for Mrs. Burnham's comfort before departing. So now, although it was nearly eleven o'clock, Ruth was waiting for him and had met him with the sentence I have given you. He waited to adjust the collar of the handsome dressing gown to his mind before he answered, speaking slowly, coldly, "I should think there could not be two opinions about that."

"No," said Ruth, controlling an almost irresistible impulse to burst into tears; "I should not expect anyone to think it right, and I am very sorry that I annoyed you."

"As to that," said the judge, putting his feet into some bright slippers that were waiting for them, "I must bear my own annoyances as best I can; but I regret that a friend of mine should be rudely treated in my own house at the hands of my wife. It was not, of course, what could have been possibly foreseen."

Wasn't it a graceful way of telling her that no one could have foreseen that she would lay aside her ladyhood and descend to rudeness?

Silence for a few minutes, and then the gentleman

made what he intended to be a gracious statement: "However, I made what apologies I could for you and am glad indeed that the spell, whatever it was, is over, and you are returned to reasonable ground once more."

Then was poor Ruth dismayed. Had her attempt at undoing the mischief of the day been construed into a concession of principle for the future? She must explain, at the risk of being misunderstood.

"Judge Burnham, I am afraid I have not made my meaning quite clear. I regret exceedingly the manner of my explanation today, but not the explanation. That is, it will be necessary for Dr. Whately, or any other person who wishes to call on me, to understand that I do not receive on the Sabbath; but I know that I could and should have made it apparent in some other way and in a different spirit."

"Mrs. Burnham, suppose we dismiss the subject and retire. We are not likely to agree, however long we may discuss it, and for myself, I confess that I am weary of the whole thing."

And this was the outcome of her attempt at reconciliation.

A polite gentleman's displeasure can be manifested in unmistakable ways, even toward his wife. The very extreme punctiliousness with which her husband attended to the minutest detail of whatever pertained to her marked his cold dignity. There were none of the little carelessnesses which are sometimes permitted, even enjoyed, where there is perfect familiarity and perfect confidence.

Still, as the days passed, the episode was not without its fruits, which were apparently healthful. The lady of the house struggled to show that she confessed herself, in a sense, in the wrong, and was willing to do all she could in the way of concession. She came to the parlor now each evening of her own will, not waiting to be summoned there by callers who inquired for her. This was a comfort, even to the young ladies; for there were always among the guests those whom they considered it a bore to entertain; and to have Mamma in the front parlor to do the honors, leaving them free to saunter into the back parlor or the music room with favorite ones, was as it should be, in their estimation.

Judge Burnham viewed the change with satisfied eyes and was by no means unmindful when his wife made her entrance in a dark blue dress, instead of the black which she had so long worn. He complimented her on her appearance—took a rose from the vase and pushed it through the meshes of soft lace which she wore. During the evening he watched her with satisfied eyes as she entertained his friends and, not having any marked interest in Dr. Whately, confessed to himself that he didn't know but he "owed the fellow a vote of thanks, if this was to be the result of his impudence." For in his secret heart Judge Burnham thought that it was bordering on impudence for a comparative stranger to send a special request to his wife to receive him socially on Sunday afternoon out there in the country, where Sunday calling was the exception and not the rule.

The next thing was a dinner party; not a general and massive affair, but a little gathering of Judge Burnham's special friends, whom he delighted to honor; such a gathering as had not been in the house since Ruth's father went away. And Judge Burnham, watching his wife, who exerted all her powers of entertainment, and overhearing one of the judges of the Supreme Court pronounce her "an unusually brilliant woman," assured himself that he could endure the momentary embarrassment of that Sunday afternoon proceeding very well indeed and was heartily glad that it had occurred; that probably Ruth needed something of the sort to bring her to her senses. She was certainly a queen among women. Now that the ice was fairly broken, society should see what a jewel he had in his keeping.

So, altogether, it was a much-mollified and very well-contented husband who lounged among the cushions in the library after the fatigues of the successful evening were over and watched his wife while she unfastened and placed in water the flowers which she had worn and which he had himself selected and arranged for her.

"They were very becoming," he said; "I had no idea that simple flowers would fit your style so well; but there was a charming contrast which just suited me. Your style is rather regal, you know, and I have always thought of diamonds in connection with it. Ruth, you were quite like your old self tonight, the self I used to admire before I appropriated it; only more matronly, of course, as became your years, and more beautiful, really. I think you ought to be grateful, my dear. Few women of your age retain their youthful beauty as you have done."

Ruth laughed in a pleased way. She cared extremely little for youthful beauty, but she did care for her husband's admiration; and it had been so long since he had expressed any that she felt her cheeks flush under the spell of his words. She was glad over having pleased him. She told herself that she ought to have done these things before; that she had been selfish and hateful; that it was perfectly natural for a man to desire to receive his friends in his own house; and that if she had realized how much he desired it, she would certainly not have waited so long.

She put herself into a white wrapper that was almost more becoming than her dinner dress and came and sat beside him. And he reached for the tassels of her wrapper and toyed with them, tossing them back and forth on her hand; and finally, possessing himself of the hand, bent the shapely fingers back and forth at his will while he chatted with her about a dozen careless nothings, as they had not chatted together actually for years; and Ruth's eyes were bright and her heart was glad. She began to see her way out of the mazes of discomfort which had surrounded her. She was somewhat astonished that the door of comfort seemed opening to her by way of the society which she had so much dreaded. But why not, after all? She had enjoyed the gathering herself; she knew how to entertain people, and she knew how to manage her domestic concerns so that that portion of the entertainment could always be a success. What had she been thinking about, all these months, not to take matters into her own hands and bring to their house, with her invitations, such people as she would enjoy meeting? Scarcely a name on the list which her husband had given her but it was an honor to entertain.

Suddenly, into the midst of her complacent musings, came her husband's voice:

"By the way, Ruth, have the girls spoken to you about having a social gathering here, chiefly of young people?"

"Well, they will," in response to Ruth's negative reply; "they have had it in mind for some time and have been quite patient, I must say, for girls. I told them that of course while the lady of the house was in mourning, anything very general in the way of company would be in bad taste; but that as soon as we could comfortably bring it to pass, they should be gratified. We must do something especially attractive, I suppose, in return for their long waiting. I believe I will have Tarrant's band come out; that would be unique and save an immense amount of trouble. What is your judgment about the floors? Would you rather have the carpets taken up or simply covered for the occasion? If you are proposing to make any changes as to carpets in the spring, perhaps they might as well be taken up now as at any time."

To all of which Ruth listened with great sinking of heart; she was evidently supposed to be making ready for a dancing party, and on a somewhat magnificent scale. She waived the question of carpet and launched another.

"Judge Burnham, don't you remember that I do not endorse dancing parties?"

Her manner was timid, almost appealing, as one would speak who dreaded exceedingly to broach an unpleasant theme; but the master of the house neither frowned nor growled; instead, he laughed:

"I don't remember; there were so many things that you didn't endorse, you know. How could I be expected to bear them all in mind? However, the girls will not require you to endorse their amusement, I fancy; they need you to play the lady hospitable to their guests. You need not be bored for more than an hour or so, you know."

Poor puzzled lady of the house, trying to walk two opposite ways at the same time! She glanced at the handsome man who was resting so luxuriously among his cushions, then looked down at her prisoned hand and sighed; the way was certainly bewildering.

She tried again.

"But, Judge Burnham, you do not understand; how can I receive guests to my house and provide for them an entertainment of which I do not in the least approve? Would there not be something dishonorable in that? Besides, I would be placing myself in a false light before the world."

"But, my dear, you are not expected to approve. If one had to approve of all the silliness which goes on under one's own roof, even during the giving of a dinner party, it would be a tremendous strain on one's common sense. You cannot manage society, my queen, however much you may grace it; and I am willing to own that few women can match you in that."

She knew he had answered her with sophistry and with flattery. Never mind, she would put the question in another form:

"Judge Burnham, ought one to offer to others that which one believes may be a temptation and a snare? If I think there is actually harm in dancing, ought I to have anything to do with providing it as an amusement?"

"You needn't," with a good-natured laugh; "I will engage the band and have the house put in proper array, and you may retire to your room with the first strain of gay music. I will even engage to lock you in, if you fear the temptation to indulge will be too much for you."

What reply could she make to this, other than to look steadily at him with sorrowful eyes? When his laugh was over, he added, still good-naturedly and with a careless yawn:

"What about dancing, my dear; wherein lies the

harm? Did you ever post me? If so, I have fallen from grace. I can not recall a single argument for your side. Do you want to refresh yourself by putting me through a course?"

How instantly was Mrs. Burnham carried back to the days when she was Ruth Erskine; to Marion's dingy little upper room in the boardinghouse; to Eurie Mitchell's merry words, half on one side of the question, half on the other; to Flossy Shipley's sweet young face. How earnestly, Bibles in hand, had they discussed this very question years ago! How easily, in the light of Flossy Shipley's Bible verses, they had settled it! She could seem to hear Marion's voice again saying: "Girls, we have spent our strength vainly. It is our privilege to get up higher; to look at all these things from the mount whereon God will let us stand, if we want to climb." And they had climbed, those girls; they were standing, at least so far as these trying little beginnings of religious experience were concerned, away above them, troubled by them no more. All save herself; here was she, after the lapse of years, sitting beside the one with whom she had spent the most of them, and he had gotten no farther than the old worn-out query, "Wherein lies the harm?" The solemn question was, Did this tell something of her own spiritual state?

9

THE OLD QUESTION

SHE looked at him curiously, half pitifully. How should she answer the question in a line with his moral development? Her look seemed to amuse and interest him.

"What is it, my dear? Do you feel in your soul that I haven't enough mental calibre to comprehend the argument? I'll promise to give the full powers of my mind to it if you will try me."

"Judge Burnham, do you want your daughters to be on such familiar terms with the gentlemen whom they meet in society as the dance necessitates? Is your knowledge of human nature such as to make this desirable, or even wise?"

He frowned slightly, and his voice was graver than it had been.

"That sounds badly, Ruth; it sounds as though you might be unpleasantly familiar with a human nature that is below you. You must have learned that sort of talk from people who think they must always drag the slums into argument."

"I am not talking about the class of people who are

recognized in society as 'the slums.' I mean the Tracys, the Markams, and Mr. Peterson. Do you want your daughters to dance with them?"

"Oh! as to that, there are degrees, even in good society; I shall want the girls to exercise common sense, of course, or, failing in that, I will exercise it for them. I do not advocate indiscriminate dancing; if that is what you are after, you are entirely welcome to the admission."

"Yet the girls dance with these persons; I have heard them mention their names in such a connection. The sole point before us just now is whether we desire to stamp with our approval amusements which are liable to such dangers as these, and which may lead astray young girls who do not understand enough about the wicked world to see any danger ahead."

"Mrs. Burnham, has it ever occurred to you that possibly our daughters may have been led into dangers because they were left, in a large degree, to face this society, which, it seems, is such an ogre, quite without the presence and guarding counsel of their parents? I have a vivid recollection of a time when invitations were accepted by them, and declined by you, by the wholesale; while I, being a loyal and well-brought-up husband, of course, remained with my wife and left my girls to dance with whom they would. What about that responsibility?"

Her cheeks were growing unbecomingly red, but she answered steadily:

"You could not expect me to do what my conscience disapproved, even though you allowed the girls to go where I could not accompany them. You knew when you married me, Judge Burnham, that I professed to be guided by my conscience. Did I do wrong, do you think, in following its dictates?"

"That depends; a fellow in court the other day argued that his conscience would not let him see his wife and children go hungry, so he stole a watch in order to feed them. This question of conscience is very obscure and miserably misunderstood. If you were a lawyer, you would know that the conscience is perverted every day to meet the demands of some crank."

Her old friends again, how fully they had discussed the responsibilities of conscience and the necessity for educating it. Did her husband suppose that she had not studied and prayed over these matters? She was silent, because she did not know how to reply to his pretense at arguing. His words seemed beneath her notice. After a moment's silence, he commenced again.

"I do not quite understand how you came to be such a slave to fanaticism, Ruth; it does not seem like you. Your father had a touch of it, to be sure, but I think he must have caught it from you, since you go so far beyond him. It must be an outcrop from some ancient Puritan. Really, my dear, you ought to study these questions; such narrowness is beneath you. Take, for example, that statement which you are so fond of making—about leading others astray. Can't you really see that if it proves anything, it proves too much? How many people do you suppose injure themselves every day of their lives by gormandizing? Yet you would not, because of that, conclude that it was your Christian duty to give up the use of food."

Oh, astute judge! To suppose that such babyish sophistry as that could pass with your keen-brained wife for reasoning! He waited for her reply with an air that said: "Now, my fair fanatic, haven't I put you in a corner?" But Ruth was in no haste to respond;

busy memories had hold of her tonight; she had gone back again into that upper room. She could see Flossy's grave, sweet face; she could hear Marion reading from her little old Bible. Were the dear girls with her in spirit tonight, trying to help her, that they appeared to her inner consciousness so constantly?

"I should think," she said at last, "that the answer to your question would depend almost entirely on the importance of food to our bodies. If the habit of taking food is one that we can lay aside at will, and still hold our place in the world and do our work, ought we not to carefully consider and decide whether we should in this thing set an example which would lead to the injury of others? Will you let me quote a few words to you from an old book on which I feed my conscience?"

And without waiting for a reply, she quoted the well-remembered words, not as Marion had done, but making her own substitution:

"'But dancing commends us not to God; for neither if we dance are we the better; neither if we dance not are we the worse. But take heed, lest by any means this liberty of yours become a stumbling block to them that are weak. For if any man see thee which hast knowledge join the dance, shall not the conscience of him which is weak be emboldened to dance also? And through thy knowledge shall the weak brother perish, for whom Christ died? But when ye sin so against the brethren, and wound their weak conscience, ye sin against Christ. Wherefore, if dancing make my brother to offend, I will dance no more while the world standeth.'"

Judge Burnham turned himself entirely on his cushions and gave his wife the benefit of a prolonged stare of astonishment.

"Are those words to be found in your Bible exactly as you have quoted them?"

"Exactly as I have quoted them, save that, of course, I substitute dancing for Paul's word—'meat'—which was the question at issue when he presented the argument."

"Oh!" spoken in a very significant tone, "quite a substitute, I should say. Of course, if your conscience allows you to read the Bible with free substitutions, you can make it prove anything."

"But, Judge Burnham, really, have I changed the force of the argument in the least, if you admit what you and I know to be the case, that there have been people even this winter, in this city, led astray through the social dance?"

It was almost impossible for her to keep her lip from curling just a little in indignation. She could seem to hear Marion's voice again as she said:

"Now, Eurie Mitchell, you are too bright to make such a remark as that."

Her husband was also "too bright" for that.

Judge Burnham yawned and turned one of the pillows and said:

"What time is it, my dear? Haven't we discussed this interesting subject long enough? You cannot make the world over if you try ever so hard. My candid advice to you is not to try. You will have your peculiar views, I suppose, to the end of time. Don't let us quarrel about them. The girls haven't a drop of Puritan blood in their veins. I'm afraid they will dance to the end of the chapter, but I will see to it that they choose partners of perfectly immaculate character. We have gone a long way astray from our starting point, which was whether we should have the carpets removed or covered. However, you can decide that at your leisure.

Oh! by the way, if I were you I would have that little room which we have been using as a sort of annex to the music room cleared and fitted up with card tables. There are always some who prefer a quiet game to any other method of passing the time, and that seems to me the most convenient place for tables. And now, my dear, don't you think it would be well for us to close this day? It has been rather a fatiguing one; I'm afraid I shall need another dinner if we talk much longer."

He smiled pleasantly on her, even stooped and kissed her as he rose up to light the gas in his dressing room. His manner was certainly very kind—kinder than it had been for months. But there was a painful little air of triumph about it, as one who said:

"We have begun life on a new basis, my dear. It is true you insulted a friend of mine, but you thereby got your eyes opened and have discovered that you live in the world and must live in it; and you have taken your place in society once more, and society will show you that she has a groove in which you must walk. You are her prisoner, whether you will or not."

And Ruth, as she went slowly, wearily over to her dressing case and began to draw out pins and let down her hair, sighed heavily, not because she was subdued, but because she was perplexed.

"I am not a prisoner," she told herself firmly, "nor a slave. I am the Lord's free woman. I am responsible only to Him, and I will not bow my neck to this yoke of fashionable life. I will not appear to countenance what I do not approve. But, oh! I see discord and weariness of soul before me, and I do not know which way to turn first. If only——"

Just here she stopped; she must always stop at that point, even in her thoughts. What good to say now, "If only my husband and I were agreed as to these matters"? But there did float through her tired brain the old, solemn question, "How shall two walk together except they be agreed?"

Away into the night she studied the problem and arose the next morning somewhat lighter of heart. She had resolved to see what genius and culture could do toward supplanting the usual amusements of the day. She would petition her husband to let her give the young ladies a surprise—an entertainment that she would promise should be altogether unique and more brilliant than anything the region had known. She would do this with the understanding that every detail should be left entirely in her hands and should be entirely secret until the eventful evening arrived. Thus guarded, she would see whether it was not possible for time and skill and money to evolve an evening's entertainment, even for fashionable people, which should have no objectionable features. Much engrossed by her scheme and ways of developing it, she roused from a half-dreamy attention to the usual dinner-table chatter, to alertness and caution.

"Robert," the host had ordered, "unpack the case which came out with me this afternoon and bring a bottle of it to the table."

"It is a very choice orange wine, my dear—"this to his wife, as Robert departed to do his bidding— "something new about its preparation. I did not give sufficient attention to understand what, but Dr. Westwood was enthusiastic over it. And the point which I did notice was that he thought it would be excellent both for you and for Erskine. It seems he has noticed the boy lately and thinks he needs toning up. And he says you need to enter on a regular course of tonics. He recommends the use of this orange wine at every meal, and a little of it as often as you feel any thirst."

"Erskine is not sick!"

The mother's voice was not only startled, but almost pleading in its notes as she studied the face of the fair boy at her side.

"Oh no! not sick, but pale and frail-looking. I told Dr. Westwood that I thought he was too closely housed; however, I have no doubt that the wine will be good for him. You shall make the first test of its quality, Mrs. Burnham."

By this time he had poured a glass two-thirds full of the liquid and was himself holding it forward for his wife.

"Thank you," she said, trying to speak in a perfectly natural tone, "I never use stimulants of any sort, you remember; I feel not the slightest need for them," and she made no movement toward the offered glass.

"But, my dear, you must allow the physician to be the judge of that last. I assure you, he was quite emphatic in his statements; so much so that I ordered a case of the wine before going to my office after meeting him."

"It was very thoughtful, certainly, and I will be grateful for the intention; but indeed, I must decline to drink it. If I am really in need of medicine—a point which I by no means yield, even on Dr. Westwood's testimony—I prefer to take it in the privacy of my own room, where I can make all the wry faces I wish over offensive doses, not to mix it with my food. No, thank you," for he was still holding forward the glass; "I must really decline it; I have studied into the merits of orange wine somewhat and am not an admirer."

Judge Burnham set the glass down at last, not quite gently, and his face was slightly flushed; both the young ladies laughed lightly, and Seraph said:

"Why, Mamma, where did you study medicine?

You have one accomplishment which I did not know you possessed. How convenient it will be for us; we shall not need to summon a physician from the city."

Mrs. Burnham made no reply; indeed, she only half heard the voluble tongue. She was watching Judge Burnham with an anxiety which he might plainly have read, had he chosen to look at her.

He had filled a smaller glass about two-thirds full of the wine and was passing it to his son.

"Here, my boy," he said in decisive tones, as though he were issuing a command instead of offering a luxury, "drink that."

"Erskine, wait!" His mother's voice, as decisive as the father's, but lower and more controlled. Then she addressed the father:

"Judge Burnham, may I beg you to excuse Erskine from drinking the wine? There are special reasons why I would like to talk with you about it before he takes any."

Judge Burnham was very angry or he would not have allowed himself to be guilty of the rudeness which followed.

"After he has obeyed me," he said in haughty tones, "I will be ready to talk with you. Drink that, my son, immediately."

The startled boy received the glass in his hands, but his mother's hand was placed quietly over the top, while she spoke quickly:

"Erskine, Papa will certainly excuse you if we explain to him that in obeying that direction you will not only be breaking a promise made to Mamma, but to God."

It was his son's questioning, half-frightened gaze, and the certainty that he was sitting as judge over the scene and would be sure to agree with his mother, which was finally the controlling force in Judge Burnham's mind.

He struggled for outward composure and presently, with a forced laugh, said:

"Oh! if the case is as serious as that, of course nothing further can be said at present. But really, Mrs. Burnham, I think as a family we are a success in getting up unexpected scenes out of very small capital. I had not the remotest idea of rousing a moral earthquake when I went a mile out of my way this morning to see that the doctor's prescription was properly attended to. I think it would be well for us to come to some understanding in private about the management of our son."

"I beg your pardon for the publicity of the scene," said Ruth; "it was nothing that I could have foreseen."

It was the humiliation of this Christian woman that there were times when silence would have been golden in which she could not resist the temptation to sarcasm.

10

COMING TO AN UNDERSTANDING

OF COURSE the question was not settled. Mrs. Burnham knew this and was anxious to bring it up again that there might at least be a full understanding with regard to Erskine. She began it unwisely as soon as they were alone, before her excitement had had time to cool. However, she was quiet enough at first, repeating with a little more care and courtesy the statement that she had been sorry for the public discussion and had not thought to tell him that she and Erskine had been talking of these things but a few days before and that they had together taken a pledge never to touch anything that could intoxicate—a pledge which her husband interrupted her to say he thought was an "exceedingly foolish and mischievous one. Pledges were serious things and should not be mouthed over by a child, ignorant of what he was about"; and then, with delicious disregard of logic, added that he should have supposed she would have had more wisdom than to have herself set up a barrier in the child's conscience in regard to the medicine which the family physician had prescribed. Ruth ignored the logic and the implied compliment to herself, and held to her point.

"I do not mean to pledge him against the use of alcohol for extreme illness. Personally, I believe that medical skill can, if it choose, supply a substitute for alcoholic poison even in cases where it used to be considered a necessity. That was what Papa thought, you remember, and I know that we have very high medical authority to sustain the belief; but I am not prepared to set up my judgment against that of an attending physician where I know there is extreme danger. I do not know yet what I should do under such circumstances. I am afraid I should obey the doctor, but in little everyday aches and pains and the weaknesses common to childhood, I am sure there is no necessity whatever for resorting to alcohol, and that feature of the subject was decidedly included in our pledge."

"And I repeat that I think you have been very foolish in playing with pledges and all that sort of nonsense; the word of parents should be the highest law a child touches. However, you made a most unnecessary scene in this case, for orange wine is free from the ingredient which has come under the ban of your displeasure."

His wife turned fully toward him then and regarded him searchingly. Was this man ignorant, really, or did he suppose that she was?

"Do I understand you that there was no alcohol in the preparation of the orange wine which was on the table today?"

"Well, of course it was fermented, else it would not be fit to drink; but the proportion of alcohol was so slight that a baby might have indulged in it without harm."

It seemed unnecessary to make any reply to this, so none was offered. The significant silence seemed to vex Judge Burnham.

"Suppose we try to understand each other," he said, speaking more haughtily than before. "Am I to conclude from the exhibition we have had today that whenever you choose to countermand my orders to the child, you consider yourself quite at liberty to do so in his presence, to say nothing of the presence of others? If you have any such impression as this," he added, growing more angry as he proceeded, "it is quite time we came to an understanding. I am not a household tyrant and have never obtruded my views in regard to the child; indeed, while he was a baby, it was my policy and my practice to leave him almost entirely in your hands. Perhaps I have carried this policy too far and led you to misunderstand me. But once for all, let me say that I expect full and implicit and prompt obedience from him and, failing to receive it, shall certainly require it. I excused him today, because the nature of your interference was such that no gentleman could do otherwise, but for the future, you, being fairly warned, will not, I hope, force me, at least in public, to the painful necessity of pressing my commands contrary to your expressed will."

If he was angry now, and he had grown more so with each spoken word, how shall his wife's state of mind be described? Her blood seemed fairly to boil in her veins. This entire harangue was so unlike her husband—was so uncalled for. Had she not striven earnestly and successfully to instill into Erskine's mind the importance of unquestioning obedience to his father? Had she not put away her fears and anxieties many a time with stern hand in order to carry out some scheme of the father's over which the mother's heart trembled? How utterly unfair and unkind was all this! Why should she be spoken to as though she were at best but a faithful nursemaid who could be trusted with the care of the child while he was a baby but who must resign her control as he grew older? There was no time for careful thought, for schooling herself to the use of the right words; she spoke hastily, almost fiercely:

"Judge Burnham, I have done nothing to merit such language as that. I have always taught Erskine to obey you quite as unquestioningly as he did me. You know this to be the case and also that I appealed to you today to excuse him from the command, giving you what I thought was a sufficient reason. Since you are so anxious that there should be an understanding between us, I will try to speak as plainly as you have. I do mean that my boy shall be kept from the taint or the touch or even the smell of alcohol, if determination and vigilance on my part can accomplish it. I tell you solemnly that, much as my life is bound up in his, entirely as I seem to be dependent on him for what happiness I have, I would rather stand beside his open grave and see him buried in his childish innocence than that he should live to be even a fashionable drunkard. And I warn you that I will not tamely submit to any tampering with him in this direction; to any scheme under pretext of medicine, or tonic, or whatever name Satan has planned to have the mixture called. I will take my boy and run away before I will endure anything of the kind."

She turned from him the moment the last word was spoken and left the room, but not quickly enough to escape his reply:

"Well, upon my word, this is the most astounding exhibition of Christian fanaticism that I have seen yet."

The words pierced her; not because of their intense sarcasm, nor because of the emphasis on the last word, which was equal to saying that he was now prepared, however, for anything in that direction which could be imagined, but because of that one word—*Christian*. It brought her suddenly back to the recollection that as she lived religion before her husband, so he would judge of its power in her heart. Oh! miserable life that goaded her by the very force of her conscience into daily exhibitions that were a disgrace to the name she wore!

Moreover, when she was quiet enough to think about it, she began to realize how very difficult she had made the way for her projected entertainment, which was to supersede and outshine the fashionable world. Had she not made the attempt well-nigh impossible? Yet what could she have done? She tried to assure her conscience that she had no business with results; that she had but stood squarely up for her principles, as she was in honor bound to do. But her conscience was altogether too well educated to be lulled in this manner; it insisted on assuring her that it was not the standing up for principle which could be criticized, but the manner of doing it.

The next complication came the next morning. Mrs. Stuart Bacon sent up her card and would be glad to see Mrs. Burnham for a few minutes on important business. Ruth knew her but slightly and, being in no mood for strangers, was tempted to declare herself engaged. But that phrase "important business" conquered, and she went reluctantly to the parlor.

Mrs. Bacon was a middle-aged lady with an earnest face and pleasant voice. Looking at her from across the aisle of the church, Ruth remembered, she had dreamily told herself that sometime she would like to become better acquainted with that face. Perhaps this was her opportunity. Yet this morning she did not think she wanted to become acquainted with anybody. It almost seemed to her that if she could go quite away from everybody she had ever seen before and stay a long time, she would be glad.

Mrs. Bacon expressed her thanks at being received, though the hour was early for calls, and said she would not abuse the kindness by unnecessary detention but would proceed at once to business. In the first place, would not dear Mrs. Burnham join their organization? Her name had been on their list for several weeks as one whom they meant to petition, but she believed the opportunity had not heretofore occurred. Still, they confidently looked for her name and support.

"What was the organization?" Ruth questioned, struggling with the apathy she felt and trying hard to bring herself into line with women who were at work in the world.

"Why, the W. C. T. U., you know," spoken confidently, as though she would know the meaning of the magic letters in an instant. "Your old pastor, Dr. Dennis, assured us that he believed we should find in you a most efficient helper."

But Ruth had been living out of the world. She could not remember what the letters meant. Dreamily, she recalled her Chautauqua experiences, where the air was full of initials, and tried to fit some of their meanings to the letters that flowed so glibly from Mrs. Bacon's tongue, but they would not fit. The caller must have observed her blank look, for she hastened to the rescue.

"The Woman's Christian Temperance Union, you know. I beg your pardon for speaking in abbreviations;

we women do it so much in our work that we forget it is not quite the way to speak to outsiders. Still, I don't regard you as an outsider; I know you are one of us; an intelligent Christian mother, in these days, is to be claimed as a matter of course."

"The Woman's Christian Temperance Union." Ruth repeated the words aloud, slowly, as if fascinated by them, her face aglow with interest. It sounded like fellowship and oneness of thought and feeling.

"Yes," Mrs. Bacon said heartily, feeling the sympathy in her hostess's voice; "I knew you would be interested. We have quite a flourishing branch here and have accomplished some very desirable results"; and she launched forth into an eager account of their late experiences.

Ruth, listening, felt her enthusiasm die slowly, and her heart grew cold; it was of no use to think of joining these women in their work. She had never heard Judge Burnham mention the name of the organization, yet she was as sure as though he had talked for hours about it that he would regard their methods of work, and even their work itself in some of its branches, as unladylike and uncalled for. He had a very pronounced horror of women whom he regarded as having stepped out of their sphere. It would be foolish to widen the breach which was already between them by identifying herself with anything of this sort, but she would like to do it. She knew, of course, a great deal about the workings of the organization and had been more or less interested in its movements in the years gone by. As soon as she had roused from her dazed condition she knew what the initials meant very well. Some of the doings of the society she had regarded with disapproval, she remembered, but as she swiftly looked back on them now, she said perhaps the women were justified in all that they did. No doubt many of them were mothers.

None of this, however, was revealed in her words. When Mrs. Bacon reached a period, having closed with a renewal of her invitation, Ruth's reply was a brief, almost cold negative. She could not join the organization. She was in sympathy with them, of course, and respected their work; every Christian woman must do that; but there were excellent reasons why she could not enroll herself as one of them.

Mrs. Bacon was disappointed. She had evidently heard, either through Dr. Dennis or from some other source, that about Ruth which had made her confident of success. However, the refusal had been given in such a way as made it almost impossible for a lady to urge further.

"Well," she said, after a moment's dismayed silence, "I am sorry. Perhaps you will see it in a different light at some other time. Now, let me come at once to the special business whose need for haste precipitated, perhaps unwisely, the invitation I have just given you. I feel very sure, my dear Mrs. Burnham, that you will not put me off with a negative here. You know, of course, how earnestly we have struggled to keep the sale of liquor out of this corner of the world; and because we do not as yet belong to the city, and because it is a factory region, we have succeeded; even the enemies of total abstinence do not think it wise to have liquor freely sold where their workmen can get it, you know. For their sons, strange to say, they have not so much regard! Well, up to this time our young men, if they use the stuff, must go to the city for it. It is true enough that with our constant trains back and forth, this can be very readily accomplished; still, it is a sort of safeguard to those who have not yet been caught in the enemy's toils. But now a new danger menaces us; it is said that our largest hotel, the Shenandoah, has discovered that the law can be interpreted in such a manner that it will have a right to offer liquor to its guests, even though none can be sold elsewhere within our limits. What do you suppose we mothers think of that? We have sons, you know, who mingle freely with the guests at the Shenandoah and are frequently entertained by them. Are we to sit quietly by and see poured before their eyes daily that from which we have pledged our lives to keep them, if possible? Do you believe we ought to do it, Mrs. Burnham?"

She was strongly excited; her eyes fairly blazed with the intensity of her feelings, and every muscle of her face spoke for her. Ruth remembered that she had heard this woman's son mentioned as a young man who was unusually gifted. Was he also unusually tempted? She made haste to answer, her heart throbbing in sympathy; suppose Erskine were nineteen.

"Assuredly I do think so, my dear madam; and if there is anything which you can do, I should think you would allow no obstacle to prevent your doing it to the utmost."

"Thank you. I knew you were true at heart. Mrs. Burnham, if there is anything which you can do for us, will you do it?"

"After what I have said, you can hardly doubt the heartiness of my reply to that question; the only trouble is, I realize only too well my own impotence. I have no influence whatever with the managers of the hotel; I have not even a speaking acquaintance with them; and if I had, it would not give me influence. How is it possible that I could accomplish anything which you, who have worked in these lines and understand the methods so well, could not do much better?"

"Oh! my dear, we are far too well trained in our work to hope anything from hotel managers as a rule. The men who can consider such a proposition at all are not of the class that can be urged through their moral natures. Liquor-dealing hotel proprietors have no consciences, I verily believe. Nothing less impossible than a 'thou shalt not' is going to effect anything in that direction. Why, one of these very gentlemen has a son who drinks to excess every time he goes to the city; and his father wants to make it more convenient for him, it seems."

"Then what can you think it possible for me to do under such circumstances? If they have the law on their side, or if it has been twisted so that it can appear to be on their side—and I have no doubt of that last; for nothing seems to be easier than to secure a lawyer who is skillful in misinterpreting law to suit his client—what is there left to do?"

"Everything, dear Mrs. Burnham. I am so glad to hear you speak in that eager way. Don't you suppose we recognize you as the power behind the throne? I told the ladies I felt sure you would be on our side; for, though your boy is only five, the years go fast; and they make drunkards of them now at fifteen; this is a hurrying age, you know. I feel sure you will save us from this curse in our midst, dear madam, for the sake of your boy and mine."

Ruth looked utterly puzzled and also pained. What wild scheme had this excited woman in mind, which she fondly imagined would tide them over this present danger?

She spoke low and gently, in the hope of calming the evident excitement of her guest:

"I have not the remotest idea what you mean; believe me, there is nothing that I would not do to help, were it in my power; but how I can do anything, I cannot imagine."

Mrs. Bacon regarded her curiously, evidently puzzled in turn.

"Why, my dear Mrs. Burnham," she said at last, "is it possible that you do not know that your husband is the owner of the Shenandoah? And that by the terms of the lease, his consent must be obtained before any liquors can be brought into the house?"

11

NO, Mrs. Burnham had not known this. Her husband's business interests were so extensive, and the pressure of care upon him so heavy, that even had he deemed it worth mentioning, he might not have thought of it at an opportune moment. And, indeed, he was so decidedly a man who threw off business cares the moment he reached his own door and who never even thought of such a thing as chatting confidentially with his wife about them that to have remarked, "The Shenandoah property came into my hands today, through the failure of the firm of Bell & Pealer," would have had an absurdly inappropriate sound to him.

So Ruth sat silent and appalled before the news. Her husband the owner of the Shenandoah! This, then, was why she might naturally be supposed to have power in the question at issue; and her cheek paled over the realization of how powerless she was. Her instant change of manner was not lost on Mrs. Bacon, who shrewdly said to herself: "She didn't know it before, and it evidently makes a difference into whose pockets the results are to go. Oh, me! who would have supposed that a Christian woman, with a son to rear, could stop over considerations like these." And she was as correct in her conclusions as the majority of persons are who sit in judgment on the acts of their brothers and sisters.

Mrs. Burnham spoke at last, slowly, choosing her words with care; she had no mind to show the sorrowful secrets of her home to Mrs. Bacon.

"You give me credit for altogether too much power, dear madam; gentlemen are noted, I believe, for supposing that their wives know nothing about business, and, in my husband's case, it would be fair enough; I profess to know very little in that line. Besides, Judge Burnham is preeminently a man who does not discuss business out of business hours; in proof of which I might tell you that I did not know he was the owner of the Shenandoah. The utmost that I can do is to repeat my assurance of sympathy and willingness to help in whatever way I can, at the same time reminding you that I may not be able to accomplish anything."

Yet as she went wearily up the stairs after her caller had departed, she thought that nothing could be more unpropitious for her schemes in regard to the evening party than these questions of conscience which seemed to be pressing in on every hand.

Nevertheless, as she thought more about Mrs. Bacon's petition, her courage rose. Judge Burnham might not be a total abstinence man, but he despised drunkenness; and being a lawyer well versed in the ways of the world, he must know how disastrous to the interests of a place which boasted of itself as a safe country home for young people would be the introduction of that which did more than anything else to make life unsafe. Besides—and on this she built strong hopes—Judge Burnham's pride would be at stake. Would he want it to go out through these earnest women that he feared for his rents to such a degree that he was willing to introduce wines and brandies as security? It would certainly have an offensive sound if she put it to him in that light. She thought so constantly about it and went over her arguments so many times that she worked herself into a state of feverish haste to have the interview over. She dreaded it but went steadily toward it with much the same feeling that one has in laying vigorous hold of any cross which must be borne: "If this thing must needs be, let me get through with it as speedily as possible."

Judge Burnham was in his worst mood—courtly, suave, and sarcastic. Yes, he had met some of those interesting females who went about attending to other people's business; one always wondered who attended, meantime, to their homes. "Women's Constant Talking Unions" they ought to be named, the tendency to talk steadily for an unprecedented length of time on subjects of which they knew nothing seeming to be a marked feature of their organization, so far as he had observed it. He had always thought that if he had been so unfortunate as to choose a wife with no more brains than to join herself to such a company, he might be justified for once in returning to the old Blue Laws and confining her on bread and water until she came to a better mind. Which particular member of the troop had honored her with a call? Oh yes! he had the honor of a speaking acquaintance with Mrs. Stuart Bacon. He had supposed her to be remarkable for nothing but a very ill-shaped mouth, but it seemed she had other accomplishments; no wonder the mouth was ill shaped, since it had such ungraceful work to do. Yes, he had the honor of being the owner of the Shenandoah; it had not entered his mind to object to the lessee's proposition. Of course, the law sustained him; it would be a return to the Dark Ages with interest if a man must be dictated to as to what he should have for his money at a hotel. There was nothing unpleasant about it; nothing that reasonable people could object to; merely light wines, such as orange wine and the like—wholesome and refreshing beverages for refined people. The class of guests that patronized the Shenandoah would not be likely to demean themselves in any way; they took care to keep the prices too high for the common people. Oh yes! the same law admitted light wines to the other, more common hotels of the place, of course; but he didn't own them and had nothing whatever to do with their affairs. As for his influence, he imagined that he should succeed in conducting himself in the future as in the past, in such a way as to be above reproach, at least outside of his own family. Of course Mrs. Stuart Bacon and a few gossiping women of her clique would talk; that was their special forte, as he had intimated; probably he would come in for a share of the censure that they distributed so liberally, but he believed he was able to endure even that.

In short, Ruth knew, long before the interview was concluded, that her plea was utterly hopeless. The very pride on which she had depended seemed to be a weapon turned against her. His pride would not permit him to seem to be swerved from his position one half inch by what he was pleased to term "gossiping interference in what did not concern them." I have not given you an idea of the half he said. Through the entire interview he maintained his ironical tone and careless manner, omitting no opportunity for using the keen sarcasm in which nature and education had made him an expert. Maintaining also his air of exceeding politeness and courteous attention, even bending to draw a wrap closer about his wife when he saw that she shivered, and himself rearranging the open-grate fire, which he knew was one of her luxuries. And finally paring with much care an orange, half of which he presented to her on a fruit plate in the midst of one of her earnest arguments, with the smiling statement that perhaps she would not object to orange juice in that shape, although she had spurned his other offering meant for her refreshment.

Altogether, Ruth went from the room more utterly humiliated than she ever remembered to have been before.

That she had signally failed was only too evident; that she had nothing but failure to report to the waiting and hopeful ladies was mortification enough; but there were deeper reaches to it than this. How had it happened that she, who had been so eagerly sought after, so earnestly and persistently wooed, chosen without a doubt because she was beloved, how had it come to pass that after a lapse of years she really had no more influence with her husband than this?

Failing in appreciating her conscientious scruples, why did he not, at least in a matter of this kind, involving only money, take pleasure in yielding to her whims if he pleased to call them so? She knew husbands who gratified their wives from no higher motives than such as these. Why was not her wish in these matters a law to him, which it gave him pleasure to follow? Long into the night Ruth questioned, and wept, and prayed, and mourned. Nothing was plainer to her than that even the Christian life for which she thought she was all the while contending had been largely a failure.

She had succeeded only in irritating her husband by her display of it. It had brought no sunshine into her home or life. She had not yielded in places where she could have done so as well as not. She had consulted her tastes instead of her husband's, even where conscience had had nothing to say. She had been a painstaking mother, but even here she had failed. Had she not often let her morbid fears of what might happen, not to the soul, but to the beautiful body of the boy, push in and thwart some cherished scheme of his father's?

Was it, after all, any wonder that when she suddenly confronted him with her opinions and almost demanded from him actions in accordance with her ideas that he should resort to sarcasm and irony and hold his ground?

Never had poor Ruth's insulted conscience read her a sterner lecture than on that weary night. Humiliating failure! and the humiliating confession to her own heart that she was, in a sense, to blame. And the very hardest of it was that she saw no way out. She could not explain these things to her husband, because he was on such a different moral plane from herself that he would utterly misunderstand her; he would think she had confessed herself as wrong in principle and would immediately, as indeed he had already done, plan for the most impossible concessions to his views.

But in the meantime, she must put aside all these burdens and decide just what to do. She had promised to report the result of her effort. How should she do it? She would write to the ladies; would explain that her husband had given his word before she knew anything about the matter and could not withdraw from it honorably. He had said as much. Could she not repeat it? And was more detail than this necessary? Yet her honest soul revolted from such a statement; for she knew at this moment that the matter was still not so fully settled but that, had it been made to appear for Judge Burnham's interests to change, he would probably have done so. The furthest she got at last was to determine to wait another day until her intense excitement and pain had had time to dull a little before she attempted any report. Afterward, she wondered whether even that had not been a concession to the enemy, which had caused her more trouble.

In point of fact, two days passed, and still she had made the waiting and anxious ladies no reply. As she went down to dinner on the evening of the second day, she assured herself that she would write that letter the next morning before ten o'clock; but she did not. Life had gone with her during these two days much as usual. She had seen almost nothing of her husband, he having been detained in town late by reason of some professional perplexity. The young ladies were busy with their regular routine of society life; the week had perhaps been unusually gay, and Ruth and her boy had spent much time alone.

Was it fate, she wondered, or providence that led her that evening, as they were on their way down to dinner, to say with sudden fervor of appeal to the impressionable boy the words she did? They had been standing by the window watching for Papa and had seen reeling by a young man—scarcely that; a mere boy in years—well dressed, with the air even then of the well bred about him, but with that painful swaying in his walk that can mean but one thing. And the boy had been startled, dismayed, and had questioned eagerly, and returned to the subject again and again, and the mother, with a terrible pain in her heart, had recognized the young man as Mrs. Stuart Bacon's son. On the way downstairs Erskine had put his other question, and then she had turned to him with this appeal:

"My boy, promise your mother that you will never touch a drop of anything that can possibly make you walk as that young man did!"

"Why, Mamma, I have promised, you know. I promised you, and I promised God."

"I know it, my darling; promise again. Mamma loves to hear the words: Whatever happens, whoever asks you, unless you are very, very sick, and the doctor, and Mamma, too, if I am there, say it is right."

She could not help that little proviso. And the boy promised again. Then they went into the dining room, and that miserable orange wine was on the table. It had been on several times since the first scene connected with it, and the judge and his daughters had drunk it when they would, but none had been offered to Mrs. Burnham or the child.

Judge Burnham was not in an amiable mood. Heavy wrinkles made seams across his forehead, and his eyes had an irritable glitter in them. Truth to tell, he was not so indifferent to the tongues of a few gossiping women as he would have his wife imagine, and the Woman's Christian Temperance Union, while waiting for their report from Mrs. Burnham, had by no means been idle, and sentences not complimentary to his name had reached his ears several times during the day. These, in connection with certain other business perplexities, served to make him less ready than usual to throw aside care.

I am afraid it must be admitted that it was pure

maliciousness on the part of Minta that made her suddenly exclaim, looking at Erskine, "How thin and pale that child is growing! He needs tonics, I believe. Here, Erskine, take a swallow of this, and see how nice it is; it will be good for you." And she held toward him her glass of wine.

It was maliciousness, I suppose, but not very deep. She was rather fond of a little scene such as would call a flush to her stepmother's face and give them the benefit of a sharp passage at arms. She expected nothing more; but almost in the same breath with Erskine's "Oh no! thank you; I don't want any," came his father's stern command:

"Erskine, do as your sister tells you, at once!"

Then Erskine, trembling under the weight of the sternness—he had never been spoken to in that tone in his life before:

"Oh! but, Papa, I can't; please excuse me: I cannot drink any wine."

"Obey me immediately!"

"Oh! but, Papa, I can't, you know; I promised."

"Erskine, either obey me immediately, and take a drink from that glass, or go to my dressing room, and wait there until I come."

Trembling, frightened, half blinded by the rush of tears, the little boy did not hesitate even for a second but went across the room and out of the door.

It was well that the meal was nearly concluded, and the servants had left the room. The mother felt that though her life had depended on it, she could neither have eaten another mouthful nor have spoken another word.

As for Minta, to do her justice, she was half scared and wholly repentant.

A messenger came just as they left the table with a

business telegram for Judge Burnham. He detained the boy while he wrote a reply, and Ruth went with swift steps to his dressing room.

"Mamma, Oh, dear Mamma!" said the frightened child, "what made Papa speak so to me? Was I naughty?"

"My darling, did you not keep the promise that you made to God? How could that be naughty?"

"But it made Papa angry. Oh! dear Mamma, what will he do? Will he whip me, do you think, like the boy in the picture?"

"My darling, that was a picture of a drunken man; you have no such father as that. Papa does not understand; he will let you explain, I think. I will see him myself if I can."

And to the baby's urging that she would stay with him, she turned resolutely away, assuring him that that would be treating Papa rudely and that she would try to see him and explain what Erskine meant. But she did not. He went directly to his dressing room by way of the library staircase and let himself in at the back door with his key.

12

◆━◈◆◈━◆

THE DEED FOR THE WILL

MRS. BURNHAM, failing in her intention to waylay her husband, returned to her own room, which opened into the dressing room. Too nervous to take a seat, she walked the floor, anxious, irresolute, miserable. She longed to go to her child, but would not insult her husband by seeming to be afraid to leave his son alone with him. Ominous silence reigned in the dressing room. Judge Burnham had opened a drawer somewhat noisily on the moment of his entrance but had spoken no word so far as his wife could hear. Suddenly on the quiet air came the sound of a blow, accompanied by a little wailing cry:

"Oh, Papa, dear Papa, please don't! Mamma said you wouldn't; she said you would let me explain that I couldn't, because I have promised God."

No reply at all from the angry father, save of the sort which seemed to scar Ruth's very soul. Her little sheltered darling, who had never before known what physical pain was except as sickness had shown it to him! How could his father strike the little delicate hand, and for such a reason! The wife's whole soul rose up in rebellion.

"Please, Papa, let me tell you about it. Oh! Papa, you hurt me very much."

But there was no reply. Should the mother rush in and, before her child, demand that this insulting demonstration of passion should cease? All her ideas of wifely loyalty rose up to object to this course, but she paced the floor like a caged lioness and said aloud:

"I cannot bear this; I ought not to bear it."

It was well, perhaps, for all concerned that the scene was short. Judge Burnham spoke at last a few low words, which his wife could not catch, and then immediately entered her room.

Erskine's punishment had been neither prolonged nor severe. The average boy would probably have minded it but very little; would perhaps have been used to such a mode of correction. But Ruth knew that her cherished son, with his unusually gentle and easily ruled nature, had inherited from her such a shrinking horror of anything in the form of a blow that she felt sure he must be quivering from head to foot, not with physical pain, but with a sort of nervous terror which he did not understand and could not control. She was not, therefore, in a mood to receive her husband's words quietly.

"Mrs. Burnham, I request as a favor that you will not see Erskine again tonight; I have punished him for disobedience and told him to go immediately to bed."

He had seen his wife in various states of mind in the course of the last half-dozen years, but had never felt before, and may never again, the blaze that was in her eyes as she turned them fully on him and spoke in low, quick tones:

"It is a favor which will not be granted. You have been cruel and unjust. If you have a moral nature, you must by this time be ashamed of yourself. I shall go to my child at once and make what reparation I can for his father's injustice."

Then, before he could recover himself sufficiently to detain her even with a word, she had disappeared through the door which led into Erskine's fair little room.

As she had supposed, she found the child sobbing violently. He had run to his room by the dressing-room entrance the instant his father released him and, burying his little blonde head in the pillows, was trembling and moaning, so that one who understood him less than his mother would have supposed him in mortal pain. In an instant he was gathered to her arms, covered with kisses and caresses, and overwhelmed with loving words. But he could not yet control the tempest of surprise and pain.

"Oh, Mamma!" he sobbed, "Oh, Mamma! he did—he did like the man in the picture. You said he wouldn't, and he did. Oh, Mamma! what can I do? Oh, Mamma!"

If Mrs. Burnham should live to be a white-haired old woman, she will never, I think, forget the experiences of that evening. It was not because the boy had been made to suffer physically. She had sense enough, even in her excitement, to understand that the punishment had been what people accustomed to such ways of dealing with their children would have called slight; but there are pains much deeper than those which the flesh can endure. She knew only too well that her child had lost faith in his father. How was it possible for the thoughtful boy, wise beyond his years, to think that he had been treated other than unjustly, especially in the light of the questions he asked, and the answers she felt obliged to give?

"Did I do wrong, Mamma? You said I didn't. But if I didn't, why did Papa punish me? You said they punished people who did wrong."

"My darling, I cannot think that you did anything wrong. You had made a solemn promise. Papa did not know it, did not understand; he thought you were disobedient."

"Oh! but, Mamma, I told him. I told him that I had got down on my knees and promised God that I never would, and he didn't listen at all. Oh, Mamma, Mamma! will he punish me every time I try to keep my promise to God?"

Do you wonder that the troubled mother set her lips hard and said in her heart, "No, he never shall"? But she had grace enough not to say it aloud. Yet what must she say?

She drew up a low rocker and took the still trembling child in her arms, dipping her hand in cold water, and then making with it soft, cooling touches over the heated face and head, and speaking low and soothingly:

"My darling, Mamma's darling, there are some things that I cannot explain; when you are older you will understand. I do not think Papa will punish you in this way again. When he thinks it over, he will see that you meant to do right."

Silence for a moment. Then the voice went on firmly. Her decision had been made.

"Erskine, Papa does not think about some things as I do, and as I believe God does, and as I want you to think. Someday I hope he will, and you and I must pray every day to the dear God to make Papa his follower in all things. In the meantime, my darling, what you and I find in the Bible that God has spoken, we will try to do always, whether it is hard or easy. Shall we not?"

She had never said so much before; questions innumerable she had evaded or half answered, after the manner of loyal Christian wives in divided homes; now it seemed to her that the time had come when she must plainly say, "There are things, solemn, all-important things, about which we are not agreed." But what an admission for a wife to make! Will she ever forget the pain of that last question, asked with a little sobbing sigh, before her baby went to sleep, "Oh! dear Mamma, why do not papas and mammas both think like God?"

At the earliest possible hour when a call was admissible the next morning, Mrs. Burnham's card was sent up to Mrs. Stuart Bacon. She had determined to give her answer in person. She made no attempt at circumlocution, but came directly to the point:

"Mrs. Bacon, I have failed in the work given me to do; perhaps you know from your experiences of life that husband and wife are not always as one where business matters are concerned; I think my husband believes his word to be pledged. No words of mine will express to you the regret that I feel at my failure. I have not shown myself so skillful a worker that you should care to have me join your ranks, but, at the same time, I want to say to you that I have changed my mind since Tuesday. I want to join your Union, and I pledge my personal support and effort in any direction where I can be made useful."

So much, at least, for the cause Judge Burnham had accomplished. He was not a very self-complacent man during the days that immediately followed. His wife's cold, stern words had burned deeply, and as soon as the first storm of passion was over, he could not but acknowledge to himself that there had been a shade of truth in them.

What a surprising thing that he who had always prided himself on his liberality of thought and feeling, who had always good-naturedly argued that the veriest cranks of society should be allowed to ride their hobbies according to their own sweet wills, so long as they injured no one; that he should have so far forgotten himself as to command a child to do that which was not only contrary to his mother's teachings, but contrary to the baby's notions of what a Supreme Being demanded of him!

Judge Burnham was by no means a Christian man; at the same time he was very far removed from being an infidel. He often smiled, and occasionally he sneered, at some of the ideas belonging to Christianity; still, he explained to himself that his smiles and sneers were for the outcroppings of ideas belonging to ignorant fanatics, not to the actual verities themselves. He assured himself that certain forms of worship were eminently fitting as offered to the Creator by the creature; also that certain outgrowths of Christianity were elevating and worthy of all respect. He assured himself that he had never objected to his wife's position as a member of the church. That was eminently a fitting position for a woman; it was the unreasoning submission which she gave to the demands of fanaticism that disturbed him.

But that he should have so far forgotten himself as to allow his child to see that there was a difference of opinion between them was, he admitted, ungentlemanly.

Especially was it offensive to him that the difference of opinion should have shown itself in the line of a mere appetite, a thing which should, of course, be subordinate; as he thought of it, he actually could not help curling his lip at himself. It was of no use trying to restore his self-respect by saying that the issue between them had to be met, and disobedience punished, no matter how trifling the occasion; he was perfectly aware that he had himself made the issue, made it unnecessarily, in a way that he would not have done had he not been irritated about something else; and that, while it was a trifle to him, it was an intensely serious matter to the child.

On the whole, the gentleman did what might, perhaps, be called somewhat profitable thinking during the days that followed.

To his wife he was unfailingly courteous, even kind, despite her cold, quiet dignity; he made no attempt to resent this; on the contrary, he even respected her for it. She had spoken some very plain words to him, words which had stung deeply at the time; but he could not help the admission that there was truth in them. You will remember that he was a successful lawyer, accustomed to weighing questions carefully and giving decisions, and his judgment had given a decision in this case which by no means acquitted himself. He was not the sort of man who could frankly say, "I was in the wrong, I beg you will forgive." Such a statement calls for a very high grade of character; calls, perhaps, for Christian character, though there have been men who knew how to say "forgive me" to mortals, not yet having learned to say it to Christ.

Judge Burnham was not one, but he knew how to act the words gracefully and persistently. His little son helped him also to a smaller opinion of himself; no trace of resentment lingered on the child's sweet, bright face. A little touch of shyness there was, a questioning, half-startled glance each time he met him afresh, as though he were wondering in his child-mind whether he had unwittingly given occasion for offense, but, receiving his father's smile, he sprang joyously into his arms and lavished kisses as before. They were inexpressibly sweet to the father's heart. Ruth, too, was glad over them. Her own soul had been hurt, but she did not wish the child to feel a lasting sting. He had settled the question for himself with the next morning's sunlight. "Mamma," he had said, with his brightest smile, "I've thought it all out; he did not want me to disobey you and God, but he had to punish me because I disobeyed him; don't you see? I don't mind it now; it didn't hurt me much, only it was so dreadful, you know. But now that I understand it, it doesn't seem bad."

It was baby logic; Ruth had to smile over it, albeit behind the smile there was a tear; but she made no attempt to reason the thought away. In fact, as the days passed, there seemed to be method in the reasoning. The objectionable wine was on the table once or twice, but none was offered to the child; and, on the third day after the dinner-table scene, Ruth overheard this order given by the master of the house:

"Robert, you need not serve any more of that wine at table; Mrs. Burnham doesn't care for it, and it isn't what I thought it was; pack it away in the cellar; it may be needed sometime."

It was nearly a week afterward that Judge Burnham came home earlier by several hours than was his custom and found both his wife and son in the library, intent over a new book that had many illustrations. The child sprang to meet him as usual. Ruth tried to make her greeting cordial; she did not want to continue the wall of reserve that she had raised between her husband and herself, but she did not know how to lower it. That he had pained her unutterably was not to be denied, but that because of it she was henceforth to show only cold displeasure was, of course, folly; the more so because of the boy's constant lesson of confiding love.

So now she closed her book and made some general inquiries as to the day's experiences, trying to make her voice sound free and social. But Judge Burnham was preoccupied. He set Erskine down after a few kisses and, throwing himself into a vacant chair across the room from his wife, drew from his pocket a formidable-looking document, bristling with seals, and tossed it to the child.

"Here, my boy, is a new plaything for you."

"A plaything! Why, Papa, what is it for? Is it sealed? Why, no, it is open, and it is all written over. How funny! Is it a great big letter?"

"Not exactly; in law we call it a deed."

"And what is a deed?"

Judge Burnham laughed and glanced at his wife.

"It means, in this case, a transfer of property."

"Papa, I don't understand."

"Don't you? That is surprising. Let me see if I can explain. A deed, this deed, at least, is to declare that I am no longer the owner of a certain piece of property; that I have given up all right and title to it from this time forth."

"Why have you done it, Papa? What property is it, and who has bought it?"

"For good and sufficient reasons. I am to answer your questions in course, am I not? You ask three. The property is the house on the corner of Markam Square, known as the Shenandoah; and it now belongs to a person by the name of Erskine Powers Burnham. Are you acquainted with him?"

The flush on the child's face was pretty to see; but Judge Burnham was looking at his wife.

"Papa that is my name, my whole name; but of course you can't mean me!"

"Why not?"

"Because—why, Papa, could a little boy have a great big house for his own? Would you give it to me?"

"So it seems. That deed says so; it needs only the addition of your mother's name to make it complete, and I have an idea that she can be persuaded to sign it."

"But, Papa, what will I do with it? I'm not big enough, am I?"

"You will be; meantime, you can consult with your mother as to what you will or will not have done; and you might retain me for your legal adviser; I will act in that capacity to the best of my abilities, under your and your mamma's directions."

"Mamma," said Erskine, "did you ever hear of anything so nice? A whole big house!"

And Ruth, looking past the boy, said:

"Thank you; thank you more than words can tell!"

13

THE WISDOM OF THIS WORLD

AFTER that there was a lull in the Burnham house-hold. The various excitements of the days just passed seemed to have been somewhat like storms, which left the air clearer.

There was, about this time, some letting up in the pressure of Judge Burnham's business affairs, and he was more at home and exerted himself to be enter-taining to both wife and son. As for Ruth, she made many concessions in the way of society life; she went with her husband to several state dinners that bored her exceedingly, and even to an elegant breakfast or two, and to one massive and oppressive evening party, where the crowds were too great either for dancing or cards; and she tormented her conscience, when once more at home, by asking it in what respect the evening's entertainments had been lifted higher be-cause of the absence of these amusements, or whether it would not have been better to have danced than to have indulged in some of the chitchat which she overheard; that old pretense of logic which she was too tired, just then, to cast aside, paralleled in folly by the statement, "It is better to lie than to steal," while one forgets or ignores the fact that if such a statement could be proven, it would prove nothing, unless, indeed, one were driven of necessity to a choice between those two employments.

As for the young ladies, their life flowed on in an endless stream of parties, concerts, private theatricals, and whatnot. Ruth was indebted to them for some letting up of her burdens. It was their choice not to have the elegant entertainment which was being planned until toward the close of the season; Seraph, who was more outspoken on many subjects than her sister, announcing frankly that their object was to see what the Everetts and the Wheelmans were going to do before their turn came, as there were hints in the air of something very unique from those quarters, and they, the Misses Burnham, were fully resolved that nothing more brilliant than their own party should be possible that season.

So Ruth breathed more freely because of this respite and kept her plans concerning the gathering to herself; time enough to bring them to the front, to be perhaps sharply combated, when the occasion for action was at hand. Meantime, in her leisure hours, she had some interests more to her mind than society furnished. She was now a member of the Woman's Christian Temperance Union; and in their weekly gathering for prayer she found herself surrounded once more by an atmosphere of earnest Christian life that rested and encouraged her. She had been so long among people who did not know how to pray that she had almost forgotten how busy some women were in their Lord's vineyard. It was inexpressibly comforting to be greeted as one of their number and to hear her name mentioned gratefully in their prayers. It being utterly foreign to her nature to live ever so slight a deception, she had told her husband at the first opportunity of her joining herself to this organization; but it was at a time when he was undergoing that sharp self-questioning which I told you was not without its good results, and though he winced a little at the information, and shrugged his shoulders, and said he had supposed such organizations were not in accordance with her taste, yet, on the whole, he bore the news very well; there were no crusades in the air at present, and although it was never safe to prophesy what a band of women would do, still, when it came to the point, he felt that he could probably trust his wife's elegant, highbred nature to do nothing incongruous. That they should meet to pray each week certainly could not harm anybody, and, while it was peculiar, of course there was nothing low about it; so, if they enjoyed such occupations, why should they not indulge themselves?

Judge Burnham realized that he was just now in high favor with the leading spirits of this Union. Their smiles were bright and their bows most cordial when they met him on the street; two or three, indeed, had offered him personal thanks for his intervention in behalf of their homes; and though he had gaily disclaimed any complicity with their schemes and assured them that he was no longer the owner of the Shenandoah and therefore not responsible for any of the whims which had brought about the present state of ill humor on the landlord's part, they accepted this as a graceful joke and were grateful all the same. As for the little new owner of the Shenandoah, it had not taken him an hour to learn how to "instruct his legal adviser" in such a thorough manner that the guests of that house had still to look elsewhere for their choice wines.

Matters generally were in the condition of lull which I have described when Judge Burnham came home one evening later than usual, with the announcement that he must leave by the morning train for a long and, he feared, tedious business trip that would detain him for perhaps two months. He spent half an hour in trying to convince Ruth that she could accompany him, leaving Erskine in charge of the young ladies; but, finding her steadily determined to do no such thing, he abandoned the idea and gave himself to the business of making ready.

Frequent journeys had been common experiences of his business life; but this was a more extended absence than he had of late been obliged to make, and Ruth, as she turned from the platform where, with Erskine, she had watched until the smoke of his departing train was lost in cloud, felt an unusual sense of loneliness. Life had been pleasanter, during these few weeks, than in a long time before; it seemed hard that the pleasantness must be so soon broken. Erskine begged to wait and watch the eastbound train, which was even then whistling in the distance, and among the passengers who hurried from it his mother saw young Hamlin. His California trip was concluded, then; would his intimacy with Minta be renewed, she wondered, or had she already found some greater attraction? And then she told herself resolutely that she need not worry about that; she had done what she could in regard to it; if they chose to be intimate friends now, they need not fear interference from her.

In the leisure from wifely duties which now came to her, she found herself turning more and more to the society of the women who composed the Christian Temperance Union. The prayer meeting, never very largely attended, was yet the gathering place for the choice spirits of the Union, and Ruth found herself rested and uplifted whenever she came in contact with them. She grew more and more interested in their plans for meeting the enemy and began to take an earnest part in some of them. She might never have made the proposition, but she warmly seconded it when one of the ladies said she thought they were strong enough to sustain a gospel temperance meeting on Sunday afternoons. Ruth had very little idea what sort of gatherings these were, but the name sounded inviting. The first meeting was a revelation to her. People came who she thought never went to meeting; and behaved, some of them, in such a manner as to make her half feel that they would better not be there. Wasn't it a sort of sacrilege to permit such conduct in a religious gathering? However, she rose above this; if they did not know how to behave in a gospel meeting, or, knowing, did not care, surely they needed the enlightening and refining influences of the gospel in an unusual degree. Besides, some of them sat quite still, chewed no tobacco, and listened, especially when Mrs. Bacon prayed, as though there was a new power about them whose influence they felt. Ruth grew intensely interested.

Meantime, home life went on much as usual. The young ladies were out every evening and kept closely to their rooms during the day, when not riding or paying visits, so that the lady of the house saw very little of them. She was relieved from even the semblance of supervision over their goings and comings by the installment of one who was supposed to have the right to protect them.

Mr. Jerome Satterley deserves, possibly, more than a

passing introduction; yet I find that I have heretofore not remembered to give him even that. You are to understand, then, that he had quite recently come into the family life as Miss Seraph's accepted suitor. Ruth, when informed of it, had realized once more that she certainly was not the mother of these girls; had she been, with what an utter sinking of heart would she have given one away into the keeping of such a man as Jerome Satterley! As it was, she smiled a faint smile, which had in it the slightest possible curve of the upper lip, as she said to Judge Burnham, "People must choose according to their individual tastes, I suppose."

Yet Mr. Jerome Satterley, in the eyes of the fastidious, fashionable world, was considered unexceptionable. He belonged to one of the old families of the city; had a reasonable fortune in his own right and an unlimited one which would probably come to him in the future. He was elegant in dress and manner; his mustache was carefully waxed, his shapely hands were cared for tenderly, and he knew how to hold a lady's fan or parasol, or attend her to the piano, or the carriage, or the refreshment room in the most approved style. In fact, the girls in that stage of development, when such phrases are used, said his manners were "perfectly lovely!" Yet Mrs. Burnham, unreasonable mortal, regarded him with feelings which were on the very verge of dislike. He had been well enough when she could pass him, along with others of his clique, with a cold bow or, at most, a dignified "good evening." But to be on such terms that he felt privileged to toy with the spools in her workbasket and say inane nothings to her while he waited for the young ladies, or to saunter in just before the bell rang and announce that he had come to stay for dinner, and to be obliged to accord to him not only the attention of a polite hostess but a semblance of the familiarity which his position in the family circle demanded, this was, to the last degree, an annoyance to Mrs. Burnham.

It was all the more trying, of course, because Mr. Satterley remained in blissful ignorance of his inability to entertain or interest his prospective mother-in-law. Truth to tell, he believed himself to be irresistible to all ladies, of whatever age and position. He considered himself posted on all subjects, whether in art, literature, or music; and unhesitatingly expressed his opinions with an air that was intended to quench any opposing views from any source whatever. Indeed, so entirely satisfied was he with his own wisdom that I do not think he would have hesitated to dispute the most eminent scientist which the world has produced if he ventured a scientific statement not in accordance with Mr. Satterley's preconceived opinion, though that opinion might have been adopted because of a chance remark that he had heard someone make at the breakfast table that morning. In short, Mr. Satterley had an abundance of the conceit which is the visible sign of superficiality. You will, perhaps, be able to imagine how trying, to a woman of Mrs. Burnham's stamp, was anything like familiarity with such a person. She confessed to herself, with cheeks that burned over the thought, that such things had power to annoy her; that when he began with an, "Oh! my dear Mrs. Burnham, I assure you, you are utterly mistaken," about some matter, trivial in itself but about which common sense would suppose her to be better posted than he could be, she felt, sometimes, like throwing her book at him.

Especially was it trying to her when he discoursed learnedly on religious topics, making the wildest statements, which were without even the shadow of a solid foundation, and proceeding gravely to argue about them as the accepted standards of the Church. Of course he was a young man, holding "literal views" and "advanced ideas," and whatever other term may be coined to disguise indifference or antagonism. And the patronizing way in which he would sometimes say, "Why, my dear Mrs. Burnham, I assure you, you are too cultivated a woman to hold to any such ignorant absurdities as are involved in that belief," made Ruth resolve, more than once, that she would make no reply to any of his platitudes, on any subject whatever.

"He is in his very babyhood as regards conversation," she said to herself with curling lip. "Of what use to try to talk with such a person?" But when a man asks a point-blank question, it is very difficult to make no reply.

It was just after one of these emphatic resolves that Ruth sat, silent and annoyed, listening to Mr. Satterley and Minta while they merrily chattered over a sermon that they had heard preached the night before. Mr. Satterley was waiting to escort Seraph to the theater, and this was Minta's method of amusing him while he waited. The text of the sermon had been quoted in a tone which would indicate that that, too, was food for amusement: "It is appointed unto all men once to die, and after that the judgment." After much merriment at the preacher's expense, Mr. Satterley attacked Ruth's grave and silent protest.

"My dear Mrs. Burnham, don't you think such themes are entirely obsolete in these days?"

"What themes?"

Determined not to discuss this question with him, the only way seemed to be to ward off his questions.

"Why, the themes which have to do with old

superstitious ideas of the judgment, and the attempt to frighten people into some sort of mysterious preparation for the same. I confess that I thought all such ideas were obsolete among people of culture."

"Do you think that death is obsolete, Mr. Satterley?"

"Oh! death—why, dear madam, that is but a debt which is paid to the laws of nature."

"Then is there any objection to learning how to pay it gracefully? If you are very familiar with death-beds, you must be aware that there are different ways of meeting this law. By the way, did it ever occur to you that it was a somewhat bewildering law of nature which takes the little child today and the old man of threescore and ten tomorrow; and it may be a young woman or a young man in his prime the next day? I could understand it better as a law if it were held to times and seasons, and meddled only with ripened grain."

He seemed puzzled by her reply—quite different from what he had expected—and hesitated for a moment, during which Seraph entered in all the dazzle of full dress.

"It is well you are come," Minta said; "Mamma and Jerome are quarreling about death and kindred cheerful subjects. There is no telling what the outcome would have been."

"It is suggestive, to say the least, Seraph, that your dress is very thin and your throat even more exposed than usual; and the night is cold. If I might be allowed to advise, I should say you ought to wear a warmer garment than that, unless you desire to court the presence of some of Death's attendants."

"Mamma," said Minta with mock seriousness,

"that is almost a pun; and about so solemn a subject as death. I am really shocked!"

Then Seraph: "A warmer dress would be more comfortable, I admit, but the trouble is, it isn't fashionable to wear high-necked garments in full dress. And you know, Mamma, you trained us to a very careful attention to fashion in all its details. We want to do full justice to your early teachings. As Madame Dupont used to say, 'A young lady who is not *au fait* in all that regards the demands of fashion is dead already.'"

It was a keen-pointed arrow, and it struck home. Ruth sat and thought about it after she was left alone, as she had sat and thought many a day since her work for these girls began to develop in ways of which she had not dreamed.

She had been careful even of the minutest details; she had labored to impress upon the minds of the uncouth, careless girls the importance of things, and shades, and widths, and shapes, and perfect fits. How could she know that they would come to mean so much more to these girls than she had meant? So much more than they had ever meant to her?

She recalled the day when, Susan having done for them all she could, the question of boarding school was discussed and the claims of Madame Dupont's establishment were urged by some of Ruth's fashionable friends. Susan had said quietly:

"I know Madame Dupont's girls; they all learn how to dance and dress."

Then she, the one who had stood in the place of mother, had replied:

"I know her girls have the name of being superficial, but that depends, after all, more on the girls than on their teachers. And really, Susan, it seems absolutely necessary that Seraph and Minta should go to a school where they give special attention to grace of movement and refinement of manner; they are so deficient in these respects. Beside, they teach dancing in all boarding schools, I suppose."

Susan had said no more, and after further discussion, the choice was made in favor of Madame Dupont, and to her the girls were sent for two years. And Madame Dupont's teachings had been: "A young lady who is not *au fait* in all that regards the demands of fashion is dead already."

Ruth's memories ended, as they nearly always did, with a sigh.

14

A Troublesome "Young Person"

ALMOST immediately after Seraph's departure with
Mr. Satterley, Minta had followed with Mr. Hamlin,
leaving Mrs. Burnham to the troubled thought of
which I told you.

Mingling with her anxieties was this one which
had to do with young Hamlin. It was all very well for
her to assure herself that she had no responsibility in
the matter, that she had done all she could; the fact
remained that people were looking to her to interfere
in this intimacy, which seemed to have been renewed
with tenfold vigor since Mr. Hamlin's return.

Marion had sent her a little note, assuring her that
the very worst might be believed of the stories which
were afloat concerning him and begging her to use
her influence with Judge Burnham before it should
be too late. "I have no influence," declared Ruth; she
was quite alone when she said it and would not have
repeated it in any person's hearing for the world. But
in her heart she believed it to be painfully true. At one
time she resolved to include Mrs. Dennis's note in her

next letter to her husband, without comment of any sort; but she shrank from doing this in the belief that only harm could come of it, and in her miserable vacillation as to what was best to do, she did nothing.

Even though Mrs. Stuart Bacon said to her one day, "Dear Mrs. Burnham, do you know it is probable that that young Hamlin may be arrested for securing money under false pretenses? Isn't it sad, and his family connections have always been so eminently respectable?—" not a word said Mrs. Stuart Bacon about the young man's intimacy in her family, but Mrs. Burnham's cheeks glowed over the thought that this, too, was a warning.

It was in the evening of that day that Mr. Satterley said to her: "I doubt whether the Judge, if he were at home, would care to have Minta's name coupled with young Hamlin's as much as it is; there are some ugly stories afloat concerning him."

"Then why do you not warn her?" Mrs. Burnham had asked irritably, angry with herself that, by so much, she must seem to accept his relations with the family and also that she must, by this, admit to him her own powerlessness. But Mr. Satterley had shrugged his shoulders, and laughed, and asked her if her experiences with Minta led her to believe that that young lady was disposed to receive warnings very graciously. And then they had been interrupted.

These two last things Mrs. Burnham did report to her husband, with the information that the young man was becoming marked in his attentions; that on some pretext or other he and Minta were together nearly every evening, and that, as he was well aware, there was nothing which she could say or do to prevent it. This letter was sent after Judge Burnham had been absent for six weeks, and his wife hoped that the hints it contained might hasten his movements.

Meantime, on the evening in question, she was not left long to solitude. Kate came to her in the library with a puzzled air. "Mrs. Burnham, there is a young person in the hall who asked to see you on special business and inquired particularly if you were alone."

"What sort of a young person, Kate? Some friend of the young ladies?"

"I don't think so, ma'am; oh! no, I am sure it isn't. She is neat-looking and civil spoken enough, but she doesn't belong to them."

"Then I suppose it is someone in search of employment; you might take her name and address and tell her I will see what I can do for her, though I am not on that committee."

"If you please, Mrs. Burnham, I don't think that will satisfy her. I asked her if there was a message, and if it was something I could do for you and not trouble you; and she said, Oh no! she must see you, and see you quite alone."

"Poor thing! it must be someone in distress. Let her come to the library, and excuse me to any callers while she is here."

But the "young person" who presently appeared before her did not look in the least as Ruth had immediately planned that she should. She was a girl of perhaps twenty, with a face which under favorable circumstances might have been beautiful; as it was, framed in clustering, natural curls and set off by eyes which, when they were not red with recent weeping, must have been very lovely, she was strikingly interesting. Her manner was so much that of a lady that Ruth half rose to meet her with the ceremony of society customs, though the exceeding plainness of the young woman's dress showed that she was not making an ordinary society call.

"Mrs. Burnham, I believe," she said in a clear and not uncultured voice.

"That is my name," said that lady. "Be seated, please. You have the advantage of me; your face is familiar, but I cannot think where I have seen it."

"I belong at the lace counter in Myers & McAlpine's store; you have seen me there."

The tone was very assured; evidently this young woman remembered her customer. A sudden light appeared on Mrs. Burnham's face; she recalled the pretty young girl who had interested her by courteous and unselfish ways.

"Be seated," she said again cordially, with a wave of her hand toward the low rocker nearby. "I am glad you have come to see me; is there any way in which I can serve you?"

"Mrs. Burnham, may I ask you a question which may seem very rude? I do not mean it for that."

"The poor child is in some trouble," thought the lady; "some difficulty between her employer and herself, probably, in which she thinks I can help her. Well, if I can, I will."

"Ask me whatever you wish," she said aloud, "and I will answer it if I can," and her smile was intended to be reassuring. But the question was utterly unlike what she had expected.

"Mrs. Burnham, is the taller of your two daughters engaged to be married to Mr. Jerome Satterley?" Then as the look of astonishment on her hostess's face deepened into displeasure, she added in nervous haste, "I knew you would consider me a bold, insolent girl, but I have indeed good reasons for asking; and I thought I ought to come to you rather than to anyone else."

"Perhaps, if you could give me your reasons for asking so strange a question upon a subject which cannot in any way concern you, I might be able to judge you more leniently."

Mrs. Burnham's voice was coldly dignified now; she had an abundance of what, for want of a better name, we may call family pride; but the girl made haste to respond:

"Oh! indeed, madam, it does concern me most bitterly; if it did not, I could not have come to you with it. If you will answer me just that question, I shall know better how to tell you the story, and I am sure you will say that I ought to have asked it."

Mrs. Burnham was puzzled, but the girl was evidently intensely in earnest.

"We do not usually speak of such family matters, save to intimate friends," she said; "but it is no secret, I believe, and I see no reason why I should hesitate to tell you that Mr. Satterley and Miss Seraph Burnham are engaged to be married."

"Then, madam, I ought to tell you, so that you, her mother, can explain to her that he is not to be trusted."

Even at such a time, Ruth could hardly restrain a smile of sarcasm over the thought that she was supposed by anyone to be the person to advise with and care for Miss Seraph Burnham. But nothing of this thought showed in her words.

"Indeed!" she said with lifted eyebrows. "That is a serious charge; one should know exceedingly well what one is saying who uses such language as that."

"Oh! I know; I know only too well what I am saying. I can give you proof of it; I did not come here because I wanted to, or without knowing what risk to my own reputation I ran; but I thought I could talk with you, because, Mrs. Burnham—" She broke off suddenly, and then, before Ruth could speak, began again, working the fingers of her ungloved hands together nervously while she spoke: "I need not make it a long story; I have been engaged to that man for nearly a year, and we were to have been married very soon. When I tell you this, and then tell you that he left me without a word of explanation, without any cause, so far as I know, beyond the one that he found a face that suited him better, do you not think I am true in saying that your daughter cannot trust him?"

"Engaged to you!" These were the only words Mrs. Burnham seemed capable of speaking.

"Yes'm; engaged to me. It sounds strange to you; I knew it would. You cannot see how it is possible that the name of a poor girl like me, a clerk in a fancy store, should have the right to be coupled with that of Jerome Satterley. I do not wonder; I used to think so myself; and I said it was because he was unlike other men—nobler and better. Mrs. Burnham, you will want proof of my story; I can give it. Look, I still wear the ring he gave me. I am a poor girl, but we are respectable; we were not even poor always; Papa was a wealthy merchant, and Mr. Durand, of the firm of Durand & Parkman, is my uncle; Mamma is a widow, and we are poor enough now. I have been a clerk in a fancy store for three years, helping to support her and the younger ones."

"And you met Mr. Satterley where?"

"In New York; I was a clerk in Jennings', at the silk counter; I met him at my uncle's here in town one evening, and then, when he came to New York, he called on me and was good to Mamma and the children—better than anyone in the world, I thought—and in a very few weeks he told me that he had come to New York on purpose to get acquainted with me, that he did not care how poor I was, that he had money enough for both of us, and that Mamma should live again in the style to which she had been used. He stayed in New York for four months; his uncle, Mr. Telford, is the president of the Grand Street Bank, and he stayed at his uncle's. When he went away he was to come again in the spring for me; I can show you many letters from him which say so. Oh! I could prove it by witnesses if it were necessary. He talked frankly to Mamma; she did not trust him, and he took it hard, and so did I; but Mamma knew."

She drew from her pocket a package of letters, carefully tied with a blue ribbon, and began with eager haste to untie them, while Mrs. Burnham questioned her as one in a dream.

"Let me understand; I thought you were a clerk here in town."

"I am, madam; I have been here two months. I secured a place; Mr. Jennings recommended me. I had not heard from Mr. Satterley in weeks, and I was so miserable, so sure that he was sick or that some serious trouble had come upon him, that I could not rest without trying to find out; so I came here; and I have found out. He does not know that I am in the city, but I have seen him almost every day for two months, and I have watched him with your daughter until I know she is going through just what I have been, and I want to warn her. Believe me, Mrs. Burnham, that is all I want; it is not money that I am after. I never mean to bring any trial for breach of promise, though the promises were plain enough and often repeated; read that," and she thrust before her hostess an open letter, which at first glance could be recognized as Mr. Satterley's very peculiar writing. As the girl said, the promises were plain enough and repeated oftener than for an honorable man would seem to have been necessary. Ruth, as she read it, could not help thinking aloud, "This reads like a man who is not accustomed to being believed."

"Does it? I did not think so; and I believed him utterly; I almost quarreled with Mamma because she could not fully trust him. I used to lie awake nights, thinking how we—he and I—would heap beautiful coals of fire on her head. He told me I should furnish her room myself, with all the elegances that money could buy, and that I should make it exactly like the one she used to have, if I chose."

What an evening it was! The doorbell rang several times, and Kate came once with a message from one of the ladies of the Union, who was importunate; but Ruth waved her imperiously away, with the assurance that she could see nobody, no matter whom. Late into the evening the talk went on. Proof piled on proof, incontestable, that the elegant Mr. Satterley, with the date of his wedding day actually set, had turned in swiftness and silence away from his deliberately chosen bride and set himself vigorously to wooing another.

"But I do not understand," Mrs. Burnham said at last; "I do not see how he expected to manage; he must know that you will hear of it and that you can make him serious trouble. Why does he not at least try to win you to silence?"

A deep blush overspread the young girl's hitherto pale face, and she shook her head as she spoke quickly:

"He knows that I will not give him any trouble in the way you mean; he trusts me as fully as I trusted him. If I cannot respect him, I want nothing of him. But could I let him deceive another as he has me? In the sight of God, Mrs. Burnham, all I want is to save her; I ought to have spoken before, but I could not believe it possible. He may be in earnest this time, but what proof can he give her that he has not given me?"

Over another question of her visitor, Ruth felt the blood roll in waves up to her very forehead.

"Mrs. Burnham, do you think a person who is a Christian ought to marry one who is not?"

"No," said Judge Burnham's wife steadily and without hesitancy; and then that telltale blood had mantled her face.

"Mamma thinks the same," said the unsuspecting girl, intent only on her own story. "And, oh! I thought so, too, once, but I gave it up; I was so sure I could win him to Christ, and here I could not even—"

She stopped abruptly, as she had frequently during the evening. There seemed to be some sentences that she did not trust herself to finish. The voice was lower when she commenced again:

"Sometimes I have thought it was God's punishment upon me, for putting another in the place of him."

"It is God's love to you, my friend, in saving you from a miserable life." The words were impulsive, but they came from the heart's depths.

She sat and thought long about it all after her guest had gone; sat even until she heard the merry voices of the returning young ladies and their attendants. Then she gathered in haste the work and the magazine that had long before dropped from her hands and made a retreat to the privacy of her own room. She had much to think about. What part was she to play in this pitiful tragedy of human life which had been so unexpectedly thrust in upon her?

She had promised the poor little clerk at the lace counter that she would do what she could toward warning, or, as she phrased it, "saving" her daughter Seraph.

Her daughter! What a miserable mockery of words! If she were in very truth her daughter, if her spirit burned within her, would not the girl recoil in horror from a life so utterly false as this? Yet did she expect it of her?

She sat late into the night, trying to plan how it would all be: what she should say to Seraph, and also, more important, what Seraph would say to her, and what the outcome of it all would be.

Would it humiliate the girl more, she wondered, to have the knowledge of her promised husband's false nature come through her lips? Yet who could tell it if she did not? The father was away, and there was certainly need for haste if anything was to be accomplished. Though what could she hope to accomplish? Yet in the name of their common womanhood she could not let this one, to whom she stood before the world in the place of mother, go on in ignorance of the hollowness of the staff she was trying to lean upon.

Ruth pitied her and pitied herself for the part she was to bear in the drama, and fell into a troubled sleep at last, still uncertain how to perform her task.

Still uncertain, in fact, the next morning when, opportunely alone with Seraph soon after breakfast and mindful of her promise to let not another day pass without warning her, she began with a hurried "Seraph," spoken in a tone of such evident perturbation as to cause that young lady to turn from the flowers she was arranging, and answer a wondering and inquiring, "Well?"

And then Ruth wished she had not spoken and knew not what words to put next.

15

"ALL COME!"

"DO YOU know a young girl by the name of Hollister—Estelle Hollister?"

"Never heard of her." The reply was made in that tone of easy indifference which says, "She is nothing to me, and I have no interest whatever in her story."

"She is in charge of the lace counter at Myers & McAlpine's."

"Oh! a pretty girl, with yellow-brown hair? Yes, I noticed her; I remember somebody called her Estelle; she admires me, I fancy," with a little half-conscious laugh at this tribute to her beauty. "She waits on me as though I were a queen."

"Did you ever hear Mr. Satterley mention her?"

"Jerome? Certainly not. He has no special interest in pretty girls in the abstract, I believe." Again that indifferent tone and half-conscious laugh.

"He knows her," said Mrs. Burnham, and the tone was so significant as to cause an angry flush on Seraph's face and a haughty inflection in her voice as she said:

"What do you mean?"

It may not have been a wise way of commencing; Mrs. Burnham, as she thought it over afterward, felt sure that it was not, but at all events the subject was fairly opened; there could be no waiting now for a more favorable time. She went through the story steadily, with admirable brevity and yet with telling distinctness; she had studied the points which could not be challenged and presented them clearly, yet with as few words as possible. If she had been a very tender, real mother, she might have made the statement more tenderly, with pitiful, loving words slipped in between the wounds she felt obliged to make, but she could hardly have done it more skillfully with a view to letting her victim know the truth with as little torturous circumlocution as possible. She was conscious of a great pity for the girl to whom she was speaking; if she really loved the man, it would be a terrible blow; in any case, it would be galling to her pride.

She did not know whether to be glad or sorry that they were interrupted by the sudden entrance of Minta, before there was opportunity for a word in reply. Then Ruth went away to her own room to think it over and wonder what sort of an explosion she had set in train. She found that her knowledge of Seraph was not sufficient for her to determine with any feeling of certainty what her course would be. That she was capable of being very angry was unquestionable, but on whom her anger would be visited was a matter of doubt and more or less anxiety. It was, therefore, in the expectation of some sort of moral upheaval that Mrs. Burnham passed the remainder of the day; and she might be said to be prepared for almost anything when Seraph's voice held her in the library that evening just before dinner.

"Mamma, we were interrupted in the midst of your

exciting tale this morning. I was sorry, for I wanted to ask you whether you intended to take Jerome into your confidence, also."

"I do not understand you," was Ruth's cold reply; the extreme flippancy of the young lady's words and manner led her to expect nothing but rudeness from this interview.

"Why, I thought my language was plain. I mean, do you intend to tell him about the young woman with whom you are on confidential terms, or have you engaged to enlighten only me?"

"Do you not intend to tell him?"

"I! Why should I? My lady did not take refuge with me; it was you she honored with her confidence."

"Seraph, there is really no reason why you should speak of the subject in this manner. I told you a sorrowful story this morning, because I thought it must be told; and I did it with as little pain to you as I knew how; and only because, judging you as one woman of honor judges another, I felt it was your right to know it."

"And what do you expect me to do?"

"I do not presume to dictate, or even advise; I promised the poor girl that I would warn you, and, as well as I knew how, I have done so; there my responsibility ceases. You will do, it is to be hoped, what you think you ought. If I thought I would be understood, I would express to you what I certainly feel—my deep pain that you should have been so deceived; but as it is—"

Seraph interrupted her hurriedly. "But as it is, there is no need for anything of that sort; I am sure I feel grateful for your sympathy, but I think it misplaced. You and I look at a great many things from different standpoints; this is one of them. I do not think Jerome is the worst man in the world merely because he has had a little flirtation with a shop girl; I do not suppose it is by any means so important a matter as she has made you believe. Girls of that stamp always think a gentleman wants to marry them if he lifts his hat to them in passing; in any case, it is all over now, and I do not see why I should make him and myself uncomfortable by mentioning it. You say the girl doesn't want money, but a handsome present will go far toward making life brighter to her, I have no doubt, and one of these days I will see that she receives it. I tell you this that you may see I can be sympathetic as well as yourself. What I want to say to you is that I would prefer your not mentioning the matter, even to Papa; I don't see any occasion. If the silly girl had come to me with her complaints, it would have been much more sensible in her, I think."

What was a woman of Mrs. Burnham's character to reply to a woman of such a character as this? She stood before her dismayed; she really had not supposed that society could build in a few short years so fair and false a structure.

"I have nothing further to say," she replied at last; "I did not promise to tell the shameful story to anyone but you; whether I ought to do anything more I have not yet decided; it is not so pleasant a theme that I shall like to dwell upon it. I will only remind you that it may not be wise to keep your father in ignorance of it, in view of your approaching marriage; the poor girl may have friends who will not be so considerate as herself, and your father's services as a lawyer may be needed, in which case it might be well to have him forewarned."

A swift look of mingled pain and anger was the only reply that Seraph had opportunity to make to this, for her mother passed her and went immediately to the dining room. Dinner was served at once, and Jerome Satterley was one of the family party, Seraph chatting with him as gaily as usual while the woman who had been acquainted with the fashionable world for years found herself too shaken, and distressed, and angry, to talk with anyone. The only comment on this was made by Mr. Satterley as the door closed between them, while Seraph and he made their way to the music room. "What is the matter with Mrs. Judge? Have I displeased her more than usual, in any way? It seems to me that the word *glum* would about fit her disposition tonight." And Seraph's gay, sweet laugh rang out as she said, "There's no accounting for Mamma's moods, as you will learn when you come to know her better."

Mrs. Burnham did not know what Seraph did, but for herself she knew she avoided even the street on which Myers & McAlpine's store was located; it made her heart throb with indignant pain even to think of the sorrows and wrongs of the fatherless young girl who toiled there.

And the days went by, and still Judge Burnham did not return. Ruth did not even know whether or not he received her words of warning; he was constantly moving from point to point, and his letters had great difficulty in finding him; he wrote frequently, always with the same story—unexpected delay and the hope that his exile was now nearly over. Matters were in this state on a certain Sabbath afternoon in March, when Ruth left her home to go to the "gospel temperance meeting" in a state of great perturbation. The reason for this was twofold. In the first place, much to her own astonishment, she had been persuaded into allowing herself to be named as leader of the meeting.

You who were well acquainted with Ruth Erskine will remember that this would have been a startling innovation to her, even in her girlhood, and the matron had not developed in those directions. It had been a very great trial to her to consent to taking her turn with the others; rather, the few among the others who were willing to share this responsibility. Still, she was not lacking in moral courage, you will remember, and her conscience, being closely questioned, could give her no sufficient reason why she should refuse to share in a work whose object she approved. Once pledged, she made what preparation she could for the formidable work.

The second source of anxiety she tried hard to hold in the background until the hour of her trial should be over. It grew out of a briefly worded, bewildering sort of note from Marion, brought her by a special messenger but an hour before.

> *Dear Ruth:*
>
> *Forgive my importunity, but the time has come when you must really interfere in regard to that intimacy, even to the extent of issuing commands if need be, until her father returns. I will not trust myself to be more explicit on paper, but Mr. Dennis wishes me to assure you from him that he believes it will be a matter of lifelong regret with you if you do not protect her now. Do not delay another day.*
>
> *In great haste,*
> *Marion*

"Protect her!" As if she did not know that Minta would tolerate no attempt at protection from her! What was she to do? If Judge Burnham were only at home! If Mr. Satterley were— But of what use to mention him! Ruth had only contempt for him. But it was the hour for the meeting, and she must put this thing away for a little time longer; when the strain of the next two hours was over, she would have time to think.

As she hurried along the street, a little late and much annoyed thereat, her eye fell upon something that caused her added annoyance. The committee of arrangements were but mortals, and, therefore, mistakes of judgment as well as of taste ought to have been pardonable; but Ruth was in no mood to grant pardon as there flamed at her from the lamppost, in what seemed to her painfully conspicuous letters, the announcement:

> GOSPEL TEMPERANCE MEETING
> AT BURNHAM HALL
> TIME, 3 O'CLOCK SHARP.
> ALL COME!
> MRS. JUDGE BURNHAM WILL PRESIDE.

To Ruth's excited fancy, it seemed as though her name was shouted at her by those great staring letters. From every lamppost it flamed out. This was entirely an innovation; no leader's name had been announced before. Why should those hateful capitals be forced upon her? On the whole, she reached the hall in a very excited frame of mind, and it took all the influence of the opening hymns and prayer to reduce her to something like composure. The hall was unusually full; Ruth thought there were more men present than she had ever seen there before. Her voice sounded strange to herself as she read the Bible verses which she had selected as the foundation of her talk, but the listeners, to judge by the entirely quiet, respectful attention they gave her, were satisfied. It was a novel situation. At first the leader seemed able to think only of the loud beating of her own heart, and while she was reading the last verse but one of her selections, she realized that she could not recall a single word of the sentences that she had prepared for the introduction; but the very last verse took hold upon her thoughts, stilled her wild excitement, helped her to feel that she was permitted to be God's messenger to these men and women, many of whom showed plainly by their faces that they knew him not. "'Thus saith the Lord, Stand in the court of the Lord's house, and speak unto all the cities of Judah, that come to worship in the Lord's house, all the words that I command thee to speak unto them; diminish not a word; if so be they will hearken, and turn every man from his evil way . . . and thou shalt say unto them, Thus saith the Lord.'"

The wonder and solemnity of the fact that God had given her a message to deliver here held her by its power. The one thing she now desired was to speak just the words which he commanded. Her language was very simple. She not only could not recall the carefully prepared phrases which she had meant to use, but she ceased to try. Out of the fullness of her conviction that they were men and women who needed God and that he was waiting to receive them, she spoke. The room was very still. The women who were with her on the platform listened with a sort of hushed awe. They forgot to be nervous; to wonder whether that young man in the corner who was chewing tobacco meant mischief; to whisper together as to what had better be sung when the speaker was through; or to do any of the little restless things that in their nervous anxiety they were generally led into doing. Suddenly Ruth, in the middle of a sentence, her whole heart, she thought, centered in a desire to lead someone to feel the need of the Savior, came to a dead pause. Every vestige of color fled from her face, leaving her white and motionless, like a marble statue.

Mrs. Stuart Bacon half rose in alarm. Was she going to faint? Oh! what would they do? Down near the door, or at least not more than three seats from the door, at the extreme end of the long hall, seated between certain rough-looking men who had crowded in late, was Judge Burnham. Mrs. Stuart Bacon had seen him when he came in. She had nudged Mrs. Parkman's elbow while Ruth was reading those Bible verses and had whispered that she did not know Judge Burnham had returned, and she must say it was a very beautiful tribute to his wife's influence for him to lay aside his prejudices sufficiently to come and hear her. But Ruth had not seen him until that supreme moment, when the sight of him took from her the words she was about to speak and brought her with a rude shock back to earth again. It all passed in a moment, and Mrs. Bacon sank back in her chair with a relieved sigh.

Ruth had forgotten the sentence she was uttering. Never mind; that strange power as of God took hold of her again, said to her, speaking low, so no ear but hers could hear:

"You are God's messenger; you are to speak to these men all that God has commanded you; you are to diminish nothing; you may never have another opportunity. What human being ought to influence you now? Say unto them, 'Thus saith the Lord.'"

It takes much longer to tell it than it did to think it. Before some had even noticed the hesitation, the clear, cultured voice went on:

"Young man, God is speaking to you; he wants you; wants you today; wants your brains, and your strength, and your influence, for himself, for himself. Why do you wait? You know you need him."

There was a movement on the very last seat; a sort of undertone disturbance: two young men pushing each other, chuckling, speaking almost aloud in their amusement. Judge Burnham arose, went with a light tread over to the last seat, and sat down close beside the rougher of the two young men. The disturbance ceased. The clear voice went on, gathering firmness. The movement had not disturbed her; neither had the muttering of the two bent on mischief. She had for the time being gotten above it all. The women seated on the platform looked at one another and nodded in satisfaction. They could see each other's thoughts: "It was splendid in Judge Burnham to do that; he is not going to have his wife treated rudely." They should not wonder if he could be won into coming every Sabbath. What a stroke of genius it was to have secured Mrs. Burnham as a co-laborer! Besides, who had imagined that she could talk like this?

So much we know about people's hearts. Judge Burnham was never in a more rebellious turmoil against his surroundings and environments than at that moment. He could have told them a curious story about his coming to that meeting.

16

On the Mount and in the Valley

IT WAS Ruth's own letter of warning reaching him at a late hour on Saturday, having been sent after him from various post offices where he had left addresses, that finally brought him home on the Sunday express instead of stopping off at Shoreham and waiting for the midnight train, as he had planned.

A few hours, more or less, might not make any difference; but then possibly it might; and being a businessman, accustomed to weighing with scales that were turned sometimes by very slight causes, he resolved to postpone his business at Shoreham and go home at once.

On the journey he had been more or less annoyed: several political discussions with other Sunday travelers had ruffled him considerably; then he had been obliged to listen to and explain away a very much distorted edition of the story connected with the Shenandoah and its change of owners. Very wild, and what he considered very silly, reports about his having changed his political basis came to his ears, and he was obliged to refuse congratulations from one side and smooth the feelings of a ruffled constituent on the other. Altogether, when he stepped from the platform of the train at his own station, he was in the mood to wish that he had not been such a fool as to cater to his wife's whims and so make all this talk about the Shenandoah, and to wish especially that he had never heard of such an organization as the Woman's Christian Temperance Union.

Imagine him, then, walking rapidly uptown, making an effort to throw off his ill humor and be ready to greet his family graciously, confronted by those flaming letters on the lampposts, the bulletin boards, in every conspicuous place possible:

GOSPEL TEMPERANCE MEETING
AT BURNHAM HALL
TIME, 3 O'CLOCK SHARP.
ALL COME!

"They even have my name dragged in, because I happen to own the building. I'll have that hall named something the first thing I do tomorrow," muttered the irate man; and then he rubbed his eyes and shaded them from the glare of the afternoon sunlight and looked again. Those large letters—could he believe his eyes or his senses?

MRS. JUDGE BURNHAM WILL PRESIDE.

It was hard on him, really. I will not have you entirely unsympathetic with him; if you do not try to understand the people who are of another world than yours—to, in short, "put yourselves in their places" occasionally—how do you expect to be other than narrow and cold in your charities?

This was entirely contrary to all his preconceived ideas of propriety, as well as utterly out of line with his sympathies. It was also very unlike Ruth; no one understood that better than she did herself; she, as you know, had been through a conflict on account of it; she had taken up the work as a duty, a cross from which she shrank. Her husband, having neither word in his vocabulary, could not be expected to understand how it was possible for this sentence to refer to his wife. Yet what other Mrs. Judge Burnham was there in the city, or in the world, for that matter? This mystery must be looked into without delay. He drew out his watch; it was not fifteen minutes past three, and that odious Burnham Hall was but four blocks away; he must go and see for himself. And this was what had given Mrs. Stuart Bacon a chance to nudge her companion's elbow and smile her surprise and approval when the great man entered the hall.

He went forward the moment the closing hymn was sung, with a smile of greeting on his face and a hand held out to Ruth. "You did not expect me in your audience, I fancy?"

"Hardly," said Ruth, "since I thought you still hundreds of miles away; but you do not need to hear me say I am glad, though the surprise, for a moment, nearly took my breath away."

She seemed not in the least embarrassed and was giving only half attention to him, her eyes, meantime, following the movements of a roughly dressed young man, who appeared to hesitate, in doubt just what to do. He advanced a few steps, then turned and stood irresolute. Just as Judge Burnham had possessed himself of his wife's heavy, fur-lined cloak and had said, "You would do well to wait until you reach purer air before you don this," she turned abruptly from him, made a quick dash forward, and laid her hand on the frayed coat sleeve of the young man. "May I speak just a word with you?" he heard her ask, and then he stood and waited, with what grace he could, while the voice dropped too low for even his strained ears; and he could only watch. The young man's eyes were bent on the floor, but his face was working under the spell of some powerful emotion; he even put up his hand and furtively brushed away a starting tear as Ruth talked and her husband chafed. What an insufferable piece of folly it all seemed to him! His wife standing there in eager, low-toned speech with an uncouth fellow smelling of tobacco and cheap whiskey; actually keeping her light hold on his arm with that shapely hand of hers! More than that, at some response of the fellow's given with apparent energy, and a lifting of his eyes, a light such as even he had never seen before broke over the face whose every expression he thought he knew, and then the ungloved hand met that hard, red one in a firm and evidently cordial grasp. It was but a few minutes, though it seemed almost hours to the waiting husband; then she turned to him again, the peculiar light still in her eyes.

"I am ready now," she said; and they went down the stairs with the noisy crowd and had walked nearly the length of a block before Judge Burnham broke the silence.

"It occurs to me that this is an entirely new departure."

"Very," said Ruth gently; "I never did such a thing before in my life; I did not imagine that I possibly could."

Even now she was preoccupied. She was hardly giving a thought to the one to whom she was speaking, or to the probable effect of the entire scene on his nerves. The simple truth was, she had just been brought face-to-face with a new and solemn joy which is unlike any other joy to be experienced this side of heaven, which is understood only by those who have experienced it and which can no more be described than one can describe the air we breathe or the heaven to which we are going. She had been permitted of the Lord to speak such words as had moved the soul of a young man—a young man who was in peril—whose widowed mother was even now mourning for him as one lost to her and to God. He had been moved more than merely emotionally; that tremendous potentate that rules destinies—the human will—had spoken.

"I will do it," the young man had said, and the tone and the look that accompanied the words, and above all the answering witness of her own soul, made her sure that the decision which had to do with time and eternity had been made.

And she had been the instrument! It was the first time in her life that she had ever been so distinctly chosen and used. Was this a time for wondering what a man who belonged outside the camp would have to say to her, even though that man was her husband? There were humiliations enough ahead, but this was her moment of exaltation.

Her manner irritated Judge Burnham. How could it be otherwise? He did not understand it. Was she trying to show him how utterly indifferent she was to his wishes?

"We should have agreed perfectly in that opinion," he said with marked significance. "I confess I had not the least idea that you could possibly do anything of the sort. Is it a proper time to ask how you came to make such an unpleasant discovery?"

"As what?" she asked gently, but with infinite stupidity. She had not been following him enough to understand him. She was thinking what an evening it would be to that boy's mother when she heard the news.

"As that you were endowed with the peculiar qualities which make it possible for a woman to step onto a public platform and harangue an audience of coarse men and lowbred women?"

Certainly these words were not easily misunderstood. Ruth flushed under them, but still her voice was gentle, unusually so:

"I did not harangue them, I think; I was only talking to them about the power of Jesus Christ to save, and I felt so keenly that they needed saving as to forget all other considerations."

"What do you think of that?" he asked, almost fiercely.

They were passing one of those odious posts, with its flaming letters. They looked as much as a foot in length to Ruth as her eye caught them now.

"I do not like it at all," she said hastily. "I do not understand why they did it. At first I was really angry, but I do not mind it so much now."

"I am sorry to hear it. Will it impress you in any degree if I tell you that I mind it very much indeed? It was the first greeting which I received on my arrival, and if I had caught the fellow putting one of them up, I should have kicked him into the road. I know why they did it. They like to have your name bandied about the town, as it will be tonight, in the mouth of every low saloon keeper and the drunken habitués of his house. It adds to their importance to know that they have done something which will set the vulgar world agape. 'Anything for notoriety' is their motto."

The flush had died away from Ruth's face; she was growing very pale. This was a rapid descent from the mount whereon she had been standing. Only a moment before she had felt as though earth and its commonplaces could not touch her again, because she had been permitted for a moment to stand face-to-face with Jesus Christ. Yet here was the keen, cruel world at her very elbow.

They had been walking rapidly. Unconsciously Judge Burnham had quickened his pace with every angry word he spoke and by this time they had reached their own door. He applied his night latch, held open the door with his accustomed courtesy for his wife, then closing it quickly, stooped and kissed her, and held her with his arm while he spoke:

"Ruth, I am angry; I don't think I was ever more so. It seems to me I have been unfairly treated; as if you must understand me better than this afternoon's scene would indicate. But I have been long away and have missed you sorely. I have been looking forward all day to the pleasure of meeting you. It was hard on a man to have to meet you where and as I did. But I do you justice, even now, in my indignation. I give you credit for not being of the same spirit with this notoriety-loving crowd, though you have somehow fallen among them. I know the power of religious fanaticism. I have studied it more or less as I came in contact with it in the line of my profession; I even know that it has been carried to such excess before now that the doors of lunatic asylums have had to close on its victims. I trust I may have strength of mind enough to shield you from great harm. You will bear me witness that I have not often laid commands on you of any sort; that in theory and practice I believe in the utmost freedom of individual will between husband and wife that is compatible with true dignity; but you have really forced me, unintentionally, I fully believe, but none the less really, to say to you that it is something more than my request—much more, indeed—that you should never enter the doors of such a place again as that one in which I found you this afternoon. Now let me beg that you will make a complete change of dress, both for your sake and mine. Let us get rid of any reminder of the offensive scene. Positively, Ruth, even the lace on your sleeve smells of bad tobacco."

Mrs. Burnham went up the winding staircase with a slow, weary air; all the pulses of her life seemed to have stopped beating. Yet thought was all the time very busy. She had been brought suddenly down to the level of the commonplace again, with questions to settle which must be thought about.

Just how far was she bound to obey her husband's dictation in this matter? For, though courteously phrased, it amounted to nothing less than dictation. Was she bound in honor to withdraw from this bit of Christian work to which her soul had responded? Must she even give up the hour spent with those Christian women in their place of prayer? Had not the Lord called her to the work? Had he not honored her in it, and were her husband's claims to be put before his? If she had really been the human means of saving a soul this afternoon, was not that return enough to enable her to endure all the disagreements of life and the discomforts arising therefrom?

But on the other hand, had the Lord called her to do just this thing, whether her husband approved or not? There were so many things of which he did not approve which she knew she must do nonetheless. Of course, when it was possible to yield, she ought, perhaps, to do so. She did not know, and found that she could not decide, just where the "ought" came in. It was easy to tell what she wanted to do. She would like to go down to her husband that moment and say to him that she was sorry their two ways did not agree, but that in this way which she had chosen, and which had its reward, and which she loved with all her soul, she should certainly walk. Ruth Burnham of yesterday would have done so, but the Ruth Burnham of today had been on the mount with God for a little while, and found somewhat to her bewilderment that all her judgments of men and things were softened, and that even such questions as these must be looked at in the light of unselfishness.

Meantime, she slowly made the entire changes in her dress which had been called for. This much, at least, she could do; she was glad there was no question in her mind about it. She smiled somewhat curiously over the discovery that her recent experiences had made her look at even so trivial a thing as this in a different light. Yesterday she would have said that she was sorry her dress did not suit him, but it really was the most appropriate garment she had for the hour, and she must ask him to be content with it. Today such a response looked humiliatingly hateful. Had she really been a disagreeable Christian through all these years?

At last she came to this conclusion: that no decision in regard to the other matter was possible now; she must put it aside with steady will until such time as she could be alone to think and to discover just where that solemn "ought" belonged. At present there was other work for her—disagreeable work; there was that letter of warning from Marion in her pocket. Must it be shown to her husband? She shrank from this with an aversion of which she was ashamed, though she recognized the reason; it was because she did not want to hear these friends of hers criticized, sneered at, perhaps; but what a humiliating thing that she must expect for them such treatment at her husband's hands!

On the whole, you will not think it was a pleasant homecoming after her hour of exaltation.

Yet I want to tell you that the last thing she did, before joining her husband in the library, was to kneel in her place of prayer and thank God for the clasp of that rough, red hand, and the decision in the voice as it said to her, "I will do it." Above all the turmoil of conflicting anxieties rose the note of joy for this new soldier added to the ranks of her King.

Erskine was in the library in full ride of joy over his father's return. There could be no doubt as to the heartiness of this welcome, and Judge Burnham was enjoying to the full the eager kisses and extravagant delight of his boy. There were no vexed differences of opinion here to mar the pleasure; at least, there were none which appeared on the surface.

He arose on his wife's entrance, smiled as he gave her a swift survey and noted that she was dressed in his favorite colors, said "Thank you" in a very expressive tone, and drew an easy chair for her close to his own. Evidently he considered the matter that had come between them already settled.

The talk flowed on, on different topics, during Erskine's presence, he taking a liberal share in it all. From the music room came the hum of voices, interrupted frequently by a sharp, dry cough. Judge Burnham glanced anxiously in that direction from time to time and once interrupted himself to say, "It seems to me that Seraph's cough is worse than usual."

"It is much worse," Ruth said; "she has exposed herself cruelly during the past two weeks and today is quite feverish."

"Who is with her in the music room?"

"Mr. Satterley; I think no one else. Have you not seen her?"

"Oh yes! she came to me for a moment."

He arose as he spoke, lifted Erskine to the ceiling and down again, then said with a sigh, "Well, popinjay, run away now to Joan; Mamma and I must do some talking without your interruption."

17

A Plain Understanding

"WELL," he said again, as the door closed after Erskine, "I received your letter with its inclosures, which were as clear as the reports of professional detectives and reminded me somewhat of them. What do you gather from it all? What are the reports, and from what source do they come?"

"I know very little, Judge Burnham, save what that letter tells you. People do not speak plainly to me; the air seems to be full of vague rumors; even Mr. Satterley, as I told you, is disposed to offer a warning."

"Even Mr. Satterley! You speak as though he were the last person from whom you would expect propriety. We, as a family, seem singularly unfortunate in our choice of friends; none of them suit your tastes. What does Satterley mean? At least, you could question him."

"You are mistaken; I was less willing to question him than I would have been some of the others; and he did not choose to enlighten me further than I told you."

And by this time Ruth had decided to say nothing

about that letter from Marion, which lay hidden in her pocket. What did it tell, more than he already knew?

Judge Burnham shook himself impatiently, as though he would give much to shake off the whole disagreeable subject.

"I suppose I must look into the rumors," he said, taking long strides up and down the room. "I worked myself into almost a panic last night, thinking it over, and rode all night, and lost perhaps a thousand dollars or so by not stopping off at Shoreham. I had a sort of impression that there might be a crisis pending, though I am sure I don't know why; but the reports were so vague as to afford ample food for the imagination, if one gave them any hearing at all. I suspect I was foolish to notice them; but tomorrow, after I have looked into matters at the office, I will see if I can find out whether it is a case of blackmail or simple meddling. It is hard if a man cannot have one evening of rest in his own home, Sunday at that. Seraph really coughs dreadfully. I'll have Westwood come out in the morning and see her."

"Don't delay another day," said the warning in Ruth's pocket. She drew it forth reluctantly. "I have nothing beyond what I wrote you, save this, which came to me this afternoon. I suppose you will attach no importance to it, however."

He read it through hastily, his face glooming over it.

"Why didn't you show it to me at first?" he demanded. "How can I tell whether to attach importance to it or not? Unless Dennis is a born fool, he would not send such a message to a woman without having some show of reason. At least I will see him and demand an explanation. I'll go in on the next train."

"But Dr. Dennis will be in the midst of his evening service," Ruth said, dismayed; she hardly knew why.

"Well, evening service will not last all night, I suppose. If you had told me when I first came, I could have caught him before service began; now I shall have to wait until it closes, and then wait for the midnight train, I presume. Pretty hard on a man who has been traveling every night for a week."

Judge Burnham was rarely so ungentlemanly as this. He must be very much worried, Ruth thought, and she busied herself, without further words, in certain little attentions for his comfort. His last words as he closed the door were:

"Seraph ought to attend to that cough tonight. Tell her to take some hot lemonade and retire early; I'll have Westwood call the first thing in the morning."

But Seraph came to the dinner table half an hour afterward, looking not at all ready to retire. She was in very rich evening costume, of the subdued sort that the fashionable world assumes when it wants to do honor to the proprieties of the Sabbath and yet be as elegant as possible.

"You are surely not going out tonight!" Ruth exclaimed, rather than asked, noting the flush on the cheeks which was deeper than health produces and the quick movement of the hand to her side when she coughed.

"I surely am. If you were musically inclined, you would know that tonight is the great treat of the season at St. Peter's. Where is Papa? I thought he would want to hear Fenwood sing."

"He went to town on the six o'clock train, though I do not think he will attend St. Peter's. But, Seraph, really, excuse my persistence, but you look ill enough to be in bed. Your father heard your cough and was troubled; he wishes me to ask you to take hot lemon-ade and retire early."

Seraph laughed musically.

"I shall probably retire early; quite early tomorrow morning, unless we are so fortunate as to make the eleven o'clock train, and I do not suppose we can. It is a long drive from St. Peter's to the station."

Ruth was so thoroughly convinced of this danger of venture into the chill night air, especially as a sleety, northwest rain had set in, that she attempted a further remonstrance.

"If I were Mr. Satterley, I should protest earnestly against this exposure. Seraph, I am sure your father would not approve; he said he should call Dr. West-wood early in the morning."

"Mr. Satterley knows better, Mamma, than to inter-pose authority; even married women do not obey unless they choose, as you will certainly bear me witness; and as for failing to hear Fenwood sing just because Papa is nervous about a cough is not to be thought of. I should go tonight if I were sure of taking so much cold that I could not appear again this season."

Judge Burnham did not return on the midnight train. Ruth's cathedral clock tolled three just as he entered her room. His state of mind the next morning might have been described by Mr. Satterley's word *glum*. He made not the slightest attempt at conversa-tion, either in his room or at the breakfast table; and in reply to Minta's statement that Seraph was not able to lift her head from the pillow said he was not surprised; that she was alive was the only matter for astonishment there could be this morning; and so far forgot himself as to add, even in the presence of Robert, who was waiting on the table, that he should think if there had ever been any justification for interference in the plans of the young ladies, it would have made itself apparent last night; that he was simply amazed when he saw Seraph in town. Then he turned to Minta before she had calmed the gleam of merriment in her eyes over this public rebuke of her stepmother: "Where were you before you joined your sister at St. Peter's last night?"

"Why, I was in several places. I lunched with Allie Powell, and went from there to hear the anthem at the Clark Place Cathedral."

"With whom?"

"Why, Papa, with the one in whose charge I was, of course. I stayed in town on Saturday with Ellice Farnham."

"Robert," said Judge Burnham, suddenly returning to the proprieties long enough for that, "we do not need any further serving. Mrs. Burnham, can he be excused?"

Then, before the door was fairly closed after him:

"That answer does not enlighten me as to your escort."

"Why, Papa, you know surely, without my telling you, that I was with Mr. Hamlin. Didn't you see us together?"

"Did you leave home in his company?"

"No, sir; certainly not. I told you I went home with Ellice Farnham on Saturday. She was here to lunch, and I went into town with her."

"And met Hamlin at her house?"

"Yes, sir; he was there to dinner."

"By appointment, I suppose?"

Minta's face had grown unbecomingly red under this fire of cross-questioning. At last she spoke:

"Papa, what does all this mean? What if I had

engaged to dine at a friend's in company with other guests? It is nothing more than I do constantly. I do not understand you."

"It means that you have been warned several times during my absence against this particular young man and that you have chosen to pay no attention to the warnings, though they came, some of them, from a source which I should not suppose any young lady of intelligence would overlook. It also means that you are to have nothing to do with this individual from this time forth; neither to dine with him, nor ride with him, nor speak to him if he presumes to call."

Evidently Judge Burnham did not understand his daughter.

"Papa," she said, speaking steadily, though her face had now grown very pale, "I do not know what right you think you have for ordering me about as if I were a child. I obeyed you like a slave for years, I know, and trembled before you, even at a time when you were treating me in a way that the commonest kitchen girl does not expect. But that time is past. I discovered long ago how insufferably I had been treated; and although you have done what you could to make me forget it, I have not. I can tell the story very distinctly if I have occasion; and if you expect the slavish obedience to your orders that you used to receive when I had been kept in such ignorance that I did not know my rights, you will be disappointed; for I am of age and shall do as I please."

If he did not understand the character of his daughter, neither had she correctly gauged him. The angry and insolent address had the (to her) unexpected effect of quieting his outward excitement. The habits of years resumed their sway. He was again the watch–

ful, wary lawyer who had an enemy to hold in check and interests to guard.

"Really," he said, and a half-quizzical smile was on his face. "Ought I to apologize, do you think, for forgetting that I had a young woman to deal with instead of a naughty child who deserved punishment? I had for the moment forgotten the lapse of years. I will order my speech more carefully. You are of age, it is true; so, you will remember, am I. And this is my house, and the funds that enable you to live your free and hitherto apparently satisfactory life are mine. You are at liberty to choose. If you prefer the society of those whom I utterly disapprove, you will seek that society outside of my house; neither need you return to it after having enjoyed yourself among your chosen friends. Since you have chosen to refer to the past in a manner that would almost seem to cover a threat, I will admit that my memory is also good and that when I returned after a prolonged absence abroad to find that you were utterly unfit, mentally and physically, for companionship with me, I did the only thing I knew how to do: furnished guardians unstintedly with money and left you to yourself until my wife appeared on the scene and showed me what years of careful training could do to make you fit companions for people of culture. If you prefer now to prove that we were both mistaken and that your preferences are for the low in character and the degraded in life, you will, of course, be at liberty to make the facts as plain as you choose. The social provisions of Mrs. Burnham and myself are, perhaps you are aware, quite equal to any strain that even you may put upon them.

"After this very plain understanding, I will take the trouble to add—what you hardly deserve—that I have convinced myself of the utter worthlessness of the person under discussion, as I would have taken pains to show you had I not felt, because of knowledge that came to me last night from outside sources, that you had already received warning enough to satisfy any reasonable woman; but I will add mine. The stories that you have heard are undoubtedly true, and more are true than you know anything about. The man is not fit for a respectable woman to acknowledge with a bow. If, even after your exceedingly improper language this morning, you conduct yourself properly, we will let the memory of it drop, and your position in our home shall be in the future what it has been in the past. You are at liberty to choose. You will observe that, after all, I have not acted the part of an excused guardian to a young woman who was of age, but of an indulgent father, being willing to condone even almost unpardonable insolence, because I attribute it to the undue excitement of the moment. And now, I trust we fully understand each other."

He arose as he spoke and turned toward his wife.

"I beg your pardon, my dear, for this long detention at the breakfast table; do not expect me to luncheon; we are on the eve of an explosion in the business world which will bring ruin to both character and bank accounts in certain directions. I found last night that this matter involved more than I had imagined possible. I will send Westwood out to look after Seraph."

He had talked himself into apparent good humor. His parting bow and "good morning" to Minta were, if not fatherly, at least courteous, and he only smiled when she vouchsafed no reply.

"She will come to her senses when she has had time to think," he said to Ruth, who followed him to the hall with a face full of anxiety. "I had no idea she was so full of fire. I am afraid, my dear, you have had more to bear from her than I had imagined possible. But this miserable business, when we are well over it, will be beneficial to her, perhaps. The scoundrel will be safely lodged in prison before many days. Oh yes! it is as bad as it can be, in every way. The misery of it is that our name must be dragged somewhat into the slime. I had no idea she was so much in his society; if your friends had not been so afraid of their communications, we might have kept ourselves out of the denouement. I can furnish my lady with particulars by tomorrow which will startle her. No, money will not help him; in the first place, there is none; he has involved his uncle in utter financial ruin."

"Don't be alarmed," in answer to his wife's anxious suggestion that he did not yet understand Minta, that she might be on the verge of some desperate step; "I understand her well enough to know that she will hardly take any steps today; she is not an idiot; she has plenty of Burnham blood in her veins. Angry she is, without doubt; but solitude and time for reflection will compose her nerves."

"But, Judge Burnham, if she should really be attached to the man—how can you know what influence he may have over her?"

"Attached! Nonsense! She is attached to his fine horses and the gay life he has shown her; and her pride is roused; that is the extent of the mischief. Besides, the man will be too busy today to think of her. I tell you, there is to be an earthquake which will take him off his feet, and he is unprepared for it. However, I will add a word of emphasis to quiet your fears." And he opened the dining room door again. Minta had risen from the table and was standing at the window with her back to the door.

"My daughter," he said, his voice a trifle kinder than it had been before, "I trust you fully understand me that if you choose to remain under my roof and look to me as your father for protection, you are under commands to have no communication in any form with any person by the name of Hamlin, or with any person connected with him. I will explain more fully to you after a day or two."

She neither moved nor in any manner indicated that she had heard a word. But the moment the door was closed, she turned toward it a pair of flashing eyes and said, "Will you, indeed? No doubt you will enjoy the explanation."

18

STORMY WEATHER

FROM the hall, Ruth went directly to inquire as to Seraph's condition and found work for mind and hands. The girl was in a burning fever, her whole frame racked with an incessant cough; and she lay with both hands pressed to throbbing temples. It was evident, even to Ruth's inexperienced eyes, that she was seriously ill and that much valuable time had probably been already lost.

She dispatched a special messenger at once for Dr. Westwood and busied herself until his arrival in using what remedies or alleviations she could think of.

He came sooner than she had dared to hope, her messenger having found him on the road. He at once made it evident that he did not consider himself as having been called a moment too soon, and for the next hour Ruth was absorbed in arranging to have his minute instructions carried out. He was so manifestly planning for a very serious fight with disease that she was solemnized by the thought, and for the time being all minor matters were laid aside.

The speed with which a well-ordered house can

accommodate itself to a change of circumstances would make an interesting study for the curious. Before noon of that busy day, a large back room which had a southern exposure and was not so crowded with dainty furnishings as were the young ladies' rooms had been, under the doctor's supervision, prepared for the sick girl, and she had been carried there, and a professional nurse installed. The lady of the house drew a long breath of relief as she came slowly down the stairs, having received the final directions of the tall, quiet, self-sufficient young woman who had swiftly obeyed the doctor's summons and laid aside her things with the air of one who had always belonged just in that room. Ruth had the feeling that she had been dismissed. It brought with it a sense of relief; the responsibility was lifted from her shoulders. It brought with it, also, a touch of pain, recalling as it did the grave facts of her life; if she were in truth the mother of that sick girl, or if she held in her heart the place which some second mothers won, no hired nurse could possibly supersede her there. As it was—and then the touch of pain came again.

Meantime, there were other things to think about. Where was Minta, and how was this distressing phase of their life to end? She believed she knew the girl better than her husband did; she by no means expected a quiet yielding to his commands; but just what form the rebellion would take would depend, probably, on what advice she received from Mr. Hamlin. And then Ruth thought with a sudden start of dismay that in her anxiety and preoccupation there had been opportunity for plenty of communication between the two. Now that she stopped to think of it, it was strange that in all the arrangements for Seraph's comfort, her sister had taken no part. She went hurriedly to her room and knocked, wondering the while what excuse she should make for intruding; but no answer was returned to her knock. She went to the parlors to find them deserted; in the music room Kate was dusting.

"Do you know where I can find Miss Minta?" Ruth asked, trying to keep her voice as usual.

"She has gone out, ma'am; she went several hours ago."

"Was she alone?" The tone was hurried, and there was an eager quiver of anxiety in the voice.

"Yes'm; she was alone when she left the house. She told me that she would probably not be in to lunch. I told her the doctor was here and that Miss Seraph was pretty sick, and she said yes, she knew it; I thought perhaps she was going on some errand for Miss Seraph."

"Probably that is the case," Ruth said, turning away with a startled fear, nevertheless, that it might not be.

For the rest of the day she tormented herself with a hundred nameless fears and wonderings. What ought she to do? Was it important that Judge Burnham should know of the girl's absence? Should she telephone him? But how absurd to send him a message that Minta had gone out for a walk! How insulting to the girl, if she had really gone, as Kate surmised, on some business for the sick sister!

It would not do to telephone anything like that. Perhaps she might go herself to town and give her message in person. But it was not probable that Judge Burnham would be in his office; he had hinted of business that involved others. She did not know where to look for him; and when, with much trouble, she found him, what had she to say but that his daughter was very sick, and she had left her with hired attendants only while she came to tell him that the other daughter was out walking? Such a course was not to be thought of. Well, then, suppose she wrote him a note and sent it by a special messenger? And then she had visions of the messenger going from office to court room, to the offices of brother lawyers, asking many questions, following the busy man from point to point, coming upon him perhaps in the midst of his most distracting anxieties, interrupting him with a note which had simply to tell that Minta had gone out, leaving word that she might not be back to luncheon! The whole thing began to look absurd to her. And as later in the day Seraph grew worse rather than better and the professional nurse was glad to have her to hand this thing and remove that, she put aside the other anxiety and gave herself to helpfulness.

Nobody lunched, finally, except Erskine and the nurse. It was drawing near to the dinner hour before Ruth could get away again for a moment's rest. Her first inquiry was for Minta; she had not returned, nor had any message come from her. About these bare facts there was nothing of necessity to rouse anxiety; to Kate it had merely the air of an everyday occurrence.

Mrs. Burnham was still in morning attire; there had been no time to think of dress. Judge Burnham would not like this; it was one of the points on which he was fastidious to a fault. His wife wondered whether there would be time to make some changes before he came; and then he came. Mr. Satterley was with him, and Ruth noted that he looked worn and anxious; she wondered if he had heard of Seraph's illness and if he really cared for her enough to be troubled. Judge Burnham did not even seem to notice the morning dress. "Where is Minta?" were his first abrupt words, without even the ceremony of a bow.

"She has gone out," trying to speak as usual.

"Gone out! Where?"

"I do not know; she went while I was otherwise engaged and left no message for me; Kate says she told her she might not return to luncheon."

"Engaged! Do you know what you are talking about? Is it possible you have let her disappear without any knowledge of her whereabouts?"

He had never spoken in this manner to his wife before; Ruth controlled her voice and her feelings; he was evidently either terribly angry or terribly alarmed. "Judge Burnham, you forget; had I any right to control her movements or power to intercept them?"

"Right! Power! You do not know what you are saying! I tell you you should have locked her in her room, if need be, rather than let her slip away—"

She interrupted him. "Judge Burnham, you are speaking very loud and unnecessarily exciting the servants. I am expecting Minta every moment; you surely know it is nothing unusual for her to be late; meantime, Seraph is very ill."

At this information, Mr. Satterley gave a start of dismay. "Seraph!" he echoed. "What is the matter?" But Judge Burnham's excitement was not quieted.

"I cannot help it," he said irritably. "Illness is the very least of our calamities; if the other one were sick, with the smallpox even, we should have cause for thanksgiving. I tell you I am afraid she has gone to destruction. The fellow has escaped us somehow; just when we thought we had the net securely laid, he received information from some source and has disappeared. When did Minta go? What did she take?"

At which point he turned abruptly and strode through the hall into the library. Ruth waited only to answer a few of Mr. Satterley's anxious questions, then followed her husband. He had gone to his dressing room; the exclamation which he gave, the moment he opened his toilet case, brought her to his side. He had a sealed letter in his hand, from which he tore the envelope savagely. Ruth looked over his shoulder as he read:

Dear Papa:

I was going to tell you something this morning, but you were in such haste and so savage that I hadn't opportunity. We had planned a lovely little surprise, Mr. Hamlin and I; we didn't tell anybody about it, save the necessary persons, just for the fun of the thing. We meant to have a very original entertainment connected with it as soon as you reached home; but you have quite spoiled our plans by your fierceness. And since I am a dutiful daughter, in spite of your insinuations this morning, and want to do my best to obey you; and since it is quite impossible for me to have "no communication in any form with any person by the name of Hamlin" for the simple reason that that happens to be my own name, I will do the next best thing, at which you so kindly hinted, and take myself out of your house until such time as you may wish to see my husband and myself. If you really need proof of my statement, you might consult the Rev. Charles Stevens, rector of St. Stephen's, who lives at Southside near the Greene Street Chapel. An obscure little place in which to be married, I admit, but the fun of secrecy lay in obscurity.

Your devoted daughter,
Minta Burnham Hamlin

It was a hard blow; I am sure you will not be surprised that Judge Burnham felt it, too, in his very soul. He had not been a very watchful father, certainly, when his children were young; he had almost deserted them, with a disposition that grew out of pure cowardice, during the period of their disappointing girlhood; but he had not lavished time and attention and money on them for the last half-dozen years for nothing. As it began to dawn upon him that they were not only to be endured, but were actually subjects for congratulation, his interest in them deepened; and as the years went by and they became objects of general admiration, you will remember that his pride in and ambition for them knew no bounds. All the more this feeling seemed to sway him, because it came with the force of a discovery, after he had resigned himself to nothing but humiliation in connection with them. He did not name the feeling pride, and I have no doubt that affection had somewhat to do with it—a great deal, perhaps, during these later years; one cannot lavish so much on any person without feeling, to say the least, a deepening interest in the person; and besides, the "Burnham blood" of which this man was so fond was certainly in their veins. Still it was his pride which had received a death blow. It was bad enough to have the name of a man who proved to be not only a villain, but an unsuccessful one, mentioned in the daily papers in connection with his daughter. He had even thought, during this busy day, of making an effort to suppress the items which whenever he had a moment of leisure seemed to float before him. Such, for instance, as "It seems that young Hamlin spent the evening before the discovery in company with Miss Burnham, the youngest daughter of Judge Burnham of the firm of Burnham, Bacon & Co."; or, "It is said that young Hamlin frequently enjoyed the hospitalities of Judge Burnham's elegant home and presumed to be on friendly terms with his beautiful daughters," or any other of the dozen offensive ways of gossiping about such matters which newspaper reporters seem so thoroughly to understand. He had thought quite seriously for a few moments of attempting to make it worth the while of these leading reporters to keep his daughter's name out of the accounts but had finally abandoned the idea as beneath his dignity. "After all," he said to himself, "what does it matter? The fellow was intimate in dozens of leading families; and that he admired my daughter so much more than any of the others is not so unusual a thing as to cause surprise. I think I will let this part of the annoyance shape itself as it may; it will soon be forgotten." And he had worked the harder toward getting matters in train for the grand exposé. And then had come that sudden discovery of flight; a flight accomplished so boldly and gracefully as to awaken no suspicion in the minds of any looker-on that more than an afternoon ride with the lady of his choice had been planned. And then had followed Judge Burnham's unspoken fears that the lady, about whom there seemed to be very contradictory accounts, might be his daughter, though he really did not believe that such a thing was possible; he believed that the young lady's pride would hold her back from such a step. And then had come the rush home to relieve what he told himself were perfectly groundless fears; that a man like that of course had intimacies with women of whose very names a daughter of his was ignorant; and then had come this final blow in the shape of a half-comic, wholly heartless letter with that name attached: "Minta Burnham Hamlin"! The unsullied Burnham name linked at last with that of a gambler and a forger! Certainly the father was to be pitied! A great deal of work had to be done in the next few days. Much that Judge Burnham had labored hard all that first day to accomplish, he labored equally hard to prevent in the days immediately following. The man who was his daughter's husband, who had joined his name and story irrevocably to hers, was to be dealt with differently, if possible, from the one who had simply, under a mistaken idea of his character, been admitted to the house as a passing acquaintance. It was not that Judge Burnham felt any softening of heart, any pity for the daughter who had so wronged him; his efforts were not so much to shield her as to keep the Burnham name as much away from the public as possible. Therefore he withdrew charges which he had meant to push, and was silent where he had meant to speak plainly, and paid large sums of money to purchase the silence of others in regard to certain points. Therefore it was that by dint of tremendous effort, not only on his part, but on the part of others, friends of young Hamlin, and by processes known to lawyers, this breaker of the laws escaped the verdict of justice and was able to take up his abode in the same city where his evil deeds had largely been accomplished. Thus much settled, Judge Burnham took exceeding pains to have it understood that his motive for his share of the work had not been pity for the sinner but pity for himself; that now he was quite through with the whole matter. Mrs. Hamlin was no longer to be considered as a daughter of his. He did not want to see her again nor to hear of her in any way; she had chosen between them and must abide by the decision. He ordered certain trunks and boxes to be packed and sent by express to the boarding house where the newly married couple were now staying, and with them sent a note, briefer than the one Minta had written, but in every sense of the word dignified, in which he had distinctly stated that from this time forth all communication between her and the family to which she had heretofore belonged was to cease; that he had done what he could to save her husband from the prison life which he so richly deserved; and that in doing this, he had performed the last service for one who was once his daughter that she need ever expect at his hands.

This was hard on the young scoundrel of a husband; he had not so reasoned it out when all these plans were formed in his mind. He had not known Judge Burnham in the days when his daughters were ignored and neglected; he had believed that the father's heart was inextricably wound about this beautiful daughter, in particular; and that, after a few angry words and a few tears and a few sobbing petitions on her part for forgiveness, she would be restored to her place again, and his falling fortunes be retrieved and set on a firm basis. He had meant that this should be done without other unpleasantness than would necessarily be involved in learning that there had been a private marriage. He had intended that the Burnham wealth should save him from a public exposure; it had been the lawyer's vigorous onslaught during that one day which had brought about the end with a precipitancy entirely unnecessary. That Judge Burnham might have avoided all this publicity had been made only too plain by the speed with which he quieted the storm he had raised the moment he found that his own name must suffer—in only a secondary degree— whatever disgrace came to the name of Hamlin. It was all bitterness and weariness of soul; and Judge Burnham aged under it.

Meantime, perhaps it was almost a relief to his angry spirit that Seraph continued very seriously ill and that he had to put aside his bitter thoughts and hurt pride and think of and help care for her in many ways.

19

WAITING

FOLLOWING all this turmoil, and pain, and anxiety came a letup. The severity of Seraph's disease spent itself, or the skill of the doctor triumphed; the professional nurse went her way; she was too important a factor in this disease-stricken world to spend her time in coaxing back to ordinary health again one from whom the immediate danger threatening had been withdrawn. Other homes were waiting for her, where anxious mothers and fathers stood helplessly about, building all their hopes of happiness on the efforts that doctor and skilled nurse were making. Such a life has its compensations; one could see that the nurse was used to these experiences, hungered for them almost. From the first hour when her skilled eye detected the watched-for change for the better in Seraph, her interest in her began to abate; and when the doctor told her of a case of typhoid that was in very special need of services such as hers, she was in almost heartless haste to be gone. It was a sickly spring, and professional nurses were in demand. With her went much of the comfort of Seraph's room and nearly all of Ruth's peace of mind.

An ordinary nurse who could be depended upon to give the invalid thoughtful care seemed well-nigh impossible to secure, notwithstanding the fact that Judge Burnham offered such fabulous wages that the kitchen entrance was besieged all day with applicants. There was some hopeless objection to every one of them; of the few who were tried as a last resort, not one stayed through the third day, and still the slow convalescence went on, and the interviewing of applicants mingled with Ruth's heavier duties of trying to reign in the invalid's room. Nothing more utterly wearying had ever come to her than this period of restless waiting and distasteful working. There were days when her life seemed almost unbearable; she had had tastes of such different work; she had so rested herself in those Sabbath temperance meetings; she had been so helped by the weekly meetings for prayer; she had felt that in these directions lay work that she could accomplish in the name of the Lord whom she loved. She chafed under this utter removal from such influences and questioned wearily as to why it should have been permitted. During the sharpness of Seraph's illness, under the pressure of possible danger, she had not felt in this way; but to be obliged to spend her time in trying to play the part of nurse to an exacting invalid who did not enjoy her ministrations or, leaving Kate in charge—who was trying to do double duty— go to the kitchen and question and cross-question an applicant whom she felt, with that acute inner consciousness which a woman much disciplined in this way comes to possess, would not do at all; or, if her summons came instead from the parlor, say over again for the dozenth time that day, "We think she is gaining slowly, thank you," or, "She is not quite so well today, had a restless night," or yet another phase of the same story, "She is about as she was yesterday, thank you; we see very little change from day to day; she will not get much strength, we fear, until settled weather"; all this was wearying to her in the extreme. Neither was she when doing her utmost a successful nurse; with the most earnest desire to be kind and thoughtful, she did not understand the hundred little things that can never be taught and which help to make the difference between the successful attendant and the good-hearted bungler. For instance, she had an exasperating fashion of bringing the utterly distasteful business of eating before the sick girl by the use of that irritating question, "What will you have for your dinner today?" or that almost equally trying one, "Don't you think you could take a little chicken broth now?"

Ruth had never been sick in her life with that depressing sickness and weakness that continues day after day, though the disease has been vanquished; she knew nothing by experience about the nervous state of mind and stomach that impels an invalid under such circumstances to say, "No, I don't want any chicken broth, either now or ever; and you will be kind enough never to mention the words to me again." So she went on with her honest attempts and privately thought Seraph the most childish as well as the most disagreeable of invalids, because she was irritable and capricious over the veriest trifles.

Moreover, this choice nurse made that trying mistake of reasoning from her own standpoint instead of attempting to put herself in the sick one's place; and because when she was sick, her head ached and the light was unpleasant to her, she was always drawing the curtains, and screening the fire, and making the room dim and quiet, when Seraph's head did not ache, and her eyes were strong, and she hated dark rooms, and one of her employments which she best liked was to watch the glowing coals in the open-grate fire. All these little things made it harder, both for Seraph and for Ruth. The latter had still another anxiety that was in its way harder than any of the others. During these days she saw comparatively little of Erskine; she could not even attend to his lessons, which had been one of the pleasures of her life; it was useless to undertake to interest a child in a reading lesson when she was liable to be called three or four times in the course of the half hour to the kitchen, or the sickroom, or the parlor; moreover, the half hour, even, in which to commence this pleasant work was very hard to secure. It was not that there was so much to do; if there had been crowding employment for hands and mind, it would have been, in a sense, easier; it was the wearing thought that when she was downstairs she ought perhaps to be up and that when she went for a little walk with Erskine, she ought possibly to be at home, that tried Ruth's nerves to their utmost; and there seemed to be no way out of the maze; daily was Erskine left to the care of a servant, to an extent that his sheltered life had not known before.

Neither was her husband a source of strength to this much-tried woman. She saw little of him, it is true; he seemed more than ever engrossed in business; but that little was most unsatisfactory. He was moody, even with Erskine, and disposed to be as nearly fault-finding as his habit of courtesy would allow with Ruth herself.

Despite an evident attempt not to do so, he still let his thoughts linger much over their recent family disgrace; too gentlemanly to blame Ruth in distinct language, he yet made frequent references to the misfortune of his having been from home just at that time; to the certainty that he could have discovered what was going on and been able to prevent it. He hinted that if her friends had been more outspoken, less afraid of involving themselves in uncomfortable consequences, all the misery might have been saved. He openly declared that the mistake of their lives had been in not keeping close guard over Minta on that last day.

Ruth, who had great pity for him in her heart, because she believed that the father's heart must have received a blow something akin to what it would be to her if Erskine should desert her, held herself entirely quiet during those outbursts, not even once reminding him that if he had long ago heeded the plain warnings of her friends instead of sneering at them, all might have been well; but it was, perhaps, not in human nature not to remember this fact and say it over occasionally to herself.

Nor was he particularly sympathetic with his wife over her home burdens; he did not realize what the daily strain was to her. He assured her that she was extremely foolish not to have all the help she needed; that it was nonsense to suppose that plenty of help could not be had since he could always secure as many menservants as he wanted; that there was no reason in her being so exacting; and that Seraph ought not to be indulged in her whim of taking violent dislikes to persons without reasonable excuse. On the whole, Ruth decided that the less he knew about home, at this time perhaps, the better it would be for them both. So the wearing days went on, Seraph seeming neither to gain nor to lose, and the future stretching out before them apparently as barren of comfort as the present.

Of course, some change must come to them; they

always came sooner or later; nothing ever stayed for any length of time just as it was, but what would the change be?

It came in an unexpected manner; perhaps that is the common way in which they come.

Dr. Westwood followed Mrs. Burnham from the invalid's room one morning, where he had been giving his usual sentences, intended to be cheering, to the effect that it would not always be March, nor even early in April, and that the warm spring days would come before many weeks, when housed-up people could venture forth into strength-giving air and sunshine; and then he had called for the usual glasses and spoons, and made his mixtures, and given directions, and said his courteous "good morning," and then followed Ruth as she went away in answer to a summons from downstairs, and as the door of Seraph's room had closed after him, had said, "I would like a word with you, Mrs. Burnham, if you please." And Ruth had halted, and thrown open the door of Judge Burnham's upstairs study, and followed him in, somewhat wonderingly. Dr. Westwood was not one of her favorites; they exchanged as few words as possible.

He closed the door carefully and drew a chair for the lady, then came directly to the point.

"I do not know, madam, what your views may be in regard to plain speaking under the circumstances in which we find ourselves. I always leave such matters to the family; my responsibilities are sufficiently heavy without shouldering them. I think Miss Burnham is entirely deceived. Is it your will that she should remain so?"

"I do not understand," faltered Ruth, her face growing pale over she knew not what. Was it possible that Dr. Westwood meant Mr. Satterley, and was there a new shadow coming over this much-tried home, even now?

"Why, of course you know, my dear madam, that it is only a question of time, and a much shorter time than I had at first supposed; but Miss Burnham evidently looks forward confidently to regaining her health."

"And do you mean—do you think she will not recover strength eventually? I do not know what you mean, Dr. Westwood!"

"Is it possible you do not know that the disease is what is sometimes called quick consumption and that it is making rapid advance?"

"You do not mean, Doctor, that she is going to die!"

"I beg your pardon, Mrs. Burnham; I did not know that you also were deceived. I have been very abrupt."

There was both dismay and pity in his voice, for the pallor of Ruth's face was very apparent now, and in her surprise and consternation she felt giddy and faint; she reached forward for the chair she had declined and leaned against it.

"No matter," she said. "Tell me plainly now what you mean; if I understand you, we have certainly been very much deceived."

"There is little more to tell," he said, speaking gently and evidently greatly surprised over her manner of receiving his news. "I will be perfectly frank, as is my custom, when the circumstances of the case will admit.

"Miss Burnham may linger through the late spring, but this morning I have my doubts even as to that. She is failing more rapidly than I had supposed probable, and it occurred to me that it might not be the wish of the family to have her kept in ignorance of the true nature of her disease. I had not supposed that Judge Burnham and yourself shared her hopes, and that must account for an abruptness which I can plainly see has been cruel. I beg you will forgive me, and unless I can serve you in some way, I will not intrude longer."

He was very polite, very ceremoniously kind, and he bowed himself away, and within the next hour told a brother physician that the gossip which had been afloat so long about Mrs. Burnham and her step-daughters not getting on comfortably together was all false; so far, at least, as the sick one was concerned; that he had rarely seen an own mother more overwhelmed with the news that her daughter was going to die than was Mrs. Burnham.

He was right; Ruth was overwhelmed. No thought of such a conclusion as this had entered her mind since those first days when Seraph had been acknowledged to be alarmingly ill. When the disease had reached its crisis, Ruth had supposed the danger past and, all unused to illness as she was, had continued ignorant, even in the daily presence of a disease which, to the experienced eye of the physician, was making rapid advance. She was more than overwhelmed; she was dismayed. Seraph Burnham going to die! to die soon! Why, it was appalling! Could anyone be more unready for death than she? How was it possible for one like her to go up before the judge! It seemed to Ruth afterwards that during that first half hour after the doctor left her alone, she came face-to-face with a realizing sense of death and the judgment for the first time in her life! And the thought that a soul with which she had had to do for years was going swiftly forward into those scenes, all unprepared, seemed almost to paralyze her with terror.

She could not give way to these feelings long. There

was much to be done. She had forgotten her summons to the kitchen; had forgotten also that the sick one was left alone; but she was not left long in forgetfulness. An imperative summons came to her, and sending Kate to Seraph, she put aside her strange terrors as best she could and tried to listen coherently to the voluble tongue whose owner had presented herself in the hope of being engaged as nurse and attendant. All the time the bewildered mistress was saying to herself, "She will not do; she will not do at all; if there were no other reason, she is not the person to attend one who is going to die."

When at last she had schooled herself into outward calm and forced herself to return to Seraph, that young lady threw her again into consternation.

"Mamma," she said, turning on her couch and looking full into Ruth's face, "I heard the doctor ask to speak to you this morning, and I know it was something about me; it would be a great satisfaction to me if you would tell me just what he said."

How was this appeal to be answered? Ruth had not thought about it; she had put it away sternly as something which must, among other grave things, be decided, but not until she had time to think; here it was confronting her, and it could be answered now only by dismayed silence.

"I do not want to be treated like a child," said Seraph, speaking coldly. "If the doctor had any information to give which concerned me, I think he might have given it directly to me; but since he did not choose to do that, I ask you as a favor to tell me exactly what he said."

"I will tell you," said Ruth hurriedly, startled at the sound of her own voice. "I will tell you at another time, not now; I haven't time now; that is, I have not thought how to—" And there she stopped. What a terrible bungle she was making of this terrible thing! Oh! what ought she to say? If there were only some-one else to take this awful responsibility. Still Seraph questioned her with those great beautiful eyes. "You have almost told me," she said. "You might as well finish; he says I am not going to get well. Isn't that it? Now tell me this: Does he think I am going to die soon?"

"He thinks," said Ruth, and her lips trembled, "he is afraid— Oh, Seraph!"

"Never mind," said Seraph. "I understand; you need not tell me any more. Go away and leave me alone." And she turned her face to the wall and lay perfectly still.

20

BELATED WORK

THE DAYS that immediately followed this revelation were strange ones to Mrs. Burnham. Long afterwards she looked back upon them and wondered that her overstrained brain did not reel under the intensity of the excitement.

Her life had been unusually shielded from any experiences connected with death. Her father, it is true, had lingered in his sunny room on the borders of the other world for weeks, but Ruth's daily visits to him were filled with not only the tenderest but the brightest memories; always he was in the sunshine; ready to cheer and encourage her; so full of bright anticipations for himself that it had not seemed possible to think of the word death in connection with him, and the final scene had been such a jubilant entering-in that she could only feel afterward as though she had a glimpse of eternal life.

But this was different—so utterly different. It was not that Seraph made any visible sign of fear or of rebellion; such was not her nature; but that she had a fierce battle to fight in her own heart was only too apparent.

Her face changed alarmingly in the course of the next few days; took on the worn, haggard look of extreme illness and anxiety; and wrung Mrs. Burnham's heart whenever she saw it with a pain unlike any that she had ever felt before. A human soul in peril, and she the only person near who knew the one sure way for safety yet feeling powerless to lead to it. She was made to feel, during those first days, that she had managed the trust that the doctor had imposed on her in an utterly irrational manner.

Judge Burnham was at first angrily incredulous; it was utter nonsense that a girl who had been in splendid health up to the time when she had caught a violent cold should sink into a rapid consumption. That disease was not in the Burnham family; they were, as a family, noted for strong constitutions. The thing was incredible; Westwood was nervous, or careless, or mistaken, at least; they must have counsel; he wondered that the physician had not attended to this before if he really feared danger. And a solemn council of eminent physicians was held, although Dr. Westwood assured the father that in his judgment it was unnecessary and useless. So indeed it proved; there was no dissenting voice. Dr. Westwood, on his part, expressed himself privately to Mrs. Burnham as being extremely shocked over the effect that the news had had upon his patient and did not hesitate to say that he feared she had been too abrupt. The only reply he made to her explanation that Seraph had overheard his own words and precipitated the tidings upon herself was to gravely repeat his fear that she had been too abruptly told and to wish that they had kept their knowledge to themselves. As for her husband, he angrily blamed her for exciting Seraph in any such manner; said he should have supposed her judgment might have served her better than that. But Ruth could forgive much to the disappointed father during these trying days; these were his daughters, and in strangely different and in strangely unthought-of ways he was losing them both. Meantime, there came into her heart a genuine pity for Mr. Satterley. Let him be what he would—a subject only for contempt heretofore—there was no denying the fact that the dignity of a terrible sorrow was upon him. He came and went a dozen times a day, always with that look of misery deepening about him which told of a sudden and bitter disappointment settling down on his soul.

Ruth, watching him, being waylaid many times during the day to answer his eager questions, felt convinced for the first time that at least one thing in his life had been genuine. He loved the woman who was now his promised wife. Was this swift-coming sorrow a portion of his retribution for the past? Her manner toward him grew gentle, almost, in spite of herself; he might have been guilty of that which had led her to despise him, but he was suffering now too greatly to make her want to add one feather's weight to the blow.

So she took care to speak an encouraging word when she could, and let voice and manner tell him that her heart ached over his burden, and grew nearer to liking him during these brief encounters than she had imagined it possible she ever could.

And still she carried about with her hourly a burden different from that of others, but heavy and bitter. How to reach this girl, whose life was slipping so rapidly away; how to help her with that important suggestion of Infinite help before it should be forever too late—this was the question and the longing that so grew upon her that it was becoming almost insupportable. Could she bear to live, and walk about these familiar rooms, and order their belongings, reminded all the time of one who had been with her years and years, and had gone, and feel that because of her unfaithfulness the going had been rayless of hope?

A professional nurse was installed once more, the disease having now taken a sufficiently serious form to awaken the respect of those important persons. Ruth had more leisure and less responsibility; more time, therefore, to break her heart over what she alone of all that household felt and feared. She betook herself to prayer. Such eager, longing cries for this soul as it seemed to her the Lord must hear; and of course he heard; but his answer was to reveal to her herself.

The scales that had blinded her for years fell off, and she realized only too plainly that much of the unhappiness of her life she had brought upon herself. She had done her duty by her husband's daughters, "good measure, pressed down," oftentimes "running over"; but she had never loved them, nor tried to love them. She had mentioned their names many times in her prayers, but she had never prayed for them in her life with the heart-wrung cry with which she now almost hourly brought this one to the notice of the Healer. It came at last to be almost the cry of Israel of old, "I will not let thee go except—" realizing oh! so fully her mistakes, realizing that had she lived before them a different life in every way, both of these who had made her life miserable might be today living for Christ; yet she cried out to the great Physician, "Nevertheless, for thy sake, Lord."

It was several days after she had begun to pray in this manner that her anxiety expressed itself in words. She was alone with Seraph, the nurse having taken advantage of a quiet hour to secure some much-needed rest.

She began by almost timidly suggesting that the pastor of the church at the corner had called the day before, and indeed called often; would not Seraph, some morning when she was feeling pretty well, like to have him come up and see her?

Silence followed, lasting so long that Ruth thought her question was not going to be answered; then, in a cold, constrained voice: "I don't know why I should care to see him. I do not feel in the least acquainted with him; the only time I ever saw him alone was that day he called when you were not at home and Kate thought you were; and he spent ten minutes in asking me about the last concert—which soprano, in my judgment, was the better, and whether, on the whole, I thought Miss Nelson's voice was as good as her cousin's, who used to sing that part. I don't feel any particular desire to see him. I have lost my interest in concerts."

It all came over Ruth then, so pitifully—the pale face, save for those fateful spots of crimson high on the cheeks, the hollow-sounding voice which told only too plainly that the singer would sing no more; the short breath, which made her pause frequently between even short sentences, and the apathetic voice, hinting of interest lost in almost everything. She had meant to be very quiet, very careful about exciting her charge, and she was not given to tears; nevertheless, they filled her eyes now, as she came over to the invalid chair, which was stretched back almost like a bed, and knelt beside it, and touched the white hand lying idly on her lap, and spoke low and tremulously:

"Seraph, I want to say something to you. I feel, oh! more than I can ever express, how far short of all that

I ought to have been, I have seemed to you. I have lived before you the Christian life in such a way as to lead you to feel that there was no reality in it and no comfort to be had from it—as though I cared little whether you walked that way or not. This I realize, and I want to tell you what a mistake it all is; there is a vital personal union with Christ which is able to make up for the loss of all other things; there is a heaven so glorious that we cannot even in our wildest flights imagine it; I know, for I saw my father bid good-bye to this world, and the glory on his face as the light of the other dawned upon him was not to be mistaken. Then I know, by my own experience, that Christ is able to give such strength and comfort as are to be found nowhere else; and if I, such a miserable Christian as I have been, can be sure of this, and I am, ought you not to believe it? If I could tell you how I long to have you take the rest which this Friend stands ready to offer, if I could give you any idea of the consuming desire I have to see you sheltered in his arms of love and have him undo some of the mischief which my cold and careless life has done, I almost think you would, in very pity for me, turn your thoughts and hopes to him."

It was not what she had meant to say; there was not a word spoken of all that which she had lain awake and planned the night before. It had not, at that time, seemed to Ruth wise to speak of herself at all, for she believed that Seraph was too indifferent to her to care what she felt; and here she was almost basing her plea on the strength of the pain which she felt for this dying girl!

Neither was the answer she received in any degree what she had planned for. She had thought that there might be, possibly, indignation, or sarcasm, or coldness, or perhaps no attempt at reply; and indeed this last seemed, for a few moments, what was to be.

Seraph lay back and looked at her, with no trace of emotion on her face, with apparently no quickening of her pulses; yet presently she spoke, slowly, in a half-curious tone, as one might who was making out a puzzle:

"I almost believe you have been in earnest all the time. I thought your religion was a sham; worn as one would wear a fashionable dress, because in your very high and exclusive circle it was the fashion, not to be fashionable in a worldly way, but to be religious. I did not think you cared whether Minta and I, or even Papa, ever had any religion or not; save so much for Papa as would admit him into the fashionable exclusiveness where you belonged; we didn't think you wanted us there; but I half believe we were mistaken all the while."

These sentences were spoken slowly, almost impersonally—as if she were not referring to herself and that other woman who knelt before her.

But Ruth was too intensely in earnest now to have this strange language or this utterly indifferent manner prevent her message.

"I do not wonder," she said. "I do not wonder at anything which the mistakes of my past life may have led you to think; it has all been wrong. I was never a hypocrite; I was simply a halfhearted Christian; yet halfway as I was, I tell you in all sincerity I could not have lived my life at all, it seems to me, without Christ. What I want now more than anything else in life—so much that it seems to me I would willingly die to secure it—is to have you give yourself into his keeping and learn from him all that he can be to a soul. Oh,

Seraph! will you do this? Will you forget all about me and turn your thoughts to him?"

Again there was no response. Seraph's eyes were dry and her face composed, though her stepmother's was wet with fast-falling tears. A long time it seemed to the excited woman that she waited, not daring to say more to other ears than God's, but praying, oh! in an agony of appeal for an answer of peace.

"I'll tell you, Mamma, who I should like to have come and stay with me a little while; and that is Susan Erskine." That, at last, was the answer she received.

Ruth rose up then, brushing the tears hastily from her face, and in that instant she was shown another revelation of her heart. She thought she had been to its utmost depths; but in the light of this experience she saw that she had not only wanted this soul saved, but had wanted the Master to let her be the instrument in his hands; and that it hurt her to have herself, in effect, pushed aside, and another messenger called after. It was an instant's revelation, and the sudden revulsion of feeling which it caused passed almost as quickly as it had come.

"It is a good thought," she said humbly. "Susan could help you; she always helped me. She is teaching, but perhaps a substitute could be found. I will write to her this evening; no, I will have your father telegraph, if you like. That will save you from waiting so long; I feel almost sure she can arrange to come."

"Then send for her; she is the only one I can think of in the world whom I would like to see." And Seraph had turned her head away from her mother and closed her eyes.

Then the nurse came, and Ruth went away—went to her own room, and locked the door, and went on her knees. She spoke no audible word, but knelt there long and rose up quieted.

Money is a potent factor in this world. Susan Erskine was three hundred miles away, holding an important position in an important school, and it was in the middle of the term. When Judge Erskine died and the old home was broken, many plans had been discussed as to what would be done. Ruth wanted Susan and would have been willing to agree to almost any arrangement which would keep her in the family; but no one knew better than Susan that the mother would not be at rest in Judge Burnham's household; that she did not fit it gracefully, and that she jarred on the nerves of the master and, for the matter of that, on the mistress as well, although her heart was full of grateful love toward her now. Susan did not discuss many plans; she kept her own counsel, but had, in the course of a few weeks, announced that mother and she were going back "home" to the neighborhood where they had lived so long; that her old position was waiting for her, and mother had many friends there, and in every respect she believed it would be best. And Judge Burnham had said that Susan Erskine was the most sensible woman of his acquaintance; that he had always thought so. Nevertheless, he sent the telegrams which Ruth suggested, with promptness, and added other and expressive ones about the importance of having the invalid's wishes respected and about the fact that any salary desired might be offered for a substitute, if Susan would but come; so Susan came.

To her mother, she said:

"I think I ought to go, for I used to have influence with the poor girl; and now that she is going to die, I may be able to help her."

"Of course you ought to go," said Mrs. Erskine.

"What are schools, where they teach grammar and things, when a body comes almost to the end and needs the kind of help that we were put into the world to give? Poor thing! What an everlasting pity it is that she put off the only important work in life until life was pretty nigh over. But there! I'd'a done the same myself, poor fool that I was, and would be doing it yet, I dare say, if it hadn't been for your father. And to think that maybe that girl will see him in a little while! I could most feel like asking her to take a message for me, if I was going along. I'm getting to be an old woman, Susan, and I do feel kind of homesick after your father once in a while, now that's a fact. It isn't as though I had had him all his life, you know, for I hadn't; there was a good deal of wasted time."

And Susan, who had steadily given her life to the care and comfort of her mother, smiled on her cheerily and said:

"Never mind, Mother, you and Father will have time enough together to make up for it all one of these days."

"That's the living truth," said the old lady with a smile on her homely face, suggestive of the peace of heaven; and while she trotted about, packing her daughter's trunk, she sang, in a quavering voice and on a high key:

> *"When we've been there ten thousand years*
> *Bright shining as the sun;*
> *We've no less days to sing God's praise,*
> *Than when we first begun."*

21

TRANSFORMATION

BUT because Susan Erskine came, Mrs. Burnham did not therefore find herself banished from the invalid's room. Instead, she was drawn there more than before; and, indeed, from the hour when she made her pitiful appeal to Seraph, the two had seemed to be on a different footing; no further words had passed between them, but Seraph had seemed less indifferent to her coming and going and had shrunk less from receiving attentions at her hands. She even smiled occasionally on her now, and once inquired as to whether her incessant coughing the night before had disturbed her mother. It was not usual for Seraph to appear, at least, to care who was disturbed by her.

At another time she said, smiling gratefully on Susan, who was arranging pillows in that deft way which some attendants seem to know by instinct and others never learn, "It is so nice to have Susan here, Mamma; it was so good of you to think about it, and bring it to pass."

All these little things were very unlike Seraph.

Moreover, as the days passed, Ruth distinctly saw

another change: Unmistakably, Seraph's face was taking on that look of rest and peace which can come—at least at such times as those she was rapidly nearing—from only one source. The haggard lines were being smoothed; the apparent apathy which had followed the days of unnatural excitement was also gone; she had roused to some degree of interest in the affairs of others. She inquired for Erskine, who had long been banished from the sickroom because his sister had no desire to see him, and he now made daily visits. Occasionally, his happy little laugh was heard to ring out from the sickroom, and when someone went in haste, lest the invalid should be disturbed, she would be found smiling on him. Yet these were days full of solemnity to Ruth. She had never before lived, as it were, in the presence of a soul at the time when it opened the door and let in the Heavenly Guest; she had never before watched the process of transformation go on. It might have been unusually rapid in this case, because the time was short; but Ruth stood often awed before it; this marvelous change of even the lines on the wasting face. "And the hardness of his face is changed."

She came to that verse one morning in her somewhat hurried reading and stopped over it as something which she had never seen before, and thought of it the instant she entered Seraph's room an hour afterwards. "It is true," she said within herself; "the 'hardness' of her face is changed; that exactly describes the process." Then she wondered if any infidel had ever watched this steady change in a human face and what he thought could be at work in the heart, transforming the life.

"Conformed to his image." This was another sentence over which she had lingered and which she applied afterwards, feeling awestricken.

What an amazing thing it was that this girl should be singled out from the family for such an experience, such an honor as this! "Getting to go abroad." Those words were spoken in her hearing one day, in regard to an acquaintance of Seraph's; and Ruth thought of it constantly as the days passed. "So is she," she said to herself, looking the while at Seraph; "getting ready to be presented at court! Oh! more than that; she is the bride getting ready for the bridegroom and the palace. What a marvelous thing it is! How do we ever succeed in thinking about or caring for anything else, with this in view?" And the fascinations of that room increased upon her. It was not that Seraph said much—said anything, indeed, except to Susan, in the confidential talks which Ruth knew they had; it was rather that Ruth allowed her imagination full play when she was in the presence of this one who was evidently slipping away from earth. Others beside herself saw or felt the changes; Mr. Satterley, who had obstinately refused to believe that nothing could be done for the sick one, and had hoped against hope, and begged that this remedy and that might be tried and such and such an authority consulted, followed Ruth from the room one morning when it had seemed to her that Seraph looked unusually quiet and reposeful and, dropping into a chair at the further end of the hall, gave himself to a perfect abandonment of grief. "I've given up," he said when at last he could speak; "I could not believe it possible that she was not going to get better; but I can see that she isn't. Some strange change has come to her; she is not like herself; she talks as though she did not even care to get well.

Can anything have happened to make her tired of living; to, to—change her so?"

"It isn't that," Ruth said; "it isn't that she is tired of this life, but—" And then she attempted to speak the King's language to this man of alien birth. He did not understand her; he was perplexed, pained, almost angry that anything should or could reconcile this woman whom he loved to satisfying her soul with another love; could make her willing to glide away from him into a mysterious world.

Gradually there was coming to be a very pleasant understanding between Mrs. Burnham and her step-daughter. Seraph smiled on her now, in return for service, and sometimes said, "thank you," in grateful tones; and once she caught her hand and said earnestly, "You were right, Mamma; there is one who can make up for the loss of everything else; it seems very strange that he should be willing to do it for me, but he is, and has, and I knew you would be glad."

After that Ruth looked at her and thought about her with a feeling which might almost have been called envy. This young woman, who a few days ago had spoken of Jesus as though he were an indifferent stranger, now evidently belonged to him in a sense of which she, the disciple of years, knew nothing. Why should her education progress so fast? What was there in heaven for her to do that she should be so swiftly hurried through the earth journey and sheltered in the sunny home? It was a new experience in every way to Ruth, and she studied it, and prayed over it, and spent as much time as she could with the one who had seemed suddenly to rise to heights above her; to draw closer each day to the Great Source of strength and power. They had little, half-confidential talks together sometimes, Seraph speaking out suddenly, after long, quiet moments, revealing in a brief sentence, perhaps, glimpses of the past which were very revelations to Ruth; making her understand what she had had to contend with in her hard and unsuccessful struggle with life.

"When we first went to school," said Seraph, "the girls used to laugh at us; they thought we could not be serious, Minta and I, when we talked about you and told how kind you were, and what you had done for us, and how much you planned for our pleasure. They made all sorts of fun of us when they found that we really meant it; they said we were the greatest simpletons they had ever met; that the idea of stepmothers really caring for grown-up daughters was too absurd to be credited; that, in the very nature of things, we were, and must be, rivals; that you had stolen Papa from us, and we must take the consequences, of course. But as for pretending to think a great deal of you, that was too silly for girls as old as we were, and a great deal more of that sort of nonsense," would Seraph add, somewhat wearily, as her strength began to fail. "It was most ridiculous in us to be influenced by such talk. I cannot think how we came to be such idiots, but we were. Poor Minta was inclined, I think, to have a low opinion of the world in general, and being constantly under such influences and hearing stories all the time about unhappy homes and heartless second mothers—there were half a dozen girls in the school who were stepdaughters—we actually came to believe that their experience was ours, or must be, in the course of time; and we came home prejudiced, you know, or with eyes so blinded by false lights that we could not see the real. We have been very hateful, Mamma, but we were honestly so."

She was too tired to say more, or to hear other than

soothing words. "Never mind," the stepmother said. "Don't worry over it now, Seraph. I, too, have been to blame—greatly to blame; I can see it plainly now, but I can say, like you, that I was honest. I meant to do the best for you that I could. No, I am not going to let you talk any more; you are to shut your eyes and not even think. You and I will both remember that we belong to one who understands hearts."

But when she was alone again, the stepmother went all over it in sorrowful indignation and began to realize, as she had not before, the irreparable mischief that false and foolish tongues had wrought for her.

"You had stolen Papa from us." This, in brief, was the silly and false idea that she began to understand was talked before children about their second mothers, until it was little wonder that they came to look upon the relation with blinded eyes, as Seraph had said. And she, who had rushed into it with such utter self-abnegation, such determination to make home what it should be for these two daughters, had ignored the world and its false tongues, had held herself aloof from it, and had been so determined to win by the superiority of her own plans that it was no wonder she had failed.

"I could have loved Seraph," she said, the tears falling fast; as she brushed them away, "I could have loved her, and have won her to love me, if I had held her from the false and fashionable world and held up Christ before her with such power as to win her to him."

And the confidential relations, so long in establishing themselves between these two, grew apace.

"Mamma," Seraph began one day when they were alone for a moment, "there is something I want very much, and I do not know whether I can have it. Did you ever tell Papa about that young woman—that Estelle, you know?"

"No," said Ruth quickly, her face flushing. It had been one of her anxieties in the earlier days of this sickness that she had not done so, and that she could not determine whether she ought or not; of late, she had put it aside. "No; I have never mentioned the matter to him in any way."

"And do you think—I mean, I do not know that there is any need for doing so now. Is there?"

There was a marked emphasis on the word "now." It was putting into plainer language than she had before, even to Ruth, the thought that she was so nearly done with all these things, that stories about them, fraught with solemn import but a few months ago, could be allowed to drop quietly into silence. Ruth turned toward her, her eyes dim with tears and her voice tremulous, but she answered:

"No; I do not think there is."

"Well, Mamma, I want to see her. I want to have a little talk with her quite alone and not have anyone know it. Do you think I might?"

Ruth smiled now, a loving, in fact, a thankful smile; this was to her one of the indications of discipleship. "I'll manage it," she said.

And that afternoon, having sent the nurse home for a two hours' vacation, she said to Susan, "I've no doubt you consider yourself authority here, but it is a mistake; you are under orders. I'm in conspiracy with this little girl, and she has a young friend coming to see her, with whom she wants to talk quite alone. We are both to be banished. I shall stay in the next room within sound of the bell, but you may go to the garden, or to the music room, or where you will, but consider yourself banished until you receive a special summons higher."

"Very well," Susan said, entering into the assumed gaiety of the moment with the quick-wittedness of one who understood that she was expected not to understand. "I suspected mischief when you were so anxious to have the nurse take a holiday, but I did not suppose it was so far-reaching as this; however, I am all submission."

And Seraph, as she caught Ruth's eye, smiled and said, "Thank you," in a low tone, full of meaning.

For an hour, the two of whom Mr. Satterley had asked the same momentous question and received from each a solemn yes, were alone together. But what the favored one, who yet was going away to a country whence they never return to fulfill earthly vows, said to the one who had been cast aside for her sake, is known only to him to whom all hearts are open. It was Ruth who met the young girl at the door when she came in answer to her summons, and showed her to Seraph's room; and when, an hour afterward, Seraph's bell rang, it was Ruth again who showed her guest out, noting only that her eyes were red with weeping.

No questions were asked by anyone. Kate, who had met the girl in the hall below and attended her to the door, volunteered the information in the kitchen that it was "some young thing who was fond of Miss Seraph; a sewing girl, she guessed." And Susan, who knew better than most persons when silence was golden, said nothing at all. As for Seraph, the only word she had to offer was given to Ruth as she took the glass of water from the wasting hand. Seraph's cheeks glowed, perhaps, a little more than usual, but her eyes were bright, and there was no hint of tears about her face. She laid her fingers gently on Ruth's hand and said, "Mamma, thank you." That was all.

Mr. Satterley came and went as usual, perhaps even oftener than before, and his face still wore the same haggard look of pain; and Ruth, watching them both and seeing this life tragedy drawing toward its close, felt more sympathy and sorrow for the man than she had once imagined would be possible.

He had been heartless, and yet it appeared that he had a heart and that he was being taught what it was to suffer. Not long after this there came to Ruth another appeal for help.

"Mamma, I wish I could see Minta."

And Ruth, her eyes flashing sudden resolution, yet kept her voice quiet as she said:

"I will see if I cannot bring that to pass without more delay."

She went very soon thereafter in search of her husband, feeling angry with herself that she had endured so long the present state of things.

In order to understand it, you will need to be reminded that Judge Burnham had always been a man of overweening pride, and that he had allowed himself to be so swayed by this feeling as to be at times incapable of controlling it.

That his heart had been trampled upon and rudely stung by his daughter Minta was true; and that his pride had received such a blow that he could not rally from it was also true. Smarting under this, you will remember how he had issued his stern mandate that his second daughter should never again enter his door; that she was from this time forth no daughter of his, and he would have the world know that he disowned her.

A proud man is also a very obstinate man, and

through all these weeks of suffering and fast-failing bodily powers on the part of his only other daughter, he had held steadily to this resolution, notwithstanding the fact that Seraph had herself appealed to him to be allowed to see her sister.

Anything else; nothing that money could buy, or time and care produce, was to be withheld. It seemed, as the days went by, as though he must have spent hours in studying what might tempt Seraph's tastes. He brought home delicacies which she was too ill to touch; books and pictures that she could only smile on wearily; flowers so rare and heavy of perfume that they had to be banished from her rooms to give her air; everything that a lavish expenditure and highly cultured tastes could furnish was at her command, save this one wish of her heart, to see and talk with the sister from whom she had never before been separated.

Over this petition he shut his firm lips and shook his obstinate head! Mrs. Hamlin was no daughter of his, and therefore, of course, could be no sister of Seraph's anymore.

Yet, on this morning of which I write, his wife went down to him in his private study with determination gleaming in her eyes.

22

Days of Privilege

"JUDGE Burnham," she said, beginning as was her habit without circumlocution of any sort, "I am going to send for Minta today, to come to her sister. Seraph mourns for her and ought to have her wish. I will wait until you have gone to town for the day, if such is your desire; but even that I think is unwise; however much she may have displeased you, Minta is still your daughter, and this is her father's house—"

He interrupted her hastily. "I have explained to you, Mrs. Burnham, that she is from henceforth no daughter of mine."

His wife's voice was very steady, having that determined quality in it which helps to calm some forms of excitement.

"But that, Judge Burnham, is simply nonsense; of course you and I know that the parental relation is not one which can be put on and off at will. Minta is a disobedient and ungrateful daughter, if you will, but she is still your daughter, whether you will or not; you can treat her as though she were nothing to you, but that will not destroy the relationship; it will be simply yielding to the desire to act an unnatural part. Still, I do not ask you to send for her, unless you think you ought; I simply say that I am going to let her know today how ill her sister is and ask her to come and see for herself."

"And what if I say that, as this is my house and I am supposed to be its master, I forbid any such proceeding; that I decline to allow her to be invited here on any pretext whatever?"

His wife came toward him and laid her hand on his arm with a little caressing movement peculiar to herself and not often indulged; she was an undemonstrative woman.

"Even then," she said very gently, "I should disobey you, because I know your true self better than you do; and I know how swiftly the days are coming when you would bitterly regret such words. Seraph is very ill, Judge Burnham; she is failing rapidly; it will do no good to blind your eyes to this fact. She has never been separated from her sister before, and she misses and mourns for her. It is unnatural and cruel not to allow, and even urge, Minta to come to her, under such circumstances. No one will see this more plainly than you, one of these days; it is simply that you do not realize how short the time is."

His lips quivered almost beyond his control when he spoke again. "I have not meant to be cruel, but I have been cruelly treated; any father would admit that. Still, as you say, we do not want to deny Seraph anything, though I cannot think she is so ill as you suppose; she seemed to me quite bright this morning. I will lay no commands on you, of course. I did not mean that, but there are certain things that must not be expected of me. If Minta personally cared for my forgiveness, she could at least ask it; could say that she had done me grievous wrong; and I do not think until she does so much that I am called upon to notice her in any way. The invitation to her to call here must not come from me; it must be distinctly understood that I do not endorse it; I merely tolerate it for Seraph's sake. And one command I will issue: that man whom she calls her husband must not step his feet inside my doors."

His voice had grown stern again, and as he had already made more of a concession than Ruth had expected, and as she could see no reason why any consideration should be shown the man who had deliberately carried out a plan to rob a home, she made no reply to this other than the general one that of course she would carry out his wishes as well as she could, and went away to write her note to Minta, then to tell Seraph what she had done, and to regret, for the next four or five hours, that she did any such thing. It became apparent that Seraph had missed her sister more than any of those about her had realized, and the hope of seeing her, coupled with the thought of the long waiting that there must still be, unnerved her to such a degree that the doctor, when he made his morning call, was alarmed at the state of her pulse and scolded the nurse roundly for allowing her charge to be excited about anything.

All this added greatly to Ruth's anxiety and dismay when the messenger who had been dispatched with her note returned, bringing a written reply instead of the girl for whom she was now anxiously watching. It was addressed to herself and was brief and to the point:

Mrs. Judge Burnham:
   Madam:
   I will not take time to thank you for the extreme courtesy of your remarkable invitation to my father's house, nor to explain to you how fully I recognize your

skillful hand in it all. I will simply say that the invitation must come from my father and must include my husband, or it will be paper wasted. I will venture to send my love to Seraph and to hope that she will soon be well enough to ride into town and visit me, when I will promise to give her a much more cordial greeting than I should evidently receive in my father's house.

Yours, in vivid remembrance,
Minta Burnham Hamlin

Over the contents of this letter Ruth stood appalled. What was now to be done with the excited invalid? Judge Burnham was away for the day; she did not even know just where to reach him, nor, indeed, if he were at home, could much be expected from him immediately on the receipt of such an epistle as that. While she was still in a state of wretched indecision as to how to manage, Susan came in search of her; Seraph had asked for her and seemed restless over her prolonged absence; so Ruth went at once and was immediately questioned:

"Mamma, you have had some word from Minta, I can see it in your face. Won't you just let me read the letter for myself, if she wrote? I understand Minta so well! Things that might sound strange to you would be plain to me. Will you let me have it, Mamma?"

All this was so unlike the Seraph of Ruth's acquaintance that she felt half bewildered and without more ado gave the letter into her hands. Then, during its reading, she tormented herself as to whether this were not the very worst thing that could have been done.

There was a heightened color on the girl's cheeks when she gave it back, but her voice was steady.

"Never mind, Mamma; that was a pretty hard letter for you to read, but there is more than Minta involved in it. He will not let her come; I understand how it is. He has a very great influence over her, and he is selfish—intensely selfish. I used to tell her that, before I knew that she cared for him so much; she does care, Mamma—it isn't all naughtiness. We will let it go for the present; she does not understand, you see. She thinks I am going to get well and come and see her, and she thinks if she holds out, Papa will receive him, too; in a few days, perhaps, we can make her understand how it is with me. I would not send again, Mamma, for Papa's sake. It is very hard for him, too, and I am so sorry. How very different things get to looking in a few weeks' time! We have both made it very hard indeed for you and Papa, and we did not dream it. You must remember that, Mamma; we did not understand at all. We were fools. I wonder if Minta will wait until she lies where I do before she realizes it? That was one reason why I wanted to see her."

"Never mind," said Ruth in her turn. "Do not think about it anymore now; you are tired, and I understand; I understand much better than you suppose I do. There are two sides to it; I, too, was a fool in many ways, and, like you, I did not mean it." Then she stooped and kissed the girl for the first time in years, and her eyes were filled with tears, and her throbbing heart said, "If we could only begin all over again from the beginning!"

Seraph was quieter after that. The sense that Minta had refused to come to her and had replied only with insulting words seemed to tone her impatience to see her. She counseled waiting for a day or two. "I will write her a little note myself, tomorrow, perhaps," she said, "if I am strong enough, and then she will understand better; and I do not blame Papa for not wanting that man to come. I never knew anything of his plans; I did not think he would dare to do as he has. Papa understands that, does he not?" And Ruth assured her tenderly that Papa had no words of blame for her. But Seraph thought much about it all; this was evident from the words she frequently spoke to Ruth, never to anyone else. "Mamma, people do not mean all the things they say. You know that, don't you? I don't know but you do; I have come to think so. That time you said you were sorry for me, do you remember—when you told me about Estelle? I know now that you meant it, but I didn't think so then. And I said things, many and many a time, that I did not mean. I did about her; I pretended not to care, and I said it was a little matter. There was not any of that true."

"I understand," said Ruth, and her voice was very humble. She had not understood, she told herself; she had not understood this girl at all; she had called her simply heartless, when perhaps her heart was break-ing.

There was another who insisted on knowing just what had been done about the summons to Minta, and on seeing her reply had tossed it down with a haughty, "That is just what I expected. I hope you have sufficiently humiliated us before her and will be content to let her take the road she has chosen."

"Seraph says she cannot now do as she will," interposed Ruth meekly, but her husband answered her only by a sharp "Nonsense!" And remembering Minta's determined will in the past, she said no more. It is possible that these two would both have been wiser could they have heard the words that passed between the young husband and wife on the receipt of Ruth's note. She had worded it carefully, trying not to give offense, and at the same time to make plain to the girl that she must come alone; and the husband had thrown it aside with much more vim than Judge Burnham used with the reply and had said in an angry voice: "Insufferable woman! If it were not for her, you would be in your rightful place in your father's house! The idea that she should dare to tell you that you may come home, but you must come alone! If you do not resent that with scorn, you are more of a coward than I take you to be."

"I wonder if Seraph is really very sick," faltered the wife. "Do you hear nothing about it in town? Couldn't you ask someone?"

"Sick! Of course she isn't; it is simply a ruse to get you away from me and then proceed to crushing me! That precious father of yours could do it, and would like nothing better, especially with your lovely step-mother to crowd on."

"Oh! but, Harold, you said yourself that Papa with-drew proceedings against you and that that was the reason you could stay in town."

"Yes; and why did he do it? Because I was sharp enough to get hold of you. He would have crushed me as willingly as he would a worm, but for that; if it had not been for his impertinent interference in my affairs I would never have gotten into such an intol-erable scrape. He may thank himself for the publicity of the whole thing. But his name is involved now, in spite of himself, and a man like him, who is all but consumed with personal vanity, will do a good deal for the sake of shielding one who belongs to him. I tell you, Minta, I understand all this perfectly; he has a deep-laid scheme to separate us and to ruin me; he has power enough to do it, even though I am not to blame, save in supposing that he had a heart. I don't depend on that organ any longer, I assure you, but I do on his pride. When he finds that you can be as firm as he thinks he is and will have all or nothing, his consuming desire to appear well in the eyes of the community will get control, and he will receive us both in the way he ought.

"Send back such an answer as this letter deserves and wait patiently; I know the world, and your precious father has a very large share of it grown into the place which he calls his heart. I do not believe there is anything the matter with Seraph but a severe cold; in fact, I know there isn't. She can come to us in a few days, and that will do much to smooth the way. It will not look well to have the daughter on familiar terms with us and the father not speaking to us. But there is one thing to remember—" this last sentence was added with gathering sternness, as he saw the look of doubt and anxiety on Minta's face—"mark my words, if you condescend to notice them in any way, so long as they ignore me, you choose between us and must take the consequences. I say that distinctly, knowing just what I mean, and you know that I am a man of my word."

He a man of his word and moving at large among men simply because of the forbearance of those to whom he had been false! His wife knew this, or at least knew that he was in disgrace with businessmen. He told her that he had been unfortunate and that it was her father's ill will that had forced evil upon him; but she was painfully conscious of the fact that there were men whom her father's ill will could not injure and that there was something very wrong about it all. Yet with the strange and pitiful inconsistency of the human heart, she felt for this man whom she yet could not quite respect a sentiment which in her ignorance she named love; and it held her in submission now, while she wrote, under his guidance and partly at his dictation, the letter over which Ruth had stood appalled.

Yet she cried when her husband left her alone, bitter tears, and wished she could see Seraph "just for a few minutes" and judge for herself whether she were really ill; and, altogether, was miserable enough to have moved the pity of a harder-hearted man than Judge Burnham.

For several days following these experiences an apparent change for the better seemed to be taking place in the sickroom. Seraph appeared stronger than she had for some weeks, and her appetite, which had almost entirely failed, returned; and her father, each time he saw her, remarked upon some token which was to him evidence of returning health. As for Mr. Satterley, he began to talk hopefully of the marvelous effects that a prolonged stay in California or in the far South frequently had on invalids and to hint that in a few weeks Seraph might be strong enough to take the journey by easy stages. Only the doctor and the professional nurse fully realized that they were simply passing through one of those deceptive lulls so common to the disease in question.

Meantime, Susan received an earnest summons back to her post, and Seraph agreed to her departure with a quiet smile.

"We shall miss you very much," she said cheerfully, "but I do not need you in the terrible sense that I did before you came. A few weeks make such a difference in things! Everything is different; Mamma and I can manage nicely together, if you ought to go."

So Susan kissed her—long, clinging kisses—and whispered good-bye and went away. And Ruth spent long hours, to be always remembered afterwards, in that sickroom.

There was often about the room now an atmosphere which awed her—it was growing so increasingly apparent that a Presence, unseen, yet potent in his influences, had taken possession and was steadily transforming this life.

There were moments when Ruth would stand looking at her charge almost reverently, absorbed in the thought of the coming changes. "She is going away," she said to herself. "In a few days she will see the Lord and talk with him face-to-face; and be with him forever and ever! A few weeks ago she did not know him at all; and now she has gotten so far ahead of me that sometimes it almost seems as though she already had speech with him such as I cannot understand. It is all very wonderful! And these are my days of privilege!"

And I may also make an exception of Mrs. Burnham; for she knew as well as did the doctor and the nurse that in a very little while Seraph Burnham was going away.

23

"Oh, Mamma! Good-Bye!"

THERE came a day, and it came suddenly at the last, as those days nearly always do, when Mrs. Hamlin, sitting alone and discontented in her third-story room in a downtown boarding house, received this imperative message, brought by a special messenger boy:

> If you want to see Seraph once more, you must come immediately; there is not an hour to lose.
> RUTH BURNHAM

Yet even then she was not prepared for the facts. Her husband had heard reports of the marked improvement in Seraph's case and had not failed to repeat them to his wife, without at any time letting her know the serious nature of the disease, though he himself was well aware of it and built some hope on the fact that Judge Burnham would, before very long, have but one daughter left to him.

He had taken his wife out of town with him for a few days, the better to keep her in ignorance of what might be going on in her home and also to prevent the possibility of her being urged there without him. They had returned but the night before, and he had been gone from the house but a few moments when this startling summons came. She did not believe it, but it filled her with alarm. What if Seraph were really very ill and wanted to see her—could she ever forgive herself for staying away? Besides, she longed so for a sight of her; and she believed in her heart that her husband was not only cruel but foolish in keeping them apart. What possible harm could come to him through her going to see her sister once in a while? Had she not shown him how little influence her family had over her as compared with him, when she left them at his bidding? While she was thinking these thoughts she made swift changes in her dress, having taken a resolution to go home at once and learn for herself just how much she had to fear. She was beginning to learn, even thus early in her married life, that her husband could be both cruel and false; it was possible that he was being false to her in this; she would see for herself.

So without more delay than was necessary, she stepped from the train at the old familiar station, which it seemed to her she had not seen before in years, entered her father's carriage, which was in waiting, and was driven rapidly to her former home. No one met her at the door; no one was waiting to receive her in the hall; she ran rapidly upstairs, frightened and yet unbelieving. Kate met her in the hall above, grave faced, low voiced. "You can go right in," she murmured and inclined her head toward the large cheerful room at the south end, and Minta pushed open the door noiselessly and entered.

She had thought that she would rush at once to her sister and wrap her arms about her—whatever the faults of these two may have been, they had loved each other—but she did not do as she had planned. Instead, she stopped, frightened, in the doorway, her breath coming in great heavy throbs which seemed to make her faint. Her father stood at one side of the great French bedstead, which had been drawn forward almost in front of the open window, where the soft spring sunlight was coming in. Near the foot of the bed stood the doctor, watch in hand, but doing nothing, saying nothing, impressing one by the very attitude in which he stood with the thought that all doing was done, so far as his profession was concerned, and that he was now waiting—for what? A strange woman was at the other side of the bed, looking intently, as were all the others, at the face lying quiet on the pillow, and bending over very near to her was Mrs. Burnham. All these things Minta, in the doorway, felt rather than saw; felt also the deathly pallor of that face on the pillow with closed eyes; so still she lay that she might even now be dead, for all indication she gave of life.

There was one other in the room; at first Minta did not see him. He was kneeling close to the form on the bed, somewhat shielded from view by Mrs. Burnham. He had one quiet hand clasped in both his own, but his face was buried in the same pillow on which the moveless head rested, and only the long-drawn, shuddering breath which he occasionally drew gave token that he was more conscious of what was passing than was the lovely body over which they were keeping their solemn watch.

No one spoke to Minta. Judge Burnham gave one swift glance toward her, then turned his eyes instantly back to that quiet face, his own growing perhaps a shade paler than it had been before. At that moment Mrs. Burnham noticed her and, moving slightly to make room, signed to her to approach. It was just then that the head on the pillow stirred once more; the lips parted in a smile which even Minta, all ignorant as she was, felt was not of earth. Her eyes opened wide, looked upward for a moment, as if reaching beyond the confines of the room—of the earth, indeed—then, returning, rested for a moment on her stepmother's face; the smile grew more radiant still, and her voice, always sweet, was filled now with an unearthly sweetness, but all she said was, "Oh, Mamma! good-bye!" and Seraph was gone.

Even in that supreme moment, Minta's first impulse was to turn a look of unutterable astonishment upon her stepmother. What miracle was this that the last ineffable smile and the last tender word of this passing soul should be given to her? Something like the same thought came to Ruth herself and brought with it such a sense of personal loss as a few weeks before she would not have supposed it possible she could feel in such a connection. You probably know all about the experiences of the next few days without words from me. It is a sorrowful fact that the scenes associated with the house of mourning are too common personal experiences to need description.

It was a grand and solemn funeral. I use the two words thoughtfully; the grandeur being of that subdued kind which marks the home not only of wealth but of culture. Judge Burnham was not the man to spare expense on any occasion, certainly not now; so the beautiful clay form which the soul had departed was adorned by every art known to skilled management and was almost literally embowered in flowers. It was, of course, a time of painful excitement and unrest; the very grief of one of the mourners having so much about it that was unnatural, as to wear heavily on the nerves of the others. The poor sister, you will remember, was utterly unprepared for such scenes as these. Ruth had made several efforts during the passing days to send her positive knowledge of Seraph's state, but owing to her absence from home and to her husband's wish that she should not know the truth, she had been successfully kept in ignorance. The bitterness of her sorrow and remorse was now pitiful to see. All the more terrible were they because no one seemed able to offer her a word of consolation. Ruth, of course, dared not speak at all. Judge Burnham made no attempt to do so, acted, indeed, as though he did not know this other daughter of his was in the house, yet that he was aware of it was apparent when he roused himself once to this stern statement: "Remember, Ruth, if that man dares to come to my door with inquiries, he is not to step inside on any pretext whatever. I look to you to see that my commands in this matter are obeyed to the letter, and remember that in this thing I will not be trifled with."

Then, indeed, she ventured one protest: "But, Judge Burnham, she is his wife—made so by the laws of God and man. Since this thing is done and she is to live with him, would it not be wise at such a time as this to allow him to come and speak to her if he will?"

Then she was glared upon with a fierceness that startled her. "You do not know what you are talking about," he said at last. "No; it would not be better to do any such thing. He has no right to be her husband; he is a perjured villain, and he knows it. He has deceived her as well as me, but she chose her own lot and must abide by it; so will I abide by my determination, and I repeat it: Under no pretext whatever shall that man step inside my door. If she wants him yet, she must go to him. I have no power to control her, but I have power to hold myself aloof from him and from her, since she has chosen between us, and I shall do so. And, Ruth, I would be grateful to you if you would not mention this thing to me again."

And then Ruth knew, more fully than she had before, that his fierce nature was entirely unsubdued.

It was not the time to say it, nor, indeed, was there any use in ever saying it, but it was not in her nature not to recall once more the fact that he had allowed this man, over whose very name his face now darkened, to lounge in his parlors evening after evening in friendly relations with the daughter who had finally yielded to his influence, and had not only made no sign of disapproval but had sneered at the warnings that came to him. What right had he to be surprised or dismayed at the result?

But he was destined to hear more on this hateful subject. His daughter, under the spell of a written communication from her husband, made successful effort to waylay her father while Seraph still lay in unearthly beauty in that back parlor, and with tears and sobs and pitiful appeals which were sufficiently honest to carry much weight with them, besought him to forgive her, to reinstate her once more in the home she had missed and see how dutiful and loving and comforting she could be to him. Very humble she was, and penitent. And he, with all the father stirred within him, with the memory of the fact that she was now the only daughter left him, yet resisted the touch of her caressing arms and held aloof from her, and walked the floor, his face still stern, but his chin quivered, and his eyes were dimmed with a film of tears. At last he spoke:

"I have not meant to be severe. I have believed myself to be a very indulgent father; too indulgent, I have had reason to think, during these later months of my bitter experience; had I been less so, you would never have been drawn into the toils of the man who stole you from me. You chose between us, however, after you were duly warned, and by me, and I had meant that you should abide by your choice; but there are other arguments than those you bring tonight that have been influencing me of late; some of them might surprise you if I gave them. I will not go into details now; I will merely say that I have resolved to do what I thought I should never do—offer you your home again. It is a desolated and disgraced home; disgraced by your own act, and the Burnham name never wore a stain before; but, despite it all, if you choose to come back to the home and the name and pledge yourself never to hold another conversation with the man who has wronged us all, I will receive you again as my daughter, even in the face of a gaping world. Also, I will take measures that will forever prevent your being annoyed by the man who would like to claim you for the sake of the money that he thinks will be yours. The idea of the villain's supposing that one cent of my money will ever pass through his hands!" Even at such a time Judge Burnham could not keep the subdued tones of voice that became the house, but let them rise into anger with the last sentence.

I am inclined to think he misunderstood his daughter as entirely as it is possible for a man to misunderstand a woman. She, too, lost her self-control and gave free reign to her passionate tongue. She had not been for weeks in the constant society of a bad man without having been influenced thereby, and many of the bitter things that she poured out in her wrath she believed to be true. She told her father that he was under the spell of a woman who hated her, and who had hated the daughter lying dead in the next room, and who had made both their lives bitter for them all these years; that it was she who had so prejudiced him against her husband that he would allow himself to be neither reasonable nor even respectable in the eyes of the world. And then she assured him that she knew how things looked to this terrible ogre, the world, of which he was so afraid, and that he might be entirely certain the world should hear just how a father, led around by a second wife, could be made not only to so embitter the life of one of them that she welcomed the grave as a release, but could actually bring himself to all but forcing the other to give up her husband and her married name in return for being received again into a home which she hated; and then she assured him that she had chosen and was glad to remember that she had, and that nothing ever, not even the honor of being recognized before the world as belonging to the Burnham race, should make her desert her husband even for a day; that she would go back to him that very night; and that she wanted nothing from this house or from the people to whom it belonged, from this time forth.

He listened to this outburst of mingled passion and pain at first in a kind of bewilderment; then, as she made some accusations, which in the light of his recent experiences he knew were absolutely false, his anger rose almost to white heat; but as her passionate torrent of words went on, gathering force as they were poured out, he reached the point where his well-trained self-control began to assert its power, and deceiving her by the very calm with which he listened, he waited before her in absolute silence until she paused for breath.

"Are you quite through?" he asked at last, when she had been silent for a moment. "Because if you are not,

I would advise you to continue; it might not be wise to go from here with any pent-up torrent of anger such as you have exhibited; an outburst in other places might be more dangerous than it will be here. I am glad you have told me all this; it makes plain much that I have, of late, suspected; it reveals some things to me much more clearly than I could have hoped to understand them from any source; but if you have really nothing further to say, I will add just a few plain words, very easy to be understood. You may, since you are in the house, if you choose, remain during the funeral services of my daughter. As soon after that hour as you can conveniently do so, I shall have to ask you to leave my house; and I wish you distinctly to understand that you are not to return to it at any time nor under any pretext. I understood you to say that you had chosen between us. Very well; you had the opportunity and can blame no one but yourself for having made use of it; what I require is that you shall abide by your decision. From this time forth I will not trouble you to call me by the name which has sheltered you all these years, and you need not even burden your conscience by thinking of me as your father; you have my full permission to disown me entirely, and to say to the world whatever you and your precious husband please. The probability is, you will learn in time, that my reputation will be equal to the shock of even the withdrawal of his favor. Now, as it is getting late, I will not detain you further, but will bid you good night, Mrs. Hamlin."

He opened his library door and ceremoniously bowed his daughter out. And the other daughter lay but a few steps from them—her face still glorified by that gleam from heaven which had rested on it—embowered in flowers.

24

"Next Most"

AMONG the flowers that were strewn in profusion all about the casket where Seraph rested was a single spray of tuberoses lying somewhat by itself and as close as possible to the face of the beautiful sleeper. It filled the room with that rare fragrance that belongs only to the tuberose. Mr. Satterley, who had been in the room alone for nearly an hour, taking that long last look which almost rends the human heart in sunder—taking it with the consciousness that dust and darkness and decay are now to claim this treasure for their own—had turned away at last, and then turned back, and, lifting the spray of roses, had broken a single perfect bloom from its stem and placed it within the velvet folds of a tiny case that held Seraph's pictured face, then returned it to his breast pocket and replaced the spray so that it almost touched the fair marble cheek.

Ruth, who had been about to enter the room, drawing suddenly back when she saw its occupant, had been a witness to this last act; a pitiful smile hovered about her mouth for a moment. The spray of tuberoses had a history which Mr. Satterley did not know. Did she whose unconscious clay lay before him know the story? In the world to which she had gone, did they know of all these little tender, pitiful things that are constantly happening here?

Barely two hours before had Mrs. Burnham herself opened the piazza door in answer to the timid knock of a trembling hand and had come face-to-face with Estelle Hollister.

The girl's eyes were swollen with recent weeping, and there were heavy dark rings under them, which told of long night vigils and tears.

"May I look at her," she had asked eagerly, "and may I lay this spray of flowers beside her? I know she loved tuberoses; I have seen her wear them often. Oh, Mrs. Burnham! I am so sorry for you all; and so sorry for—for him."

And Ruth, for the moment unable to speak, knowing no words, indeed, which would fit the pitiful strangeness of the moment, inclined her head in silence toward the closed door, with its significant badge of crêpe, and left the two alone together. And this was the spray of flowers from which Mr. Satterley had picked one bloom to wear close to his heart.

They had planned very carefully for the funeral hour. Mr. Satterley had been reminded that Minta would be dependent on him for care; but nothing took place as it was planned. Minta, after that last stormy scene with her father, refused to stay another hour in the house; refused to be present at the funeral services next day, but went in haste and in anger to the husband for whose sake she had left them all. And Judge Burnham was held all the dreadful morning in the grasp of relentless pain. A peculiar form of nervous headache, of which he was sometimes a victim and against which he had struggled all the previous night, increased upon him to such an alarming degree that when the hour for the public service arrived, he was under the influence of a powerful opiate and therefore mercifully unconscious alike of bodily and mental pain. So it came to pass that the stepmother attended by Mr. Satterley were the only recognized mourners who followed Seraph Burnham out from her father's house.

It seemed a strange house to Ruth to live in after that. She wandered through the deserted, silent rooms, throwing them open to light and air, caring for the many dainty and delicate things left behind with painstaking fingers that almost quivered with a sense of dread.

How was it that she, who had for years felt no responsibility and but little interest in this part of the house, had come to be the sole caretaker here? How swift and terrible had been the changes which had left her free and lonely in her own house! No danger now of being disturbed day or night by inopportune out-bursts of merriment or the sound of gay young feet; the house was still—very still.

Its mistress folded, and wrapped, and marked, and laid away package after package of pretty trifles that had belonged exclusively to Seraph; and while she worked there fell many a tear born of that most sorrowful of all sorrowful memories—what "might have been."

She had been so very late in finding out what she and Seraph might have enjoyed together! She had so utterly failed in regard to Minta; and though she reminded herself that the two were, and had always been, very unlike, yet in the light of her recent revelations, she could not but feel that possibly, had she managed all things differently, all results might have been different.

Those were lonely days, the ones which followed. She could not settle to anything; indeed she could not find anything satisfactory on which to settle. Society did not claim her, of course; there were endless proprieties connected with it to be observed, but it released her from personal inflictions in many ways. Still she did not find it by any means so pleasant to be alone as she had once supposed it would be. She was very much alone; Judge Burnham absorbed himself in business even more than usual; and when at home was gloomy to an almost alarming extent; indeed, if I should call him morose, it would perhaps be the more fitting word. That he was a rebel against all the recent family trials was only too apparent. Minta he did not mention at all. Whether he knew anything about her or her circumstances, Ruth could not determine, for it did not seem to her wise to break the ominous silence in which he chose to wrap himself. His mention of Seraph was always in the way of bitter regret. Had she been sent from home at once, when she first began to cough, all might have been well. Had there been somebody besides a deceiving idiot for a doctor, they might have known in time what was feared and prevented it. Had Seraph been properly guarded from exposure, she need never have taken such an alarming cold. He did not know, of course. How could men be expected to keep guard over these things? It was the woman's place. Girls were careless, of course; they always were; it was mothers who watched. "If—" And it was about at such a point that he usually had the grace to stop. Ruth often wondered whether, had he continued, he would have said, "If the girls had only had a mother!" But she was very pitiful toward him; she had some realization of what it must be for a father to lose, thus suddenly and thus painfully, the hold which he thought he had on two who were his own. As often as she looked at Erskine, she shuddered over the possibilities which the future might hold in shadow, waiting for her.

Then, too, she realized that the bright side to these heavy clouds her husband did not see at all. It seemed an infinite pity that he could not, at least at times, absorb himself as she could in the wonder of the thought that Seraph Burnham was today singing among the angels. She had been gone only a few weeks; yet how much she must already know about those things of which her father was totally ignorant, and concerning which Ruth herself could only vaguely conjecture. Yet the conjecturings grew daily more interesting to her. And in the leisure which had come upon her, she found herself reading and study-ing much about the possibilities of that other world which, because of the experiences in Seraph's room, had come near to her. She collated in logical order all the words which the Bible has to offer in regard to it and was, as many another Christian has been, de-lighted to find that the grand old Book told so much and amazed to think that she had not, long ago, learned all it had to tell on such an absorbing subject. As the weeks passed, and she still remained in uncer-tainty as to how to use her leisure, this method of exhaustive Bible study grew into a fixed habit.

Day after day she was occupied in familiarizing herself with proof texts in regard to this or that doctrine or duty, and in so arranging and illumining them with incident or story that Erskine would be interested and helped. If he had but known it, these were growing days for Erskine. He delighted in being with his mother—in her having, once more, abundant leisure for his needs—and it mattered very little to him how she planned to have the leisure occupied, so that he could share it with her. So the golden head and the mature one were often and often bent over the large and elegantly illustrated family Bible, and the two drank in wisdom together. "Erskine will never be puzzled as to the right or wrong of many questions which have disturbed me," Ruth said to herself with infinite satisfaction. "He will have a clearly defined 'thus saith the Lord' to settle them for him."

Meantime, the ladies of the Temperance Union were watching Mrs. Burnham with no little anxiety. The brilliant career which they had marked out for her and which had been so signally commenced had been arrested, you will remember, almost immediately thereafter.

The ladies thought that her public work had been held in check only by the series of providential circumstances which had followed each other in her home.

But Ruth knew, even as you and I do, that had not these startling experiences come into her life, her career, so far at least as regarded the public meetings, would doubtless have suddenly closed.

It was one of the questions which perplexed her now, how far she was justified in letting her husband's prejudices hold her back from work which she knew she would enjoy and in which the Lord had once given her a signal token of his approval. She held the ladies at bay and held her own decision in the background while she tried to study with unprejudiced mind the entire subject. The ladies were very hard to answer; they were importunate. "My dear Mrs. Burnham, why will you not come next Sunday and help us? You cannot think how we have missed you! There are so very few of us, you know, to bear burdens of this sort. There are plenty who are willing to give money and time; to carry around petitions, to distribute literature, and to serve on social committees; but when it comes to speaking a few words to the poor fellows about their souls, or even to leading in prayer, the only answer we can be sure of is, 'I pray thee have me excused!' I don't understand why it is," would Mrs. Stuart Bacon conclude with a weary sigh; and then, after a moment, return to the charge: "And, dear Mrs. Burnham, since that first Sabbath when you helped us so grandly, we have been depending on you. Of course we did not expect you while family cares and afflictions were resting so heavily on you, but now that the Lord has taken those duties out of your hands—"

It was very hard for Mrs. Burnham, in the face of such appeals, to make answer to the effect that Erskine needed her or that Judge Burnham, who was nearly always at home on Sabbath afternoons, would be lonely if she should leave him for an hour. She knew such words must sound painfully trivial to women at work among souls who were in immediate and desperate need.

The very fact that she was giving reasons which were not, after all, the real ones made this truthful woman wince, and stammer, and feel and appear ill at ease; and the ladies went away pained and puzzled. And the weeks went on, the summer waned, and another autumn was nearly upon them, without there having been any definite settlement in this Christian woman's mind as to what work she would do for her King.

Not that she was idle; it had been to her a summer

of study. Certainly she was furnishing her brain for some encounter with error; and because of her connection with and interest in the Woman's Christian Temperance Union, her studies had, almost without plan on her part, developed in that direction. She had gone into the hall on that Sabbath afternoon with no very clear idea as to what she thought in regard to the political or indeed any other working aspect of the temperance question. Had she been asked that day what she thought of high license, or of no license at all, or whether she believed prohibition would prohibit, or whether she thought constitutional prohibition was feasible, she could only have replied in vague general ways that she never wanted her boy to touch, or taste, or handle alcohol in any form and that if we were really to love our neighbors as ourselves, she was in duty bound to take that same stand for other boys. Thus much she knew, even in her ignorance. But on that September afternoon, as she sat with the evening paper in her hand and her fine face aglow with a feeling very like contempt for the astute member of Congress who had written a remarkable article on the folly of the proposed temperance movement, she said aloud, speaking, Erskine thought, to him, since he was the only other occupant of the room: "What utter illogical, nauseating nonsense! I'd like to reply to that man!"

"What has he said, Mamma?"

"Why, some false and silly things against the temperance movement and against the temperance workers, Erskine. They are so silly that they could be very easily answered by one who was thoroughly posted as to facts; and yet they have such a semblance of truth that they will help to lead astray many who have not studied facts."

She was not trying to make the little boy understand; she was simply thinking aloud, as she so often did during these months of comparative solitude. But the boy, being so constantly with his mother and sharing, in a degree, all her studies and all her interests, had come to understand much better than even his mother knew. What suggested to his wise little heart the next remark?

"Mamma, how do you know but God wants you to stand up in a big church or somewhere and explain all about it to people who have not studied facts?"

The rich blood glowed over the mother's face in an instant. Was the thought somewhat like a revelation to her heart? Did God want her to do anything like this? But what would Judge Burnham say to work of such a character, even in its meekest developments?

"Don't you think he may want you to do it, Mamma?"

"Do you think ladies ought to do such work, Erskine?"

She did not know why she said it; she laughed at herself for her folly even while she spoke. What should the baby know about such questions?

"Why not, Mamma, if God wanted them to? Wouldn't a true lady do anything for God?"

Certainly this was high ground. Could she, with all her added years and wisdom, hope to reach higher? Nay, was she really prepared to reach so high?

She went back instantly to the old painful query, What would her husband say? "I'll tell you what God wants," she said, speaking with sudden fervor; "he wants, and I want, more than anything else in this world, to have Papa give himself to Christ. If we could only have that, Erskine."

"Why, yes," said Erskine, speaking with slow gravity,

apparently surprised at her sudden fervor, "I know that, and I speak to God about it all the time, and he knows we want it most; but then, he wants us to think about the next most, too, doesn't he?"

And from that hour Ruth tried, with a new energy, to come to a decision as to what her "next most" ought to be.

25

A Waiting Worker

YET, in the days that immediately followed, had Mrs. Burnham been questioned in regard to her hopes for her husband's change of views, she would have admitted that they were never at a lower ebb.

Even as regarded his acquiescence in, or endurance of, almost any form of active Christian work for herself, she was almost hopeless. The question that seemed pressing for decision was, How far must she allow deference for his opinions to hold her passive? Meantime, he grew, if possible, more gloomily unreconciled to the quiet of the house; and it seemed to his wife that they could not even take an evening walk without meeting something that added to the bitterness of his unrest.

They were lingering together in the park just as twilight was falling. The walk had been of her proposing and was one of her many devices for drawing him, if possible, away from some brooding care of anxiety; she could not be sure of what nature it was, and while she suspected that it might have to do with his daughter Minta, she did not dare to question. Her sole hope was to rest him from the burden for a while. He had consented half apathetically to the walk, only stipulating, somewhat sharply, that Erskine should not be of the company, declaring himself to be in no mood for a child's incessant questionings.

So Erskine, to his great grief, had been left at home, and the two had wandered aimlessly through the park, on whose beauty the touch of another autumn was already beginning to settle. Ruth had left her husband's side and gone forward a few steps to examine more closely some gay foliage plants about a fountain, when she saw, on the opposite side of the driveway, two familiar forms. It took but a glance to recognize Mr. Satterley, but the lady she had to study carefully before she could be sure that it was Estelle Hollister.

Younger she looked, and prettier, than Mrs. Burnham had ever seen her before; and as she listened to what her companion was saying, the soft pink flush on her face could be distinctly seen. At that moment the two turned suddenly and met her eyes. Both faces flushed, and as if by common consent, they stood quite still in the walk. Ruth bowed cordially, and then Mr. Satterley seemed to recover himself and, bowing low in reply, moved on. It was but a moment afterwards that, rising up from the shrub over which she had bent, Mrs. Burnham saw that the girl had broken away from her companion and was coming toward her.

She was evidently in the habit of being as simply direct in what she had to say as was Ruth herself. She began at once, without waiting to reply to the cordial "Good evening!" that accompanied Ruth's outstretched hand. "Mrs. Burnham, do you think it wrong for me to be taking a walk with him? He asked me to come out here where it was quiet and where he could talk with me undisturbed. He has not for-gotten—we have neither of us forgotten; there are some things, you know, that people cannot forget. But he says she asked him to talk with me and tell me some things that she wanted me to understand—and I promised her to—to forgive him, you know."

Mrs. Burnham could hardly forbear a smile. It was a duty which the poor little thing was so manifestly willing to perform; yet she was so conscientiously desirous of doing only the right thing and of paying the utmost deference and respect to the memory of the one who was gone. She hastened to speak her reassurance: "My dear girl, why should it be wrong, unless, indeed, you are wronging yourself? Miss Burn-ham has gone where none of these things can touch her anymore. I should think there could be no impro-priety in Mr. Satterley's carrying out her wish in regard to seeing you; but if you would really like my advice for yourself, if I were you, I would go home to my mother without delay and be guided by her as to anything in the future; you owe it to her and to yourself."

"I mean to," said Estelle with half a smile and wholly a sob. "Good-bye! and thank you."

Meantime, Mr. Satterley had joined Judge Burn-ham, and the two had been speaking together, appar-ently of matters about which both were indifferent. He acknowledged Mrs. Burnham's coming toward them only by another low, grave bow and immedi-ately turned away. Judge Burnham did not speak a word for the next five minutes; then he said, in a voice which seemed to have taken on an added tinge of bitterness, "It seems to me Satterley has sought and found consolation very early for one who was so nearly brokenhearted as he."

"They are friends of long standing," Ruth said, simply and gently; there was no need now to say more. The grave had closed over all necessity for revealing that chapter which would be only an added sting to the father's heart. Ruth smiled to think that she could be loyal to both husband and daughter and do no harm. And as they walked on in silence, in the gathering darkness, it almost seemed to her that she could hear again that singularly flutelike voice, and once more it said, "Mamma, thank you." Their next encounter was a business friend of Judge Burnham, and an important business conference must needs be held then and there; and as Ruth stood aside and waited, there came to her presently a bit of life that was all her own. A plainly dressed young man, who looked as though he might be a mechanic but who lifted his hat to her with the air of a gentleman, stopped before her in the pathway.

"I beg your pardon, Mrs. Burnham, for speaking to you. You do not know me, I suppose, but I know you so well and have so much for which to thank you that it seemed to me I could not let this opportunity pass."

The twilight had fallen very fast; the face before her was but dimly defined. Ruth's first impulse was to draw back and step quickly to her husband's side, but he was close at hand. What was there to fear? Why not learn what the man meant?

"I think you must be mistaken in the person," she said with gentle dignity. "I am sure you have no occasion to give me thanks."

"Indeed I have; I ask God daily to bless you forever. But for you, I shudder to think what the next step would have been."

A sudden, sweet memory came to Ruth.

"You are that young man to whom I spoke that

Sunday?" she said, hesitating, throwing both hope and doubt into her voice.

"I am that young man to whom you, on that never-to-be-forgotten Sunday, made plain as daylight the way to eternal life. I thought you ought to know that I kept my promise to go straight to the Lord Jesus and claim his help. And I got it, bless his name! I belong to him now in life and death."

Was ever sweeter music than this offered to a Christian's ears? There were only a few more words after that. Inquiries as to the young man's plans and prospects. He was doing well; he had found, already, that to be a servant of the Lord meant more than a hope of heaven; it meant very much for this life also. He said this with a smile which she could feel, rather than see; it sounded in his voice. Then he had thanked her again in strong, hearty words and had told her that he knew she must be going on with her work; he felt sure God had called her to the saving of young men who were, like himself, almost lost. Only a few minutes, but when she turned, Judge Burnham was alone, waiting for her, and it did not need the firm grasp with which he drew her hand through his arm to tell her that he must have overheard the last words and was annoyed.

"You seem to have acquaintances of all sorts," he said haughtily, "and to be fated to meet them tonight. Let us get out of this park as soon as possible. Pray who was that young fellow who presumes to speak to you so familiarly?"

"He was not familiar, Judge Burnham; nothing could have been more deferential than his tone. He is a young man whom I met at the Gospel meeting."

"I thought you did not attend those meetings."

"I have not since that one Sunday, which you must remember."

"Oh! and this was the tobacco-smelling fellow with whom you were kind enough to talk. If he has not improved his habits, it is well we were surrounded by so much fresh air."

"He has improved. He is a servant of the Lord Jesus Christ, and I am glad over it, with a gladness which I wish you could understand."

"Thank you for all kind wishes; and I presume it is hardly necessary to remind you again that I will not on any account have you meet familiarly with those people, nor allow your name to be associated with theirs."

And Mrs. Burnham went home from her walk more hopeless, in regard to some things, than she had been before, but more sure than ever that she must decide, and speedily, as to her "next most."

And then suddenly, unexpectedly, Judge Burnham went away again. Another member of the firm was to go, but sickness detained him, and the business was important, and complicated, and tedious. It involved much travel and long delays, and Ruth was left more utterly alone than ever before in her life. There were no young ladies this time to almost bewilder her with their comings and goings; there were no sounds of gay society life in the great silent house. Even Mr. Satterley was not there to make occasional calls out of respect to the family tie which had once existed.

He was going to New York on business which might detain him for some time, so he told her when he called to say good-bye; and Mrs. Burnham, who knew that Estelle Hollister had gone home, wondered as to the nature of the business and was somewhat anxious and silent. It made her smile, and yet almost humiliated her, to find that even Mr. Satterley was missed. There was a painful sense of not belonging to anybody which sat heavily upon this lonely woman. As often as she wandered through the lonely halls of her handsome house she wondered what could be done with it. Since society had shrouded it in crêpe and passed it by, to what use could those large silent rooms be put which would reflect honor on the One to whom all hers was consecrated? Ah! therein lay the secret of the difficulty. She must say "our rooms"; if only she could say "all ours is consecrated," how plainly would the answer to this painful riddle glow before her! She knew a dozen beautiful things which might be done with cultured, consecrated homes. Did she not know all about Flossy Shipley Roberts, and the "green room," and all the schemes to which it was consecrated? This was certainly her "most," and though she clung to her one weapon, the power of prayer, and though she daily, even as Erskine had said, "talked with God about this," kept it before him that it was this which she wanted most, yet certainly her heart was very heavy and her faith was weak.

Her husband had gone before there had been time for that long talk with him which she had planned. She had meant to say, in all gentleness and yet in plainness, that the time had certainly come when she could no longer fold her hands in graceful idleness to please his tastes; she must find her appointed niche in the Lord's great workshop and do her part. She had meant to ask—very humbly—what there was that he was willing to have her undertake. She would like to go to that women's gospel meeting; it was there the Lord had met her and told her what to say for him; and she felt that she could do such work as this again;

but if for any reason he shrank from that particular form of work and was yet willing that she should undertake some other that would be honest work, she would not press her wishes against his will. Only this must be understood: She was bound by command and covenant to work in some direction and felt that she could wait no longer. Even while she thought it out—what she would say, and what he might possibly reply, and if so, what she could answer—there came to her that same sad memory over which she winced as in mortal pain. Her husband might say to her, if he understood these things well enough to use their language: "The Lord gave you work to do; he placed two young girls in your special care—gave you all the appliances with which to work and bade you shape, and mold, and train them for himself; and you failed him! To one of them he reached out loving arms, and snatched her from the perils of the life in which you had started her feet, and took her to himself; but the other—where is the other?" There was no danger that Judge Burnham would speak any of these terrible truths to his wife; but there was also no need; her own conscience knew how to press them home with tremendous power. Still, she was in earnest now, and she must not longer make the mistake of sitting idle, glooming over the past while present opportunities ran to waste. But there had been no time for that talk with her husband. He had been gone for several weeks when Mrs. Stuart Bacon sent up her card one morning with a penciled request that she might be seen if possible, as her business was urgent.

"I do not want to see her," said Mrs. Burnham aloud and incautiously, rising from the low chair against which Erskine had leaned while he made careful attempts over the figures which had been set him to add.

"Why not, Mamma?" said this wide-eyed questioner, who was not held to rigid rules during school hours, his mother being his sole teacher.

"Because," said Ruth, still speaking out her troubled thoughts rather than addressing Erskine, "she will want me to do what I cannot."

"Don't you know how, Mamma?"

"Oh yes!" with a half smile on her face over the question while she lingered to arrange her dress; "I may know how to do it, but there are other difficulties in the way."

"Don't you think it ought to be done?"

"Indeed I do"; this reply was given with energy. Erskine paused, pencil in hand, curly yellow head dropped a little on one side, and gravely considered this problem which was more puzzling to him than the column of figures; at last he reached a solution: "Then, Mamma, I should think if it ought to be done, and you know how, that God would want you to do it."

Whereupon the mother laughed again, albeit her eyelashes were moist, and kissed her young logician, and went down to Mrs. Bacon.

But that lady, who was generally clear-brained and hurried, delayed the special reason for her call in a most trying way. She talked about the last Sabbath's meeting with earnestness, indeed, but forgot even to hint of the pleasure it would have been to have had Mrs. Burnham's help. She told a long story about a young girl whom she had taken into her family under circumstances of peculiar distress, and how deep was her interest in the matter, and how much there was in just such lines that needed doing. Under other circumstances, Ruth would have been deeply interested in the story; but it was at this time so manifestly being told to cover an embarrassment over something not yet reached that to the listener it was simply irritating.

When her caller, having exhausted the story, went back to the weather, waxing eloquent over the beauty of the morning, Ruth felt almost like saying that if her errand was really no more important than it appeared, she would like to be excused.

And then at last Mrs. Bacon broke off in the midst of a statement that the air reminded her of a certain September morning in Italy, to say:

"But, dear Mrs. Burnham, to tell you the truth, I did not come to you this morning to talk about the weather. I want to ask you to forgive me for what I earnestly hope is unnecessary interference on my part, and then to tell you plainly what I have heard."

26

UNDER GUIDANCE

"I KNOW it is possible that you may have heard the same reports, but I told Mr. Bacon this morning that I did not believe you knew anything about it; and I was just going to try to do as I would be done by." A nervous little laugh finished the sentence, and then Mrs. Bacon launched a question that covered the ground over which she had just gone. "Do you know anything of Mrs. Hamlin's circumstances, my dear Mrs. Burnham?"

"I have not heard from her, or of her, since she left her father's house on the evening before her sister was buried," Ruth said with steady voice but rising color. The unnatural relations that now existed in the disorganized family were sources of continual embarrassment to her.

"I was sure of it," affirmed Mrs. Bacon with an air of relief. "I was sure that your kind heart would lead you to act in the matter, now that in your husband's absence the responsibility falls on you. Well, my dear, I will not make a longer story than is necessary. It is said that her husband has gone from bad to worse. He has been getting into very dangerous relations again with certain men; gambling, you know, and—well, I am afraid, forging notes. Mr. Bacon thinks it will hardly be possible to save him from state prison this time. We have also heard that he has kept his wife in a very straitened condition. They have changed boarding places several times, even in these few months, and always, I am told, of necessity, because they were in arrears with board. And only last night I heard, from what I am afraid is a reliable source, that he had deserted her and that she was really in very destitute circumstances."

"Do you know where she is to be found?"

It was the only question that Ruth's lips seemed able to frame.

"Yes, I do; I took special care to learn. She is on Court Street, away down toward the river, in one of those long houses, on the third-floor back. I don't wonder you start, Mrs. Burnham; it is terrible to think of Judge Burnham's daughter in a tenement house on Court Street, isn't it? However, you will be able to right all that. If the man must really go to prison, why, the poor thing will be rid of him, at least."

She had risen as she spoke and was drawing her wrap about her with the air of one who had done her part in the best way she knew. And Ruth, quivering in every nerve with a sense of shame for her husband's sake, yet had sense enough to feel that this good woman had done the best that the circumstances would admit; had really said the only comforting thing that could be said, even though what comfort there was must grow out of the fact of there being prisons for convicted criminals. Verily, Minta Burnham had chosen for herself!

What to do was the imperative question staring Ruth in the face, demanding immediate reply. She was by no means so clear of her course or of her ability to accomplish as Mrs. Bacon seemed to be for her. Of course something must be done. A daughter of Judge Burnham's could not be left in a Court Street tenement house alone!

Yet would she, at Ruth's request and under her care, go elsewhere? And if so, where was the suitable place for her, and what was the next step to take?

It was all bewilderment; and while she struggled with it, she could not tell whether to be glad or sorry that Judge Burnham was absent. If he were at home, he would know just what to do; but were not the chances that he would do the wrong thing? Yet what was the right thing?

Troubled exceedingly by these and kindred questionings, she yet made herself ready with all speed for a journey to town. Erskine came, questioning: Why were they not to have a geography lesson? Why was she going to town? Could he go along? He would like to go to the city very much.

No, his mother said, he could not go with her this time, because she had something to do in which he would be in the way. What was that? he wanted to know. And smiling faintly over the apparent incongruity of her statements, she confessed that she did not know what she was going to do.

"Why, Mamma!" he said, in great amazement. "Then how can you do it?"

She couldn't, she explained, not until she learned. She was to try to find out what was the wise and right thing to do in a matter of great perplexity.

Over this statement Erskine considered for a moment; then came his wise, sweet question that went to the root of things: "Why don't you ask God to tell you?"

"I will," she said, turning toward him with a smile that yet was very close to tears. It was a surprising thing, when one stopped to look at it. She, a Christian woman, hurrying to an emergency that she consciously did not know how to meet, yet taking no time to consult, not only the acknowledged Source of all wisdom, but One who had graciously said, "Ask of Me." She held out her hand to Erskine, and the two knelt in their accustomed place of prayer, while Erskine voiced the request that the dear Lord Jesus would show Mamma just what he wanted her to do.

"Do you know now?" he asked her cheerily a moment after. Evidently there had not entered the child's mind a question as to her doing, without fail, whatever the Lord Jesus wanted done. "Has he told you yet, Mamma?"

"Not yet," she said, smiling over his lesson on faith.

"Oh, well! He will, I'm sure he will, and he'll do it in time."

And in the light of this earnest assurance she went to her task.

The lower part of Court Street was not used to carriages such as the one which Mrs. Burnham summoned to her aid; there was much staring from behind half-closed blinds, and the noisy following of certain ragged little boys and girls who felt no need of blinds to hide behind. The stairs were somewhat narrow and somewhat steep; and a very slatternly girl, from whose contact Ruth carefully held her dress, toiled upward just ahead of her to show the way. Dinginess increased upon them as they mounted, and the third-story back was destitute of anything like comfort. A well-known voice answered Ruth's hesitating tap and, still uncertain what to do or how to make known her errand—

if she had one—she entered and stood face-to-face with Minta Hamlin.

"Oh! it is you." This was her greeting, intense astonishment bristling in every letter, and then the two women stood and looked at each other. Certainly the situation was striking. Several times in their lives had these two confronted each other under sufficiently startling circumstances, but neither perhaps had ever felt it more than at this moment. The beautiful girl of Mrs. Burnham's memory had changed even in these short months. Her face was almost deathly pale, even in this moment of excitement; and her hair was pushed straight back from her forehead in unbecoming plainness. She wore a dark silk dress which had once been pretty, but which was now drabbled and torn; the lace of one sleeve hung in careless frays, the skirt was daubed with something which looked like paint, and one elbow was worn to a decided hole. The furniture of the bare and cheerless room matched the dress of its mistress; shabby remnants of bygone finery, in a sentence which sufficiently describes it. And in this room Minta Hamlin, who in her father's house was accustomed to all the elegancies and to all the trained attention that money will furnish, was evidently preparing, with very insufficient appliances, to do some washing for herself. A small hand bathtub filled with suds occupied a perilous position on a slippery chair that was once upholstered in haircloth, and a pile of soiled clothing lay on the floor. That the girl looked miserably ill would have been apparent to the most casual observer; and the hollow cough which she frequently gave reminded Mrs. Burnham, each time she heard it, of Seraph.

"Well," she said at last, after that prolonged silence, accompanied by a haughty stare, "to what am I indebted for this most unexpected honor? You did not send up your card, so I was not prepared; I thought it was my landlord."

Even then there was a mocking smile on her face, as of one who could almost enjoy the embarrassment, because of the fact that it must be a very embarrassing moment to the other person. Just then came a knock at the door, quite unlike Ruth's timid one: sharp and imperative. The opening of the door almost immediately afterward threw Ruth just back of it, and the intruder did not see her. He was a young man with an impudent face and a voluble tongue.

"I have called once more for the money," he began, "and we may as well understand one another this time; I don't propose to climb these stairs again for nothing. Either you give me the month's rent now, or else you walk out of this flat without any more delay. People cannot expect to rent furnished flats with nothing but promises; and I have instructions to—"

He did not finish his sentence. All the Erskine blood, which in its way was certainly as intense as any that belonged to the house of Burnham, seemed to boil in Ruth's veins as she heard her husband's daughter thus familiarly and insolently addressed. It increased her indignation to discover that the girl-woman who confronted the man was palled with terror and evidently felt herself to be in his power. "He'll do it in time, Mamma!" Erskine's last assuring words, mingling with his good-bye kisses, seemed to sound in her ears. Did God tell her what to do in this crisis of her life? She thought of it wonderingly afterwards—the painful doubt of the moment before, the instant decision flashing upon her from somewhere.

"You forget yourself strangely, sir," she said, stepping with the air of a princess from behind the half-open door. "If you have any claim on this lady you may present your bill at Judge Burnham's office, 263 Fourth Street, tomorrow morning at ten o'clock, and it will be paid."

The alarmed young man made confused efforts to apologize, to explain; but he might as well have attempted to address an iceberg.

There could be no explanation, the lady said, which could justify the use of such language to a woman; all she wished of him was to retire. Which he did in haste and dismay.

And then Ruth speedily forgot him in the unexpected work she found for thought and hands. The poor haughty girl who had tried to be so self-sufficient and so daring in her insolence had suddenly felt her strength giving way; the room spun dizzily around her, then grew dark and wavered in that sickening fashion which is the last conscious feeling that the victim to a fainting fit remembers, and but for Ruth's sudden spring to her side, she would have fallen. It was very unpoetical, what followed. Ruth could not get her charge to a chair; the utmost that her strength could accomplish was to lay her gently on the dingy carpet, then look about for water. The soapsuds in the bathtub was the only liquid at hand; there was no help for it but to dip her hastily ungloved hand into the foam and bathe the pallid face with it.

It was well, perhaps, for all concerned that there was no disinterested looker-on to view the ludicrous side of this scene; it was really the first conscious thought of the proud girl as she came slowly back to life. She darted a suspicious glance at her stepmother and attempted to push her ministering hand away and rise to a sitting posture. But Ruth, as she splashed the soapy water right and left, was too manifestly absorbed in ministering to the best of her powers to have room for any other thought.

"You are better now?" she said inquiringly. "Oh! I would not try to move just yet; let me put my arm under your head, so; and lie still just a few minutes longer."

The tone was gentle, soothing, as she might have spoken to a frightened child. And Minta, who had never in her life, save in these five miserable weeks just past, known what it was to think of and plan for her own necessities; and who was amazed, and frightened, and miserable in every possible way, struggled for just another minute to regain her haughty voice and speak her repelling words, then suddenly covered her white face with both hands and burst into a perfect storm of tears.

"Poor child!" said her stepmother, wholly sympathetic and pitiful; "poor frightened child! I do not wonder you were overcome. The wretch, to dare to speak to you as he did! Never mind; he has gone away and will be quite sure not to return." Then, from that mysterious inner Source of Strength there came to her, not by thinking it out, but someway, entirely as a matter of course, what to do. She spoke as though the matter had been planned for weeks. "I have a carriage at the door; as soon as you are able to move, it will do you good to get into the open air. This room is stifling. We will drive directly home. I will just lock this door and send Mrs. Barnes to attend to everything. Come, Minta, I would try not to cry so much; it will take your strength, and you need it to get ready."

She had not meant to go home, this angry girl who had not yet sufficiently reached her right mind not to suppose herself ill treated in some way. She had not expected to have the chance to go, during these later weeks; but she had assured herself bitterly that if she were to have the chance, she would spurn it with scorn. She had been surprised to see her stepmother, but, true to her plans, had tried to summon the scorn. But she was utterly alone; her husband, for whom she had risked everything, had cruelly deserted her under circumstances of peculiar misery. She was entirely without money or friends; she was in a strange part of the city, the very noises of which kept her in a state of fear day and night. She was faint for lack of proper food; she had despised her supper the night before and loathed her breakfast that morning. She had not known what she could say to the landlord's agent when he called again, and she had gotten ready that tub of soapsuds and made her pitiful preparations to wash under the dim impression that when he should turn her into the street, it would be better for her to have clean clothes to carry; but as she lay there limp and helpless on the floor, with the absurd incongruity of one's thoughts in moments of high excitement, she remembered the little heap of soiled clothes, and it seemed to her that she could never, never get them washed. And then there came another knock at the door, and she had so far recovered as to make a desperate effort to struggle into the small cane-seat rocker, the only touch of comfort which the room held. It was Ruth who answered the knock and held open the door in dignified silence while the woman who had the general charge of all these flats stood and looked at her in open-mouthed astonishment, and finally said, "Oh! I didn't know." What she did not know was not explained; it might have taken a very long time.

Mrs. Burnham was a woman who, however she

might question and delay on ordinary occasions, in an emergency knew just what to say. The present seemed to her an emergency.

"Do you want anything?" she asked with gentle dignity; and the woman murmured that she thought she heard a noise and didn't know but—and then she stopped.

"You did not know but you might help us," finished Ruth pleasantly. "Thank you; you can. Mrs. Hamlin is not well; she has been quite faint, but is better now, and I want to take her away immediately. If you will see that the halls and stairs are clear of idle children, so we can reach the door and my carriage without annoyance, I will take care that you are paid for your kindness. I will lock Mrs. Hamlin's room and take the key with me. I shall send my housekeeper to attend to her property here as soon as possible, and after that you may let the proper persons know, if you please, that the room is vacant."

The miserable young wife could not have told, afterwards, how it was that she, who had meant to be so independent of her home, should have been thus easily managed. But she felt so weak and faint, and the thought of getting out of that dreary room into the fresh air was so inspiring, and her stepmother was so prompt and matter-of-course in all her movements, that really the fact was, the girl was lying back among the cushions, being whirled toward her old home, before she had rallied enough to think what she must do next.

As for Mrs. Burnham, the uppermost thought in her mind was one of surprise that there could have been any doubt as to what to do.

27

At Home

WITH Mrs. Hamlin, the feeling of irresponsibility, of yielding to the inevitable, continued after she reached home. She was very miserable, but the quiet beauty of her old room with its familiar belongings rested her nerves, though she did not know it.

She was a deserted wife, disgraced, penniless, brokenhearted, yet the bed was so soft, and its coverings were so pure, and the pillows were so fair!

She let hot tears soil their purity, but still she buried her face in their depths with a feeling that all these belongings fitted her, as those with which she had had to do of late did not. And being very tired as well as very miserable, she quite soon forgot her sorrows in sleep.

But with Mrs. Burnham the case was different. She was alone in the library, and the reaction from all the day's excitement was upon her. There was time for her to think over what she had done and to imagine some of the results which might follow. It was not that she doubted the wisdom of her movements thus far; she was still upheld by the calm assurance that what she had done was the thing to do; but she could not, even with this assurance, keep her overtired brain from surmising results. What would her husband say? What would he do? Nothing apparently was more firmly impressed upon his mind than the fact that he had disowned his daughter, and here she was domiciled in her old room! Would Judge Burnham tolerate this innovation? From his wife's knowledge of him, gleaned by many experiences during the years, she did not believe he would. And yet it had seemed to her the one thing to do.

There was nothing for her but straightforward action in the line which was plain to her. Judge Burnham's duties she could not shoulder for him. But certainly the next thing for her was to write him a plain statement of affairs as they now stood. It was not an easy letter to write; she avoided the central feature of it longer than was her fashion. She told the absent father much about Erskine and his sweet, bright ways, and much even about the common details of home life, before she brought herself to the sentence: "And now, I have something to tell that will alarm and pain you. I heard today some very startling news. What will you think when I tell you that—" She held her pen at this point and considered. She had often spoken to Judge Burnham about "the girls"; she had often, of late years, said "your daughters"; but now there was only one, and the circumstances were such that to say "your daughter" seemed almost to insult him. How should she manage the sentence? Her face, as she held her pen, waiting, and looked away into space with thoughtful yet resolute eyes, would have been a study for a painter.

Did not this woman realize that she had deliberately and of her own will introduced once more into her home that which had been its chief discordant element in the past? No; after careful deliberation I think I may say to you that she realized at last that such was not the case. Either you have been a thoughtless reader, or I have failed of my purpose, if you have not discovered that Ruth Burnham has reached higher ground than that on which her feet ever trod before.

It is not easy to explain just how much that sentence means. It was not that she had reached serene heights, where daily pettinesses could not disturb her more. It was not that she was not keenly alive to the discomforts—to call them by no stronger name—that would probably come to her through this latest movement of hers, but it does mean that she was keenly alive to her mistakes in the past and believed them to have been the chief sources of her unhappiness. One of them, she knew, had been a persistent effort to carry her own burdens, even after she had been to the Cross and professed to leave them there. And another of them had been a persistent determination to do her own planning, even after she had asked the Lord to plan for her.

These two mistakes she had resolved to make no more. And it was the thought that the One to whom Erskine had appealed for help had assuredly told her what to do that held her eyes and her heart quiet, even though, so far as her foreknowledge went, there were seas of trouble yet to cross.

Suddenly she bent over her paper, and the pen moved on. "What will you think when I tell you that our daughter Minta is at this moment in her old room, sleeping quietly? I went for her this morning and brought her home. I found her in a very third-rate house on Court Street. Think of it! She is not well; has a cough that reminds me painfully of Seraph. It seems that her miserable husband deserted her some weeks ago; left her quite without money in this wretched flat that he had rented on Court Street. Her meals were brought up to her, prepared by a woman who rented the kitchen and made her living by serving the occupants of the rooms with badly cooked food. When I found her, she was on the eve of being turned out of even this refuge by the landlord's agent, because she owed for two weeks' rent! None of them seemed to be aware of her relationship to us. Of course I knew that she must come home at once. She was very willing to do so, for she felt sick and frightened. A line from Mr. Bacon, received since I reached home, informs me that there is very little doubt but that Hamlin, on whose track detectives have been ever since he fled the city, has been arrested and is now in confinement, awaiting trial. It is forgery again. Mr. Bacon thinks there will be no possibility of his escaping justice this time. I have not told poor Minta this and do not know how to tell her. I think I will wait for advice from you. Meantime, your heart would ache for her, if you could see her. She is very pale and has grown alarmingly thin. I think the poor girl has suffered more than perhaps we shall ever know. It frightens me to think of her having been alone in that part of the city, and she so young and still so beautiful." And then had followed a few sentences expressive of her loneliness in his absence and her hope that these days of separation were nearly over. And then this weary woman closed her writing desk with a little sigh, because her heart could not escape wondering what he would say to it all.

There was also perplexity as to the very next day. She could not determine what would be Minta's line of action. Whether she would remain the pale, passive woman she was now, or whether she would rebel and insist on escaping ever so kind a control of her movements. Or, whether, indeed, she would assume that she had rights in this home equal, if not superior, to those of the woman who had brought her here.

Ruth could not but admit that this last state would be more like the Minta Burnham of her acquaintance than either of the others; and, in view of her father's present position, would work disastrously for the girl.

Having wearied herself after this fashion, imagining scenes that might take place, she suddenly remembered, with a smile of relief, that the part that it was impossible for her to arrange, she had a right to leave.

I think it was, perhaps, as well for both these women that the next morning found the younger one quite ill.

The program for that day, at least, was plain. Dr. Westwood must be sent for, and the role of decided invalidism must be carried out. It proved that the same line of action would do for several days. Minta was not alarmingly ill, but the doctor counseled quiet, and utmost care; and Ruth, in arranging for tea and toast and lemonade, and various cooling drinks, and seeing to it that her patient was made comfortable in many ways, had little time for troubled imaginings. As for Minta, the necessity for asking to have the glass or the handkerchief handed to her, or the pillow moved, and for saying "thank you" frequently, overcame much of the painful embarrassment with which the new day began; and for the most part she was quiet and submissive. As the days passed, and she grew better, and was, presently, able to sit in the large easy chair and watch the passers-by on the street below, it became evident that she was very much subdued. One circumstance contributed largely to this result. Mrs. Burnham, in looking over a trunk of packed-away treasures in search of something for which Minta had asked, came suddenly upon a little box of Seraph's that had not been opened. It closed with a spring that Ruth did not understand; but as she held it in her hand, it appeared that her fingers must have touched the hidden spring, for it flew open, and on the top lay a letter addressed to Minta in her sister's familiar writing. Ruth, much moved, ceased her search and carried the letter at once and in silence to the pale-faced girl lying back among the cushions of the easy chair. She did not know, either then or afterwards, what words Seraph had spoken for her last ones; but Minta's eyes were red with weeping when she saw her again, and her voice seemed gentler and her manner more subdued after that time. It became apparent that she also had anxious thoughts about the future. She asked often for word from her father. When was he coming? Did he know that she was there? What had he said? And once, she asked, did Ruth think "Papa would allow her to remain at home, after all that had been?" And Mrs. Burnham, whose heart was daily growing more full of pity for this deserted wife, who—even though she had sinned and also certainly much sinned against, and though her love was so misplaced yet so entirely selfish in its exhibition—had yet, in a sense, loved the man who had deserted her, felt that she would give much to be able to answer a hearty yes to this hesitating question and did not know how to reply. Her husband maintained an ominous silence in regard to the news she had sent him. His letters came as regularly as usual, but they were shorter and, she fancied, colder. He was crowded with care and some anxiety. He hoped to get the complications straightened out before very long; she did not need the assurance that he would be home as soon as possible; and then had followed messages for Erskine, very tender and fatherly, but not a word for or about Minta in any way. He seemed to have simply ignored her story. This boded no good for the future. There was nothing now but to wait, with what patience they could. Each day it became evident to Mrs. Burnham that she was settling into the position held so long ago: looked upon by Minta as the intercessor between her and an indignant father; and each day she grew more doubtful about her ability to perform her part. Judge Burnham was cruelly proud; he had been cruelly stabbed, and very publicly, too; he had publicly disowned his daughter. Would his pride ever let him acknowledge her again? More and more the wife felt that this household needed other than human power to settle it into anything like peace. Her cry for help from the Omnipotent became daily more earnest. There was notably in her experience a certain Sabbath evening when her prayer rose into the realm which perhaps might be reverently called "wrestling."

And then one morning, when all the air was crisp with frost and the earth was aglow in its latest autumn finery, came a telegram from Judge Burnham to his wife. Could she join him in Westford by the noon train, to return that evening? Now Westford was a little city but an hour's ride from their own greater one. Ruth had often been there, and there was nothing about the telegram in itself to cause her anxiety. She was frequently summoned to that or neighboring towns to meet her husband on business—to sign an important paper, to tell her version of a bit of news that had been supposed trivial, but which had suddenly, in the light of events, grown important.

It ought to have been simply a satisfaction that Judge Burnham was at last so near home as this. But about everything which could happen during these days, there was an undertone of anxiety. It was an almost humiliating fact, but Ruth felt that she was somewhat in disgrace with her own husband and dreaded while she looked forward to meeting him. Of course she must obey the summons; but she looked wistfully at Erskine, and was half ashamed to think how much she would like to be able to make herself think it sensible to take the child with her. He, too, was wistful. He never approved of his mother's absences from himself. He asked her the same question in many forms: "Was she sure and certain and positive that she would return that very truly night?" and "Would she bring Papa home with her?" Over this last Ruth considered. The telegram was ambiguous, after the manner of those two-sided messengers. Did it mean that she could return that night or that they both would? She did not know; the utmost she could say to Erskine was that she would come, unless something which they could not foresee or help, prevented; and that she would certainly "bring Papa home" if she could. And then she went away with all speed.

Judge Burnham was on the platform before the train fairly halted; his greeting was warm, but he seemed preoccupied and in great haste. He hurried her into a carriage.

"I have to go at once to an important gathering," he explained. "Will you mind coming in with me? I shall not be detained over a half hour."

"Is it a courthouse?" she asked as the carriage drew up before a large building. "Will there be ladies present, Judge Burnham?"

"No," he said, "it was not a courtroom, but a public hall. O yes! there would be plenty of ladies; but he should have to leave her and go to the platform."

There was nothing unusual about this; he had often

to go to the platform when there were gatherings for the discussion of public interests.

He seated her in the closely filled hall and hurried forward; he was evidently being waited for. He had only time to lay aside his hat and exchange a few words with a gentleman who stepped toward him, book in hand, and then Ruth watched her husband as he took the book and came forward to the center of the platform and began to read.

And this was what he read:

> "There is a fountain filled with blood,
> Drawn from Immanuel's veins;
> And sinners plunged beneath that flood,
> Lose all their guilty stains.
> I do believe, I now believe that Jesus died for me.
> That on the cross He shed His blood
> From sin to set me free."

Can I tell you anything about it, do you suppose— the tumult of amazement and of joy surging in his wife's soul?

She felt her face grow pale and then red under the power of her emotions. She held herself, by main force of will, quiet on the seat, when it seemed to her she must spring up before them all and shout for joy. Those words read by the voice which was to her the finest in the world—read with such a peculiarly marked emphasis on the personal pronouns as to tell her, even if his reading them at all under such circumstances had not done it, that he had made of this a personal matter.

"I do believe, I now believe that Jesus died for me!"

She said the lines over in exultant undertone, emphasizing the words as he had done, while the great company burst into song. This was surely the noon prayer meeting, about which she had heard much and which she had never before attended.

Almost with the last note of song mingled Judge Burnham's voice again, and he said, "Let us pray." His wife bowed her head on the seat before her, and her whole frame shook with emotion. She did not know afterwards whether she prayed, or cried, or laughed.

"I know," she said, long afterwards, telling Erskine about it, "I know I said Hallelujah! if that is praying."

An elderly lady seated beside her regarded the slight figure draped in mourning with an air of tender sympathy; and when a few moments afterwards there came from the leader of the meeting an invitation for those who would like to learn the way to Christ, to rise that they might be especially remembered in prayer, the old lady touched her arm and whispered:

"Won't you stand up, dear? It will help you ever so much."

Then Ruth turned toward her a radiant face, in which smiles were mingling with falling tears, and shook her head as she whispered back:

"I know the way. Isn't it glorious?" But she could never give a very lucid account of that noon prayer meeting.

There were other gentlemen who entered the same carriage with them, and there was opportunity for only an exchange of smiles between her husband and herself until they reached a hotel and he had ordered and secured a private room. Then he took her in his arms and kissed her, his face indicating too deep feeling just then for words.

"It is a long story, my dear," he said when they were

calmer, "or rather, it has been a long, long battle on my part, and could be summed up in a few sentences. It began, oh! long ago, but it has been marked by a few very decisive incidents. That Sunday afternoon meeting—I never forgot it, Ruth: nor your way of putting the facts; you were logical, and your conclusion was inevitable, and I was angry that it should be so. I silenced you, but not my own conscience; I never got away from it. Then came our troubles, and your attitude through them all. You were different, some way, from what you ever were before. It angered, while it awed me. I knew you were controlled by a power that I did not understand. About that time, too, Seraph told me many things that I did not know before; I began to realize something of what you had borne through the years. And then, Ruth, you know that I saw Seraph die.

"But the final appeal," he continued after a moment's silence, "the final appeal came in that letter which I did not answer. The thought that you could voluntarily open your home again, after what you had borne, and I, her father, had disowned her! I cannot tell you all that it said to me. Neither will I try to tell you now about the conflict. It is a little too recent to speak of it calmly. Yet I will tell you this, Ruth: I reached a point last Sunday night when I felt sure that the decision must be made then and there, for eternity.

"I have struggled with this question for years, and affected skepticism whenever that was the most convenient way of stifling conscience, and affected indifference when my heart was fairly on fire; and hidden behind inconsistencies of others and all that sort of flimsiness. But last Sunday evening it was as if the Lord himself stood by me and said, 'Just this one more time, my friend, I offer myself as your advocate.' It all came over me in an instant, Ruth, how often he had done it